JACKIE'S PARIS

A NOVEL

MERCEDES KING

Jackie's Paris

ISBN 978-17343927-60

Cover design and interior formatting by *Hannah Linder Designs*
www.hannahlinderdesigns.com

THE JACQUELINE BOUVIER KENNEDY ONASSIS COLLECTION

Jackie's Paris

Jackie's Camelot

Jackie's Greece

Jackie's New York

For Haylee, Ryan, Holden, Chloe, Holly & Kevin

ONE

Manhattan
April 1949

Poised and postured like the twenty-year-old debutante she was, Jacqueline Bouvier strolled into Schrafft's on the arm of her father. The scent of Sunday brunch—freshly griddled waffles and bacon—greeted them, along with curious stares from several female patrons. Jackie loved it, the charisma he exuded that effortlessly captured women's attention. There at his side, with sunlight streaming in behind them, she basked in the envy of every woman in the establishment.

As they followed the hostess to their table, her father's flirtatious glance seemingly waltzed through the restaurant, at least when he wasn't focused on the hostess's salacious saunter in her snug crème-colored skirt. Jackie took the seat her father held for her. The hostess promised that a waitress would be with them shortly, then departed with a tilt of her head and a subtle wink meant only for Jack Bouvier.

Was it any wonder? Jackie mused. Crowned with jet-black hair and sporting a thin moustache, he was often mistaken for Clark Gable. Dapper in every wool or tweed suit he wore, he never lacked for female companionship but showed no interest in settling down. His reputation as a womanizer, combined with his nutmeg skin tone, had earned him the nickname Black Jack.

"Pity that Lee couldn't join us." He draped the linen napkin across his lap.

Jackie grinned at him, attuned to his sarcasm. Friction often sparked between her sister and their father, which Jackie blamed on their parents' divorce. Lee's outbursts and penchant for drama tested and drained their father's patience. He never voiced his frustrations, but Jackie suspected he resented having to soothe and subdue her sister's cantankerous moods.

"She sends her love and regards," Jackie fibbed. Her request—insistence, really—on lunching alone with their father today had resulted with a bedroom door slammed in her face.

"Does she now? How thoughtful." Jack opened the menu and pretended to scan the selections he knew so well. For a man who had a varied and insatiable appetite for women, he remained faithful to the corned beef sandwich on pumpernickel, topped off with a shot of sour scotch. "And how is the rest of that brood, dare I ask?"

Brood was the best insult her father could hurl about the blended family of nine Jackie was part of. Quite comfortable in the lifestyle her stepfather's fortune afforded, she could tolerate her father's petty criticism and unveiled jealousy. An heir to the Standard Oil fortune, her stepfather practiced law, served in the government, and heralded a brokerage firm he'd established, while Jack Bouvier, a stockbroker himself, still hadn't recovered financially from the crash of 1929. When he wasn't gambling or bedding the mothers of Jackie's classmates, his alcoholism got the best of him. Nevertheless, nothing could diminish Jackie's adoration for her father.

"We manage." Jackie gave a feeble smile, careful not to injure her father's feelings. Her homelife held no interest for him, and she didn't want to risk putting him in a foul temperament. Not when she had such an important item to discuss.

The itch to change the subject took over. Jackie reached into her handbag and removed a folded pamphlet. Smoothing her gloved hands over the paper's crease, she did her best to flatten it before handing it to her father.

"What do we have here?"

"A fabulous opportunity." She sipped her water while he read the announcement, but her patience failed. "Smith College is offering a year-long student exchange program at the University of Paris, which would include classes at the Sorbonne. Vassar doesn't offer such a program, but I can still apply through Smith." Jackie pressed her lips together to stop her zeal from running away.

He skimmed the pamphlet, then shifted his gaze up to her.

"Paris?"

Jackie nodded.

"Are you certain this is a good idea, my love? I know you've had a taste of Europe, and Paris can be intoxicating. But living there—for a *year*—well, I'm afraid it would be frightfully expensive."

Jackie would be the first to admit that her seven-week holiday with family friends the previous summer had whetted her appetite for more of Europe. She dreamed of living there and being more than a passerby, but two things kept her from a life abroad—her parents and money.

"I realize that, Daddy, but I could board on campus instead of renting an apartment. That would save money, and I could find a job." Her enthusiasm waned with the last suggestion, though she hoped her father didn't notice.

Working held no appeal for her, not if it meant being shackled to a schedule and stuffed inside a dank building. She wanted to immerse herself in Paris, savor its art and architecture; but mostly, she relished the thought of exercising total freedom over her life—and escaping the tangible strife between her parents. If a job was required to secure her fantasy, then so be it.

Jack glanced over the paper again and set it aside. "Shouldn't you be enjoying everything Vassar has to offer a young woman of your age and standing?"

His real question wasn't lost on Jackie: *Shouldn't you be finding a husband?* Many women her age attended university as a glorified dating ritual and abandoned their studies once a proposal came along. Education and obtaining a degree were not secondary for Jackie. Though she was social, attending football games and weekend outings at Yale, her dating life had been fruitless. She often sensed her parents' growing impatience, but it wasn't her fault that she found most men dull.

"I have, Daddy, and that's the problem. Poughkeepsie is like a frumpy old spinster, who sips her gin and falls asleep in her housecoat." Jackie paused while her father enjoyed a chuckle. "There's nothing stimulating there, which is why I end up at your apartment."

Jack grinned, no doubt appreciating that his oldest daughter preferred retreating to his Manhattan apartment on weekends rather than romping on her stepfather's grand estate in Newport, Rhode Island.

"But now is your time, my dear. Why, you were Debutant of the Year. I would think that troves of worthless beaux would be salivating at your feet."

"All men are rats. Isn't that what you've been telling me for ages now?"

"No argument there." Jack withdrew his pack of Chesterfields from his pocket and lit into one.

"You see, this is the perfect time for me to go to Paris. I have no attachments, no one I'm particularly fond of, and just think, my French will become perfect while living there."

Their waitress appeared, and Jackie sensed a sigh of relief from her father, indicating he wasn't prepared to give his consent yet. He took advantage of the moment and exercised his charms with the young woman. In turn, she smiled and played coy.

As usual, Jackie mentally absorbed the exchange and envied the way he captivated women. She needed a dose of such magic since gentle persuasion was failing her.

The hesitance was because of the money, she knew. Her father wouldn't relent easily, even if his funds were abundant. Controlling the purse strings, as it were, of Jackie and Lee's lives was the only power—or influence—he still held over them. Although that was only in his mind. No trust fund would be forthcoming from their father. As it was, he barely kept up with their monthly allowance of fifty dollars each—a sum that paid for their cosmetics and little else.

But Jackie wouldn't let that pinch of resentment derail her determination. She deserved this trip, having fed her father's pride with her stellar academics and award-winning horsemanship. She gave him no grief, and her love for him never wavered, even when rumors of his gambling debts circled or when he required another drying-out spell. Now, would be her father's turn to show his love and loyalty.

"I know it's a lot to ask, Daddy," she said once they were alone again. Employing new tactics, she rested her hands in her lap and tilted her head slightly, feigning resignation. "Perhaps I've acted too hastily. Maybe going away to study isn't ideal, but I'm aiming to make changes regardless."

Jack's gaze locked on hers. "Do tell."

"Like you said, living in Paris would be expensive, but that's true of life most anywhere. I was thinking of easing the burden on you and Mummy. I'm perfectly capable of reading and acquiring knowledge on my own, which is primarily what university life entails. I don't need Vassar, or the Sorbonne, for that."

"What are you getting at?" Jack squinted and tucked his cigarette into the corner of his mouth.

"Perhaps it's time I ventured out and started making my own money. I've been thinking about becoming a fashion model, here in New York. I could get an apartment—"

"Now, now, I'll not tolerate foolish conversation." He waved a hand in the air, as if to shoo away the suggestion. "You're a rare bird, my dear, and one of the things that makes you so extraordinary is your mind, that hunger you have for history, literature. You shouldn't abandon university just so you can make money. I won't hear of it."

"Then you'll let me go to Paris?" Hopefulness swelled in her chest. "It's only for a year, Daddy."

He reared back in his chair, his expression pensive.

"What does your mother say about this idea of yours?"

"I haven't told her yet." Jackie smiled. "I came to you first."

Jack beamed. The way he always did whenever Jackie demonstrated her devotion to him or gave him an advantage over Janet.

"Tell me, then, when you *do* mention this to your mother, what do you think she'll say?"

"I imagine she'll want to talk me out of it." Elation pulsed through her. Why hadn't she thought of using her mother's disapproval earlier?

He exhaled a puff of smoke slowly, and a Cheshire grin appeared from behind the cloud.

"In that case, my pet, we'd better make sure that all the arrangements are in place before you tell her."

DESPITE HER UNFALTERING love for her father, Jackie wasn't robust with confidence in the man. She well knew that one drunken episode, one sultry dame, one called-due gambling debt could deter him from following through and providing the money she needed to secure her spot in the program. Jackie couldn't risk such catastrophe. She needed assurances.

Days crawled by, and when no receipt or bank note arrived guaranteeing the finances in her account, Jackie took matters into her own hands. She went to Grampy Jack.

Sprawling and exaggerated, Lasata, the Bouviers' family mansion in East Hampton, had been purchased by Jackie's grandmother, Maude, back in 1925. Situated on twelve acres, the estate always took Jackie back to blissful summers in her childhood, where there was church followed by Sunday brunch, collars as stiff as they were white, and peach ice cream churned by their French chauffeur.

For Jackie and Lee, Lasata had lived up to the meaning of its Native American name, *place of peace*, and provided an escape for two young girls coping with the disintegration of their parents' marriage. When they weren't plucking grapes from the arbor or playing hide and seek in the stables, they picked daises and bachelor's buttons for Grandma Maude. On one occasion they crouched in the shrubbery and watched Daddy play tennis with one of his paramours while golden trumpet flowers tickled their cheeks.

Knowing those magical summers were gone pained Jackie—though not as greatly as the loss of Grandma Maude. Since her grandmother's passing in 1940—the same year as her parents' divorce—Jackie had hardly visited her grandfather.

Panic mounted in her chest when he opened the front door. Suddenly fearful he would lash out at her for the long absence, her breath caught, and she almost skirted away.

"My Jacqueline!" Grampy Jack greeted her with an embrace that forced all the air from her lungs—and purged her worries. Equally strong was the scent of sandalwood and beeswax. The Major, as he was known to others, mirrored Lasata with a grand appearance that teetered on being obnoxious. East Hampton residents revered him, and for years he'd christened the summer season at the Maidstone Club with a speech and a toast. Although there was no crevice in Lasata where one could escape his booming voice, he had an affinity for poetry, which he only shared with Jackie.

Grampy ushered her into the family room and called his staff to bring refreshments.

Jackie took in her surroundings and noted how little things had changed. Tension seeped from her shoulders as she settled on the tufted mauve sofa. By the time warm slices of bay bread with raisins and glasses of iced tea arrived, she and Grampy were trading bits of family news and gossip. Jackie remembered not to speak too much and to let him repeat his favorite stories. She realized, as he spoke, she'd forgotten a few of his habits. Namely, his ability to guzzle drinks (two iced teas in this instance) and how he wiped his mouth on his sleeve. She had missed his unpolished ways.

Never one for sitting still long, Grampy stood. "Shall we stroll the garden?"

She nodded, though a lump welled in her throat. The garden, lined with boxwoods and adorned with Italian statues, had been Grandma Maude's retreat. Just as Lasata reflected Grampy, the garden spoke of Maude: an enduring, peaceful presence of quiet, yet tested, strength. Jackie recalled their moments together, planting flowers and listening while Grandma Maude told tales about the statues.

Jackie clenched and clasped her fingers as they made their way outside, hoping the churn of emotions within wouldn't overtake her. She threaded her arm through her grandfather's and gently squeezed herself against him. Strength radiated from the man and nourished her courage.

"Grampy, I could use a favor."

"Oh?"

She shared the prospect of studying abroad and her desire to participate in the program. Impatience and short attention spans plagued the Bouvier men, so Jackie made a passionate and animated plea.

"A trip to Paris, you say?" Grampy required hearing aids but preferred tuning people out when it suited him. "Sounds marvelous, Jacqueline, simply marvelous. We've an old ancestral home in France, you know."

How could she not? Grampy had detailed the Bouviers' lineage in *Our Forbears*, which traced the family back to French aristocrats. Whether or not his account was true and unadulterated, Jackie couldn't say. No one else in the family dared to question his narrative either.

"Yes," Jackie said, "I intend to visit while I'm there."

"I assume this relates to the favor you have in mind."

She appreciated his directness but blushed just the same. Being needy, bordering on desperate, wasn't becoming.

"I need some money for the trip."

"Ah, I see. I take it that your stepfather has no desire to give you any money, since you're not his." Grampy tweaked the waxed tips of his moustache.

A response wasn't necessary, but Jackie held no contempt toward Hughdie. As far as stepfathers went, he'd been wonderful to her and Lee. Generous, too, having funded her European excursion last summer. She couldn't hope for more and approaching him with such a request would cross the boundaries of propriety.

"Have you spoken to that father of yours?" Little respect existed between Grampy and his oldest child. In the years since the stock market crash, Grampy had repeatedly advised his son on finances and had rescued him financially more than once. Jackie believed Grampy's disgruntlement came from his fear of losing another son to alcoholism. Death had snatched William "Bud" Bouvier at age thirty-six, despite family interventions.

Jackie nodded. "We had lunch together. He seemed agreeable at the time, but..."

"But you haven't heard from him or received a dime from the cad, have you?"

She cast a glance at the ground, hating the way he made her father sound, hating that her father's actions were indefensible. Silence was best when it came to Grampy's observations. Irksome but for the best.

"I've told him, I've counseled him on the way he spends money—wastes it really! Between the women, the booze, and the gambling, he's ruined his reputation. It's his own fault, and he's downright foolish for not safeguarding his accounts better than he has. What's to become of him in old age, if he makes it that far? And should I bother with the stain he's added to our family's legacy?"

Much like Bud, Jackie thought, recalling how her uncle had been divorced and unable to provide for his ex-wife and son. Such was grounds for public humiliation on the Bouvier name.

Irritation stewed in Jackie. Her father and Bud may not have been men without weaknesses—but neither was Grampy. His affair with a household servant had devastated Grandma Maude and nearly destroyed their marriage. In addition, Grampy's two daughters were also divorced, deepening the disgrace.

"You did the right thing, Jacqueline, coming to me. Your education and exposure to all life has to offer is of utmost importance." He stopped walking and cupped her face in his hand, a rare display of affection. "I'll see to it that you leave here tonight with the funds, my dear."

"Thank you, Grampy!" Jackie threw her arms around him, an exuberant response from her as well.

"Yes, well, someone must do this family proud, and I do believe that's you, Jacqueline! Repairing the Bouvier name and instilling a notable legacy rests upon your shoulders now, my dear."

Jackie gave no thought to revamping her family's name. Not at the moment. Instead, she worried about the more formidable and immediate task of telling her mother that she was planning to leave home—for Paris.

Newport, Rhode Island

"JACQUELINE, this is the most reprehensible, selfish, irresponsible thing you've ever done!"

Irresponsible? Jackie refrained from arching an eyebrow in response.

"How could you? How could you go behind my back and orchestrate such strategies without a word to me or Hughdie?"

Hughdie kept his eyes on his dinner plate, chewed his food rhythmically, and acted as though he heard nothing. In the course of his seven-year union with Janet, he'd learned not to interrupt during one of her tirades, regardless of whether or not her viewpoint on the matter was hyperbolic. When possible, he stayed hidden behind the newspaper, which served as a useful shield from her often biting words.

Of the children seated around the table, only Lee showed a pinch of interest, darting her eyes from Jackie to her mother. The other siblings, which included Nina and Tommy, being only twelve and eleven, focused on eating. They stole occasional glances at their father, perhaps in need of reassurances that Janet's riled state would soon subside. The youngest children, Janet and Jamie, were too young at four and two, according to Mummy, to properly dine with the rest of the family and were therefore tended to by the nanny. Yusha's absence was felt but not mentioned.

Jackie glanced at Lee and regretted not divulging her news beforehand. No doubt Lee would end up in her room later, badgering her with questions and wondering how she'd pulled off the arrangements. She was probably perturbed at Jackie as well, for not confiding in her.

"Hughdie, what do you intend to do about this?" Janet's silverware clanked on her plate.

"What would you have me do, dear?" His voice remained calm and his eyes stuck to his veal.

"You'll telephone her father and tell him we won't have him interfering with our daughter." Janet gave a stiff nod.

Hughdie allowed his gaze to intersect with Janet's.

"Mummy, no!" Jackie said. "I want to go to Paris! It's only for a year and it's to study. I'll take care of myself. You and Hughdie won't have to do a thing." Normally, she wasn't one to bite-back in a public altercation with her mother; she endured Janet's harsh words and verbal corrections. If Jackie wanted to go to Paris, a docile attitude wouldn't do.

Janet huffed. Her cheeks flushed from embarrassment. She appeared to be searching her mind for an argument, only nothing came.

"I don't appreciate being undermined in my own home, Jacqueline," she finally said, though taking a cue from Hughdie, she focused on her own place setting while she spoke.

"I'm sorry, Mummy. Perhaps I should've told you in private—"

"Yes, you should have. It was hardly appropriate to bring up for dinnertime conversation."

Decorum proved to be Janet Auchincloss's primary religion. Vocalizing her staunch convictions often resulted in demeaning others, a tactic she considered an acceptable form of collateral damage.

Jackie sighed. She knew announcing her travel plans in front of the family guaranteed an outburst from her mother. But Jackie reasoned it was the only way to be fully heard. She went on to explain that she'd been accepted into the program and the money for travel had been secured.

"Why," Janet struggled to find a complaint, "I'm not even sure if it's proper for a young lady of your standing to study abroad. What about chaperones and accommodations?"

"Smith College is sending us with a chaperone, of course, and I'll be staying on campus near the Sorbonne."

"On campus hardly seems appropriate! There's no telling what a dormitory in Paris is like. Filthy, I imagine. Surely Hughdie and I must know of someone who can help us find acceptable housing. Don't you think, Hughdie?"

"Yes, dear."

"That settles it, then. I'll look through my registry this evening and make calls. I suppose if you must fulfill this...desire of yours, I can at least rest assured knowing you're well looked after...in a suitable dwelling."

Jackie grinned. She should have known that the best way to win over her mother's approval was by allowing her an element of control.

As the tension in the room eased, she wondered if she'd pulled it off. Had she convinced her family to let her go to Paris for a year? And had she pulled off the ploy, petty as it was, that Jack Bouvier wasn't as financially impotent as her mother believed? Money sourced from the Bouviers was good enough for Jackie, even though it was wrapped in a little white lie.

"Children, no slouching at the table," Janet said to Nina and Tommy. "Just think, children, we won't have Jacqueline with us. A year will seem so long. I know we'll be lonesome without her."

Jackie bit back the smirk that tried to creep across her face. Sentiment, contrived as it was, seeping from her mother was uncharacteristic at best. Beside her, Lee sat with her hand in front of her mouth as if she were about to sneeze. That only made it harder for Jackie to hold back her mounting giggles.

There would be no laughing at Mummy.

SHE COULDN'T SAY WHY, but after dinner, Jackie wasn't in the mood for her sister. Perhaps she wanted to make the news easier on her mother by not holing upstairs with Lee and recounting how dumbfounded Janet looked at hearing that Daddy had provided. Perhaps she didn't want to chance the euphoria being ruined by Lee's questions, or she feared letting it slip that Grampy was her true benefactor.

No matter the reason, Jackie didn't dwell on it. She left the main house, anxious for fresh air off the bay that edged the backside of Hammersmith Farm. Although springtime mornings were her favorite, with the sun bright and tiny orange blossoms peeking from among the rocks along the shoreline, the evening had its own appeal. Ships of all kinds, from naval vessels to tugboats, cut through the water while the melody of their horns bellowed in the dark.

She walked to the stables, an eagerness rising to check on her horse. Naturally, she never went to Danseuse without an apple or sugar cubes in her pocket. Tonight she'd swiped both as she left through the kitchen, a maneuver meant to ensure that no one followed her. Inside the stall, the mare nuzzled Jackie's palm and gingerly accepted the treats as Jackie ran her fingers through the horse's charcoal-colored mane.

"Guess I picked the wrong night to skip dinner."

Jackie turned at the sound of Yusha's voice. Two years older, her stepbrother resembled a youthful version of Hughdie with his tall, lean build. Unlike his father, Yusha didn't need glasses, and dark, lush hair still crowned his head. His playful personality served him well with the ladies, and his impish side endeared him to Jackie.

"I overheard Janet yammering on about you running away." He slid his hands into his trouser pockets. "There may have been a remark about poor manners, and a mention about living in Paris. That's the problem with eavesdropping, I suppose. Murky details. Care to fill me in?"

Ever since their parents had wed, Jackie was convinced she couldn't have hand-crafted a better brother. His wry humor matched her own, as did his fondness for staging pranks on the household staff. Few people could make Jackie laugh like Yusha did, especially when he imitated Lee's pout-face.

They took brushes and began grooming Danseuse as Jackie explained about the chance to study abroad—and how she revealed her set plans over dinner. Much to Janet's chagrin.

"So it's true, you're really going to Paris?" Yusha patted the mare and put their brushes away when they'd finished.

Before Jackie spoke, the realization welled up inside her. "Yes." She exhaled and felt the tingle of bliss cover her skin. "It means a break from being in the middle of my parents' animosity, and it means I get to be on my own."

Yusha nodded. Like Jackie, he'd survived his parents' separation and divorce. His Russian-born mother had tired of the socialite life and left Hughdie—and Yusha—for a musician. Hughdie moved on to another ill-fated marriage while Yusha was tucked away at boarding school.

"And once you're there," he said, "twirling through the Louvre and books up to your shoulders, am I supposed to believe that you'll come back?"

He had a point. Jackie couldn't deny an inner tickle that accompanied the thought of freedom from Janet's control. Would it take being separated by an ocean to diminish that hold? But in truth, one variable troubled Jackie even more than her mother's heavy-handedness —money.

"Depends," Jackie said.

"On?"

She grinned playfully. "On whether or not I find a wealthy man who sweeps me off my feet."

TWO

June 1949

As the early morning fog crept along Narragansett Bay, Jackie, mounted atop Danseuse and filling her lungs with the brisk air, couldn't be too upset with her mother. Despite Janet's flares of temper, Jackie had her to thank when it came to her own athleticism and horsemanship. Few activities fueled her soul and eased her worries like foxhunting and racing across an open meadow. The thundering of hooves underneath and the wind whipping in her face never failed to cure a foul mood.

Mornings like this, with Lee riding close behind, would be fleeting. There'd be no fresh cut hay and stables ripe with manure in France. No wide-open countryside at her back door, and no Danseuse. Jackie ached at the thought of leaving her horse for so long.

A sudden yelp and a thump tore Jackie from her thoughts. She turned and saw that Lee had been thrown from her horse. A few tugs of the reins, and Jackie had Danseuse whipped around and trotting toward her sister.

Lee stood almost immediately, as if that could make the fall less noticeable. She brushed the dust from her jodhpurs and snatched her riding crop from the ground.

"Daisy's always had a stubborn streak," Jackie said.

Lee scowled. "If I had any sense, I'd send her to the knackers."

"You know you'd be the last person to do such a thing." Jackie dismounted but held onto the reins. "Are you sure you're all right?"

Lee hesitated. "I can't believe you're leaving me. You know I'm no good at handling the two of them."

Guilt nudged Jackie. She understood her sister's reluctance to be the lone pawn between her parents, and a year was a long time to be the one to bear their disgruntlements.

"It's two more months before I leave. Besides, I wouldn't say that I've accomplished anything between Mummy and Daddy. I can't even get them to be cordial to one another."

"But you're Daddy's favorite." Lee said it with the dramatics only a sixteen-year-old could muster. "You always have been. This trip just proves it. He never gives me anything extravagant, and he groans when I want to shop at Bloomingdale's."

Jackie knew she could never make Lee understand that being their father's favorite gave her no advantages. In fact, Jackie believed, that lent her to more demands and criticisms from their mother. But this was Lee. Captive to her own viewpoint and occasionally insensitive to Jackie's hardships.

"There's still plenty to look forward to." Jackie brushed back the fallen strands of Lee's hair. "Summer's coming, which means you'll be home from boarding school and heading with the family to East Hampton. I'll visit on weekends, and we'll sneak into the lighthouse at night. And I'm sure Yusha will pop in. You can flirt with all his friends. They're crazy about you."

If she were a certain kind of sister, Jackie would point out that Lee wouldn't have to worry about vying for the attention of young beaux with Jackie not around. That Lee would have an easier time, maintaining their adorations on her own. Fortunately, Jackie wasn't that kind of sister.

Lee looked at her and smiled, though she may not have wanted to.

"I'm jealous," she said. "And I might never forgive you."

Jackie responded with her own grin, knowing how those words must've ached Lee. Being sisters served as both a gift and a curse. Experiences bonded them, but their parents' expectations pitted them against each other in everything from academics to posture. Lee came up short on most triumphs, and Jackie sensed the underlying bitterness her sister harbored toward her. Time and petty victories enabled Jackie to tolerate it.

"A week after I'm gone, you'll hardly notice."

Lee sighed. "No one lies to me better than you, Jacks." She tapped her riding crop on Jackie's nose, brushing it with dust and rousing their laughter.

JACKIE COUNTED herself fortunate for many reasons—one of them being her close friendship with Charles Bartlett and Martha Buck. A journalist by trade, Charles had known Jackie for years through their social circles in East Hampton. He and Martha had been dating for months, and Jackie expected the two would make their union official soon. In no uncertain terms could she leave for Paris without spending an evening with the couple at Charles's Georgetown home.

"Every young lady should spend a year abroad," Martha said as she finished setting the table in the modest kitchen. "It should be a requirement for finishing school. Your mother must be thrilled."

"She's come around about it. I think she'd be more enthusiastic if it were her idea from the start." Per Martha's instructions, Jackie continued icing the cake that had been baked especially for the night's occasion. She had insisted on arriving early and helping out, but Martha knew Jackie's culinary skills were nonexistent, and she couldn't be entrusted to watch the rolls in the oven.

"Sounds like your mother," Charles said.

Martha swatted him playfully with a dishtowel, then looked at Jackie. "I need a few assurances before you board that ship."

"Oh?" Jackie's brows piqued with curiosity.

"First off, you must promise you'll write regularly, and that you won't leave out a thing. I'm serious on this point, my dear, very serious.

Operas, art, romance, books, weather reports, bird sightings, I want it all!"

"I'll do my best." Jackie resumed her cake-icing duties, a grin tugging at her lips. "I am required to study while I'm there."

"Fine, but don't disappoint me." She pointed an oven-mitted hand at Jackie, apparently to stress the issue. "Secondly, you must promise me that you won't fall in love and marry some Frenchman while you're over there. I would never forgive you if you made me miss out on your wedding day."

"That's nonsense, dear," Charles interjected. "Jackie's not the impulsive type, not when it comes to a matter as important as marriage."

Jackie paused, and her grin lost its spirit. An unconventional notion had budded in her mind lately. Keeping it to herself might have been best, but the words slipped out like liquid from an overturned glass.

"Maybe I don't want to get married."

Martha and Charles froze.

"Heavens, Jackie, I do believe you'd give your mother a heart attack if she ever heard you say such a thing," Martha said.

"Perhaps my mother is one reason why I don't want to get married."

"You might have a point there," Charles mumbled and sampled an hors d'oeuvres.

"But are you serious?" Concern crinkled Martha's forehead.

She shrugged a shoulder. "Mummy keeps telling me how important it is to find the right husband. What if I wanted to make it on my own, to do as I please without having a man hovering over me?"

"I can't believe I'm hearing this." Martha sank onto a stool.

"Besides," Jackie continued, "who's to say there's a man out there for me? Most of the men who find me attractive are ordinary and tedious."

"Like Hughdie?"

She shifted her gaze to Charles. "I don't want to compromise like Mummy."

Charles laughed. "Trust me, Janet's not disappointed in being Mrs. Auchincloss, even if she is his third wife. No, your mother accomplished a feat few in her social ranking could manage—she upgraded in the spousal department."

Jackie averted her eyes and silently disagreed. Hughdie's sizable wealth and impressive lineage paled next to her father's charisma. Jack Bouvier could bed any woman he wanted, and though Jackie didn't understand why, that feature alone swelled her sense of pride in him. True, his wanton actions had led to divorce, but for Jackie, it was forgivable. Being a bore was not.

"Not everyone can quote Byron from memory or appreciate a Rodin," Martha said. "You might need to be flexible in your expectations, dear."

"I'm sure what concerns Jackie most is the money," Charles said. "You know that's why Janet pushes you toward matrimony. Personally, she has no fortune to hand down, and Hughdie's not obligated to you and Lee. *Marry well*. Isn't that Janet's mantra?"

Jackie nodded, thankful that Charles's observation didn't include a comment on her father's finances—a humiliation she feared would follow her always.

"I'll be finishing my studies soon. Who's to say I can't support myself?"

Martha grinned and shook her head. "What are we going to do with her, Charles?"

"Let her go." He said it without hesitation, which Jackie liked. "Let her get out in the world and see what she discovers on her own. She'll be better for it."

He winked.

Jackie's adoration for Charles soared. She considered him a rare confidante, one who balanced being frank and corrective with her while his genuine esteem for her remained apparent.

"Oh, no!" Martha sprang from the stool. A faint trail of smoke seeped from the oven. She opened the door and pulled out a tray. A billow of gray smoke kissed her face. With a mild cough she turned and set the baking sheet on top of the counter. "My rolls."

Dejected, Martha shooed away the smoke with her dishtowel. When she checked their faces, laughter burst forth from everyone.

August 1949

JACKIE and her father had shared their good-byes in Manhattan a week prior, an encounter that left her heart entrenched in disappointments. Not only was her father tipsy during their visit, but he was also nonchalant about her leaving, as though he'd see her in a few days rather than several months.

His main preoccupation that night had been getting Jackie to promise she wouldn't go horseback riding while she was away. A fall from Danseuse had aggravated her back, and her father insisted she not ride. Jackie, ever dutiful, gave her word. Inwardly she marveled he could press a demand on her, especially since he never asked how the final arrangements for her trip were paid for. Her disappointment reached its zenith at the minor amount of cash he handed her before she left.

Now, standing on the dock near the newly refurbished French ocean liner, Jackie drew in a breath to settle the fluttering in her stomach. Goodbyes didn't come easy for her.

Hughdie was a dear in that he saw to it that her trunks and luggage made it aboard the ship.

"I do hope you appreciate all that's gone into this." Janet brushed her hand across the shoulder of Jackie's suit.

They stood for a moment, regarding each other. Both oblivious to the sea of gaiety surrounding them as passengers and well-wishers milled around the *SS De Grasse.* Sprays of confetti flitted through the air as a balloon vendor enthralled children with his wares, while others clapped and danced to the brash notes of a harmonica.

"My dearest Jacqueline, how did we ever get here?" Tenderness laced Janet's voice and paired with a somberness in her eyes.

Such rarely displayed affection caught Jackie off guard, and she wasn't certain what her mother meant. She'd sent her daughter off on lengthy travels before, but they both knew this was different—that after months of separation, they would each be different. Whatever the exact emotion that stirred in Janet, Jackie was touched. If it were not for her mother, her strictness and discipline, Jackie knew she wouldn't be the refined lady—the equestrienne—she was. Gratefulness swelled inside her.

Janet sighed and began blinking furiously. Tears, Jackie wondered? Janet turned aside, as if the children, Janet and Jamie, suddenly needed her attention.

Lee stepped into her place and took Jackie's hands. "I'll never hear the end of it. The littles always complain when I read them bedtime stories." The sisters stole a glance at the toddlers. Jamie, eyes cast upward, endured Janet wiping an imaginary smudge from his face. Janet, wedged close to her brother, was mesmerized by the red helium balloons other children were holding. "They tell me I'm not as good as you. Now, they'll be stuck with me."

"They're lucky to have you." Jackie embraced her, then whispered in her ear, "Please be good to Daddy. He needs you now."

When they released, Lee gave her an understanding nod.

Jackie bent to collect her satchel, but Hughdie got it for her and drew her in close.

"I want you to have this." He gave her a thick envelope and waited for her to slip it into her handbag. With a smile in his eyes, he squeezed her hand firmly but lovingly. "I'm not looking forward to the day-to-day without your smile. We're all better when you're around, my dear." He swallowed hard. "If you need anything at anytime, don't hesitate to send a cable."

She thanked him and kissed his cheek. Though she couldn't admit it, not even in part to herself, it was moments like this—stolen, quiet moments that garnered no fanfare—that drew Jackie farther from her father and more toward Hughdie.

After more embraces and affection from her family, Jackie walked the gangplank and joined the other girls from the Smith program. Together with their fellow voyagers, they pressed against the ship's railing while bidding farewell to the cheering crowd.

When the ocean liner blared its horn and began drifting from the dock, Jackie, perched on her tiptoes and waving, knew she would treasure the moment always.

THREE

Unlike a few of her companions, Jackie didn't mind traveling third class aboard the *SS DeGrasse*. For the ten days it would take to sail to France, she could endure the tight living quarters. Being the lone student from Vassar and the fifth girl among the group, she had volunteered to room with a stranger. Such a maneuver would allow her a respite from the others, if needed. Not that she anticipated any disagreements, but with no stables to retreat to, it might afford her a degree of privacy.

Through the years Jackie had grown increasingly aware, perhaps too keenly, that she wasn't like most girls her age. While her classmates at Miss Porter's shared an interest in poetry and fashion, Jackie differed from her peers when it came to suitors, her own education, and, most notably, the sport of gossip. Although never one to shy away from hearing the latest rumors, Jackie noticed girls were quick-to-be-cruel to one another, which taught her that being reserved, even withdrawn at times, proved wise for self-preservation.

Still, in order to be part of the year-long program of study, Jackie knew her propensity for privacy would be challenged. Possibly sacrificed. The trade-off, she reminded herself, would be the freedom of exploring the city she already loved.

In the meantime, she settled her suitcases and belongings in her cabin. Her cabinmate had yet to arrive, so she freshened up and joined the Smith girls. They ate a late lunch together, then she excused herself from the group and explored the ocean liner. A passenger struggling with seasickness reminded her how fortunate she was that the rock and sway of the ocean agreed with her. Always had.

She found an empty row of lounge chairs and settled in with Proust's *In Search of Lost Time,* which she'd snatched from her suitcase before leaving her cabin. Later, as the sun dipped toward the horizon, her attention drifted to a couple standing by the ship's railing. Jackie guessed them to be older than her, though not by much, and judging by their behavior, their closeness and kissing, she suspected they were newlyweds. They peered overboard, watched the ship carve through the ocean and kick up spray, then turned their attention to the seagulls hovering overhead, squawking for food. The couple's simple intimacy, shared smiles, and fingers laced together captivated Jackie.

Though beyond the scope of her recollections, she imagined that her parents had been the same way together. Their love, obvious to onlookers. Words gentle between them. Jackie wondered, where had their relationship gone wrong? Her father had undoubtedly contributed with his unfaithfulness, but before that, when did he lose interest in his wife's adoration?

Trudging the recesses of her mind, Jackie recalled a distant memory of her parents. Janet tucking her in bed and kissing her forehead. Fur from her mother's fox stole brushing her cheek, and the dim light from the hallway glimmering off her mother's long strand of Tahitian pearls—an anniversary gift from her father.

"Daddy and I are going out. Goodnight," Janet had whispered, careful not to wake Lee, sleeping nearby.

Cocktails awaited them at a posh club.

Leaning against the doorway and smoking, her father whispered his affections.

Fear crawled over Jackie and tore her from the memory. She drew her legs up and pulled her knees to her chest. Her arms, now squeezed between her legs, holding her gathered up skirt. Despite the late afternoon warmth, chills ran over Jackie. Did all relationships endure the same course? Starting out with promise and swathed in bliss, only to crumble and create two injured, bickering souls? Like her parents. And like Hughdie, victimized by two failed marriages before he met Janet.

Jackie returned her gaze to the couple at the railing and watched as they kissed.

All men are rats! echoed in her mind.

JACKIE RESISTED GOING to her cabin and giving in to the melancholy that threatened her mood. Instead, she found the ship's office and asked if there was any stationary she could use, since hers was still packed. After her request was fulfilled, she entered a lounge where the lighting was fair and passengers were scant.

Dear Martha,

You wanted every detail. I'm only hours into this journey and already plagued by the advice you gave me on my last night with you. I believe you cautioned me to be flexible with my expectations in a man, correct? Well, for the life of me I cannot even state what expectations I may have. What does one look for in a spouse? What sustains a romance until death do us part? What is the ideal? Honestly, I hadn't given it much thought. Do I search for someone like me, who has at least heard of Byron and knows that Rodin is a sculptor? Someone who has an appreciation for opera, and has a passion for horses that matches my own? Or do I hope for a man who isn't anything like me? Will contrasts and differences guarantee our success? There is much to ponder. That is, if I were in fact interested in finding a husband.

Much love,
Jackie

WHEN SHE RETURNED to her cabin, Jackie found the backside of a portly woman struggling into her girdle. With her rear assets facing the door, the woman hadn't noticed Jackie's entrance. She wiggled and shimmied, withs sighs and grunts resulting as a natural side effect, until the garment was in place. After taking in a deep breath, she heaved the zipper upward and achieved a successful closure. Then she stood for a moment, her arms held out at her sides, and appeared to be testing her breathing against the girdle's seams.

Jackie softly cleared her throat.

"Oh! Lord have mercy!" The woman snatched a piece of clothing and clutched it to her front before spinning around.

"I apologize for startling you." Jackie averted her eyes while the woman pulled a dress over her head. It was a lame apology, she knew if she'd been properly endowed with manners, like every good girl from Miss Porter's should be, she would've slipped back out the door and returned later. But always one for impish adventure, Jackie had forged ahead.

She apologized again, more sincerely, and mentioned that she was her cabinmate.

"Well, I'm only sorry for you, dear girl." Cheeks flushed, the woman put forth an injured smile. "I'm Alice Harrison."

They delicately shook hands and Jackie reciprocated the introduction.

"Traveling alone, dear?"

Jackie explained the Smith program briefly, finishing with, "So I'm spending a year in Paris for my studies."

"That's impressive!" Alice moved and bumped her foot against one of the many suitcases that now occupied the room. "Sorry for the mess, dear. I don't travel often and had no idea what to bring." Her cheeks reddened again as she took stock of the clothes lain about the room.

"A girl needs options."

They traded smiles before pitching in to reorganize the contents of the small cabin room. By the end of it, Alice was winded and dotted with perspiration. She wiped her brow and put on a moss green hat with an arrangement of yellow flowers on its side.

"Should we see about refreshments?" Alice asked.

Jackie realized she'd been staring and quickly agreed.

They headed topside and ventured to the dining saloon where supper was being served. The Smith girls waved for Jackie to join them at their table. After a round of introductions, she and Alice settled in. Cumberland ham, succotash, and mashed potatoes filled their plates. Roll jam pudding awaited for dessert.

"I'm going to see my son, Arnold, in Germany," Alice shared. "He's a soldier and was with the men when they stormed Omaha beach. My Arthur and I are so proud of him." She beamed for a moment, then sighed as somberness moved across her face. "He was injured that day. Lost a leg. He hasn't returned home, not even to recuperate."

"And you haven't seen him since...the injury?" Jackie asked.

Alice shook her head. "I sent telegraphs, letters, but he wouldn't let me come. He's a proud man, you understand, and I think it was enough for him to adjust. Having me there would only complicate things for him. But now he's stronger, and with the weather so fine, I insisted on seeing him. Arthur wanted to come, but his consumption was acting up. But I need to see my boy for myself. I need to take care of him."

Jackie marveled at what their reunion would be like, full of tears and possibly regrets. Alice was a good woman, she believed, and she made Jackie wonder about motherhood. Was it easier being a mother to sons than daughters? Would Janet have been so demanding if she and Lee were boys? From listening to Alice, she wondered if the mother-son relationship was more binding or deeper on some level, the way her own relationship had been with her father over her mother.

And was Arthur too sick to come, or was he struggling with his own feelings of seeing his son so altered?

Jackie could only imagine.

That night, tucked in her upper bunk, she had plenty of time to ruminate on the family dynamics. For just as Alice had proven to be a woman with a caring heart and a fondness for gaudy hats, she also proved to be quite the snorer.

JACKIE FLED the cabin early each morning, both in a desperate mode for coffee and to avoid seeing more of Alice in her delicates. Between Alice's snoring, talking in her sleep, and thumping against the wall of their confines regularly, Jackie had no idea how the woman managed any sleep.

Reading and cat napping on the deck became ritual for Jackie, as did escaping an evening or two into the bowels of the ship. Not only did she befriend the sailors, but she got first-hand knowledge of what their work entailed. Of course, she knew men responded to the flattering attention of a woman, and she used her charms to wiggle her way into their late-night shenanigans of poker and drinking. Besides a sip of whiskey, she didn't participate in their antics. Observation was key, as was maintaining her lady-like composure.

However, she didn't limit herself to mixing with the third-class passengers and the ship's laborers. She lunched daily with the other girls from Smith and participated in a game of shuffleboard or bridge before making her excuses. Jackie was thankful no one seemed perturbed with her slipping off. On more than one occasion she dined in the first-class saloon, where she waltzed with a Persian prince and discussed French poets with a Jewish art collector.

She wrote to Lee and her father, boasting of her adventures, and again promised her father that she had no intention of falling in love with a count—or any other Frenchman for that matter.

The most fantastic impression left on Jackie was the division of the passengers. Money determined how one traveled and navigated in life. She understood Martha's—and Janet's—concerns about finding a husband, considering how his wealth would chart the course for the rest of Jackie's life. If, however, she truly embraced the notion of developing a career, what kind of lifestyle could she possibly carve out on her own? Would being a working woman also ensure that she'd end up a spinster? Worse, she'd be enslaved to a daily routine that wasn't her own design. She shuddered at the thought of being controlled—and from an acute sense of having no control over her destiny.

FOUR

After ten days at sea, the *De Grasse* reached Le Havre, France. Lengthy train rides awaited Jackie and the Smith girls, as they headed to Grenoble for a six-week language emersion course and orientation.

"Well, dear girl," Alice said from where she sat on her bed in the cabin, "you have been a delight. Not sure how I'm going to make it without you."

The cabin had grown cozy with Jackie's books on the dresser, the framed pictures of their loved ones in various places, and the gentle scent of verbena that accessorized the room. Now, their suitcases and treasures tightly packed, a cocktail of anxious excitement stirred within them both for the journeys ahead.

Jackie turned from the mirror, her hair freshly brushed. "I've enjoyed our time together so much." *Well, excluding nighttime in our cabin.* "I wish you weren't traveling alone to Switzerland."

"At least I'll be prepared." Alice held up a hat pin that Jackie had given her. "I had no idea that strange men liked to get handsy on trains."

"On overnight trains, yes. They wait for you to fall asleep."

Alice shook her head in disbelief. "Just terrible!"

Though Jackie didn't share mornings with Alice, a friendship had still forged between them. During their hours spent in the smoking lounge, trading stories about their lives and their families. Jackie had overshared. She poured out her concerns for her father and his reckless lifestyle. Hinted at her fears of the future. Exposed her worries about the never-ending rivalry with Lee. Whatever quirks Alice had were overshadowed by her skill of listening genuinely. Aside from Yusha, and occasionally Lee, Jackie kept emotional matters tucked in her heart. Speaking so freely to Alice had let her experience the merry-go-round of feelings she usually bottled up.

Jackie turned to face her. "I hope your son is well and can make the trip back with you."

"Me too." Alice nodded slowly. "I just hope they haven't ruined him. He was always a wonderful boy, and I'm a bit worried he may be feeling...hopeless. A man needs to feel useful, capable. And not having one of his legs, well, I don't want him to think his life is over."

"Of course it isn't! Why, he's a hero for what he's done. Losing a leg must be awful and difficult, but he has everything to live for. There were so many who died that day, why, he must go on to honor them. And think of all the men who overcame challenges. Winston Churchill had a lisp and a stutter, but he worked tirelessly to improve his public speaking. Your Arnold still has his mind, and with time and your support, he can accomplish anything."

Alice released the breath she'd been holding and smiled. "I'm just so grateful he's alive."

"He'll have so much to tell you, and he'll grow stronger with you near."

"Thank you, Jackie dear. I have a feeling that one day, you're going to make a handsome fella very happy and very proud. Wish I could be there to see it."

Jackie grinned and let her imagination toy with the notion of a proud, handsome husband. She wondered what it would cost her—what sacrifices she would have to make—for such adoration. Was it too much to hope—to dream—of a man who might benefit from and fall in love with who she was rather than what she could give or do for him? She decided the matter was too complex for clear solutions, especially when she had yet to meet a man she could discuss art and history with over coffee.

SITUATED IN SOUTHEASTERN FRANCE, Grenoble welcomed Jackie and her companions with breathtaking views of the French Alps and clear skies painted with wispy clouds. Grenoble, a commune rich in its own history, marked the spot for Napoleon's short-lived comeback, provided the backdrop for the Battle of the Alps, and had become renowned for manufacturing gloves.

Jackie, the Smith girls, and their chaperone settled in at the University of Grenoble, as all thirty-five participants of the program trickled in. Their dorm, an aging château, provided only three temperamental toilets and no heat. Along with wearing the Smith uniform of white-blouse, mauve skirt, and thick bobby socks, the girls had committed to speaking only French. Their days were devoted to indoctrinations of French grammar and phonetics, led by a teacher the girls dubbed Professor Plum, who stank of the pipe tobacco tucked in his cardigan.

Among her fellow students, Jackie favored the friendship of a curly-topped brunette named Beatrice, whom they affectionately dubbed Bea. With an affinity for cherry-red lipstick and unmatched stamina on the dance floor, Bea despised early mornings almost as much as her hair despised humidity. She ebbed along the edges of the group, with the stealth and slink of a panther, and had a knack for plucking Jackie from the group for a quick smoke exactly when a conversation teetered on boredom. She observed more than she participated and lacked that over-eager quality of making friends. Her sly mannerisms and rarely shared but against-the-grain opinions drew Jackie in.

"What a disgusting lout." Bea entered Jackie's dorm without knocking and plopped onto Jackie's bed, which responded with a sharp squeak. A week into their new routine, she had made a habit of joining Jackie in her room after dinner. Invited or not. "Such nerve and no manners!"

Sitting at her desk, Jackie couldn't resist smirking—and wondering if the same could be said about Bea, on occasion. "You've mentioned that. Every night, I believe, since the class started."

"Of all books for us to read aloud, *Madame Bovary* is his pick? You know he's enjoying some deranged pleasure out of it. Along with telling us to roll our tongues more and how to perk and pucker our mouths." She rolled her hand and exaggerated her French.

"Some men are naughty romantics." Jackie closed her book and set it aside.

"No, he's filthy. But I loved the way you handled him in class the other day. We all did. You stood up there and read, trying to sound just like him and mimicking that condescending tone of his. It was a riot!"

"He was the only one who didn't laugh." Jackie prided herself on causing the mild disruption, even though the joke was lost on their teacher.

"Professor Plum is a windbag." Bea propped Jackie's pillow against the wall and gave it a light punch before she leaned her back into it. "I'm no prude, but a horny-toad like that has no business having a classroom of girls as his captive audience."

Jackie agreed but felt no need to belabor the point. "Only a few more weeks, then we're off to Paris."

Bea blew raspberries with her lips as she sighed. "Oh, I almost forgot. The real reason I popped in. Miss Langley is taking us to Sassenage. Not far from here. You might want to pack a bag with a change of clothes. She says there's a grotto and a quaint restaurant we must see."

Jackie gave a half-hearted shrug. "Should be a nice break from reading about Emma and Rodolphe panting on each other."

Bea fell face forward onto the bed and muffled her groan.

THOUGH JACKIE SPENT the most time with Beatrice, she felt at ease among the group of young women. Back home, a palpable competition existed whenever she was around girls her age. From horse shows to the debutante and society scenes, girls were in a fierce pursuit. Driven by an athletic hunger for blue ribbons or the lioness stealth and cunning that infected women on the hunt for a husband, women were wary of other women. Jackie's abundance of talents and beauty posed her as a threat in East Hampton.

But not here, not among these women. Freedom from their normal lives bonded them. So did their eagerness for knowledge and adventure. Jackie reflected on this, along with how her new friends viewed her as daring and mischievous. Her own doing—which she loved—though it was still her nature to hold back personal parts of herself. Jackie had written a poem about the cold château floors against her feet and had drawn half a dozen cartoons featuring Professor Plum. She painted the landscape a dozen times in her mind and practiced in her sketch pad. Some days, a terrible pang of homesickness struck, where she missed the smell of the tack room and the glint in Danseuse's eyes when she entered the stable. None of which she'd shared with the girls or Bea.

Sassenage, a hamlet nestled into the base of the Alps, mirrored Grenoble with its countryside charm and beauty. Miss Anita Langley, the girls' chaperone, led them into the cave with a flashlight and unbridled excitement. They wound their way around rock formations the underground river had carved, careful not to slip, and on the lookout for cave spiders Miss Langley warned them about.

At the end of the path, the girls enjoyed returning to what was left of the sun-bathed afternoon. Warm temperatures kept their teeth from chattering as they dried and refreshed. Miss Langley escorted them to a nearby restaurant, which featured most of its seating outside next to a softly rolling waterfall and stream with moss-covered rocks. Trees canopied most of the patio while the aroma of fresh-bake croissants lured them to their seats.

"Ladies, have any of you heard the tale of Melusine?" Miss Langley asked, once they were settled and napkins draped across their laps.

The girls shook their heads.

"Well, I can't say I know all the particulars, but legend has it that Melusine is a mermaid-like creature who lives in the grottos here in Sassenage. She appears to be a woman like any other. Beautiful and refined, but when she takes a bath, her mermaid tale appears. When she married, she made her husband promise not to look in on her while she bathed, but he didn't keep his word. So she had to flee to protect her secret, and now she resides in the caves and is always changing from one form into another."

"That's not so hard to believe, is it?" Bea said after a beat of silence. "Men are lousy at keeping promises."

Laughter erupted, and it was then that Jackie noticed him.

A man, sitting alone at a table tucked closest to the waterfall. Judging by his confident poise, Jackie guessed he was several years older than her, and thought he had the look of a man well-educated and traveled. His coal-black hair and olive skin tone reminded her of the Romanian gypsies she'd seen in the region. Bangs had slipped from his pomade-style and curtained his eyes—which were fixed and intense on Jackie.

She pretended not to notice but her body reacted to his weighty stare. Hairs on the back of her neck stood and her pulse tapped out the Fox Trot inside her chest.

"A bit harsh, Bea." Jackie sipped from her cup. "I'm sure there are men who can stick to a promise."

"Maybe. But telling a man not to peek and then stepping into the next room to take a tub, that's just setting him up."

Miss Langley blushed the deepest among the group and whispered Bea's name.

"You have a point there," said another girl. "Men are endowed with weaknesses when it comes to women and nudity."

"Ladies, please!" Miss Langley straightened. "This is hardly a suitable topic for dinnertime conversation."

"But, Miss Langley, you brought it up." Jackie served her remark with a playful grin.

"Perhaps to my regret." She returned the gesture.

Bea gave that deep laugh of hers that bordered on maniacal. "Can you imagine if that were ol' Professor Plum"—she held up her napkin as if to cover her chest—"and his wife told him don't come in, don't look at me? Why, he'd have the hinges off in a snap."

"Oh, please don't mention Plum before we eat."

Their raking continued as Jackie's eyes wandered back to her admirer. His stare still held. A corner of his mouth tugged upward as Jackie locked eyes with him. She pictured herself leaving the girls and joining him. How she wished to slip into the seat across from him, ask him if he was with the gypsies and if he'd heard the story of Melusine and what he thought of men and their weaknesses...

"Jackie."

She turned to Bea, who was patting her forearm.

"Come on, let's dance!" Bea took her by the hand.

Jackie followed as Artie Shaw and his orchestra flowed from the radio. She stole a glance over her shoulder and caught a glimpse of the man raising his glass, as if toasting her.

By the time she and the other girls returned to their seats, the man was gone. Disappointment pinched Jackie, until she saw two sprigs of lavender resting on her chair. A swift scan of the patio confirmed he was nowhere to be found. As the others sat, she realized hers was the only chair with a token on it. Of course, she couldn't know for certain that the man was toying or teasing or flirting with her, but she savored the notion. Jackie inhaled the flowers and for once in her life regretted playing coy and virtuous.

She sighed. *Wait till I tell Martha.*

September 1949

AFTER THE SIX-WEEK intensive in Grenoble finished, Jackie's French could almost pass her for a native. No one cared for Professor Plum's sendoff: *Au revoir, mes beauties*. The girls replied with muffled snickers and deadpan farewells.

Jackie had kept an eye out for her admirer but didn't see him again. At times, she wondered if she'd imagined the whole thing. A fiercely attractive man, alone in a picturesque setting. The gallop of her heart under his intense stare. Then she recalled finding the lavender, its intoxicating scent wooing her effortlessly. No, she hadn't imagined him. But when she boarded the train for Paris, she accepted that she'd be leaving him behind. Wasn't that what made fleeting moments memorable, the fact that they were fleeting, extemporaneous, and never meant to be substantial? She fed on such thoughts during the five-hour commute.

Most of Jackie's classmates were set to room at Reid Hall, but Janet wouldn't hear of her daughter living in a porcelain factory-turned dormitory. Through her social threads, Janet had learned that the de Renty family of Paris hosted exchange students. Discovering they also held titles of nobility gave Janet the peace of mind—and bragging rights—she craved.

The Jasmin metro stop delivered Jackie to a public square across from her host family's apartment building. She took in the Parisian air, a thick bouquet of baked goods, smoke, and coffee. Located on the western rim of the city in the 16th arrondissement, the Montparnasse neighborhood featured a newsstand, grocer, café, butcher, and dress shop. Each storefront would likely become familiar to her.

Armed with her satchel and traveling case, Jackie approached the seven-story building that she'd call home for the next several months. Constructed of glazed, seafoam-green bricks and with a nod to art nouveau architecture, 78 Mozart Avenue appeared untouched by the war. She suspected the same couldn't be said of its inhabitants. After snatching another breath of the late-September breeze, she headed to the second-floor apartment.

"*Bonjour!* You must be Jacqueline!" came the friendly greeting after she rang the bell. "Welcome! Come in."

Jackie, offering her thanks, entered the parlor. Along with the middle-aged woman opening the door, two younger women and a toddler awaited her.

"I am Guyot de Renty, and these are my girls, Ghislaine and Claude."

Madame de Renty resembled Queen Victoria in Jackie's opinion, stout in figure but regal in stature. Her gray-and-white streaked hair styled in a low chignon, she radiated a winsome presence that engulfed Jackie in comfort. "Oh, and this is my grandson, Christian. He's Ghislaine's." In a lowered tone she added, "Ghislaine is divorced, left a troublesome marriage, and it wouldn't do to have them anywhere but here."

With Christian tucked on her hip, Ghislaine regarded Jackie and nodded hello. Her silence and stone-like expression appeared to be a warning not to judge her situation. Jackie understood. Though she formed no immediate opinion on the matter, she didn't mind the work ahead of earning Ghislaine's friendship.

Ghislaine's somber face contrasted against her son's bright blue eyes. With his head against his mother's chest, he waved shyly to Jackie. When she smiled and waved back, he received it like a shot of adrenaline, popping his head up and smiling wide. His sudden cheer and tiny voice as he exclaimed *"Your coat has big buttons!"* stirred an ache in Jackie for her little brother Jamie. Christian slid from his mother's hold and Jackie knelt so he could fiddle with the buttons while she traded pleasantries with Ghislaine and Claude. Jackie adored his curious energy and hugged him before he returned to his mother and waved goodbye as Ghislaine excused herself.

"Now, then, we should review the rules of the house." Madame de Renty clasped her hands together. "First of all, we share household duties, from tending to the wash to meals. Each week responsibilities rotate. Also, I prefer no smoking in the house, although I know it's fashionable for you young people. And Sunday means church. No exceptions. The rest, well, we'll figure it out as we go along. Are you agreeable, my dear?"

"Of course." Despite what most would consider a posh upbringing, Jackie wasn't new to hard work. During World War II, Hammersmith Farm had become a primary source for chickens, vegetables, and dairy products to the local naval base and military outposts in Newport. With most of the household servants and gardeners placed on hiatus, Jackie took on the responsibilities of mowing the lawn and feeding two thousand cranky chickens. When she wasn't weeding endlessly, she also collected eggs and gathered baskets of apples. Having chores at the de Rentys' didn't faze her. It meant a deeper sense of belonging to the family.

"I'll show you to our room." Claude took Jackie's traveling case and nodded for her to follow.

Our room? Jackie said nothing but darted a glance toward Madame.

"Oh, yes, I should mention that we've had a slight change in plans."

She rubbed her hands together slowly, as if the impending news were uncomfortable to share. "I'm afraid I overbooked. When I traded correspondence with your mother, months ago, I stated that we had a room for you, but things being what they are...well, economics being the way they are, and rooms hard to come by in the city these days... well, I was able to rent a room for more than double, so—"

"There's no need to explain." Jackie forced a smile, as she equally disliked discussing money. "Sharing a room is fine." She looked to Claude and hoped that settled the matter.

Claude shrugged her indifference. "Come on, then."

She led Jackie down a narrow hallway, past another parlor, dining room, water closet, and the kitchen.

"I hope you like it." Claude beamed and opened the door with dramatic flair.

Each side of the room had built-in drawers. Two beds with nightstands were separated by the slender floor to ceiling doors that opened to a Juliet balcony. Waning afternoon sunlight crept in and highlighted the peeling edges of the wallpaper. A Victorian-style dresser with a mirror and rug completed the space. Claude placed Jackie's traveling case atop a perfectly smoothed cover.

"No closets?"

"Oh, Mother said we could do this." Claude took a roll of twine out of a drawer and strung it between two hooks that were already screwed into the wall. "It might not hold much, but it should help."

"Very clever. It will work well. Thank you." Jackie took her travel case and removed a blouse she'd forced into one of the pockets. Hardly recognizable in its wrinkled state, Jackie put it on a hanger and then hung it on the line. "*Violà!*"

They laughed and Jackie continued unpacking. When the latches of her travel case clicked open, Claude eagerly peered inside. Jackie showed her the cold creams and lotions she'd brought. "You're welcome to use them, though I imagine Paris has better offerings."

"You have such nice things." Claude removed Jackie's hairbrush, a gift from her father after his travels to Cuba. She went to the mirror and ran the brush through her soft, sandy curls. "We don't usually host students who are...so well off." Claude stopped brushing and held the brush as if she'd been caught using it without permission. "I'm sorry we had to room together. I promise not to bother your things."

"It's fine." Jackie had already decided the matter wasn't worth a fuss, though Claude's nervous-excited energy made her a bit dizzy.

"Mother didn't tell you, but she's a countess."

"That's thrilling." Jackie already knew from Janet but liked hearing it from Claude.

"Mmm. We sacrificed much of our furnishings during the occupation. It was difficult on Mother, with Father and all. I think she can't help blaming herself...you know, for things she can't change, things she can't control." Claude set the hairbrush on the dresser. "Anyway, it's good that you're here. It helps distract Mother from being sad all the time." She smiled apologetically, as if she feared she'd said too much.

"I've read how terrible the occupation was. I know that can't compare to what you lived through."

"Ghislaine and I were sent to the country and stayed with relatives when things got bad. It seems like so long ago and like yesterday all at the same time. Everything's dirty now and meats are still rationed, but no one cares too much about that. No more curfew or soldiers mocking us in the streets...or people being taken away. That's what's important." Claude cast a glance toward a small, framed photo on her nightstand. She wiped the corner of her eye, leading Jackie to assume it was a picture of Claude's father. "You must also learn to ignore Ghislaine. It is true, what Mother said about her marriage being troublesome, but I know they are both embarrassed about the divorce. It's not an easy situation for a woman, and Ghislaine takes it hard."

Jackie could've mentioned that her own mother had endured similar circumstances, only with two children in tow, but the timing didn't feel right.

"I think you'll like the Sorbonne." Claude brightened as she switched topics. "I've attended there. Right now I'm at the Institut d'etudes politiques. We call it Sciences Po for short."

"That's impressive." Jackie didn't know if that were true but felt as if Claude needed the minor validation.

"You'll love the Sorbonne. The Grand Amphi is breathtaking, but the lectures are the worst. Always an hour long and always boring."

Jackie laughed softly.

"Do you smoke?"

Before Jackie could answer, Claude retrieved a pack of cigarettes and a book of matches from a dresser drawer. She lit one and opened the double doors. Though the balcony only provided enough room for two, Jackie joined Claude in the fresh air. This side of the de Rentys' apartment offered a view of only the building next door and the alley in between them.

"She's not opposed to it, not entirely." The breeze dissipated Claude's puff of smoke. "Mother worries that smoking irritates Christian." She shrugged. "I don't know if she's right. Maybe Christian is just a cranky boy. The key to it is not to smoke around her, and to keep the smoke outside."

Jackie was equal parts taken aback and comforted. Although she wasn't anxious to disrespect Madame de Renty's rules, she didn't mind skirting around the smoking ban. Just like she'd done at Miss Porter's.

As she lit her own cigarette, the fact she wouldn't have her own room sunk in. Briefly, she wondered how private her time in the water closet would be. But setting that irritation aside, she felt good about the de Rentys. Mining through their family history would require compassion and patience, as would revealing her own true self, but for now, her only worry was whether or not she could keep up with Claude's ever-shifting mood and mischief.

Surely a lifetime of living with Lee has prepared me well.

THAT EVENING, Madame de Renty commenced dinner with, "Tell us about your family, Jacq-kleen."

Jackie immediately adored hearing her name pronounced by a native Parisian. *Jacq-kleen* sounded posh, regal even. She flushed, both from being the center of attention and from the thought of explaining her complex family dynamic.

"We're a rather large brood." Echoing her father's intended insult amused her. "There's nine of us."

"My! Your poor mother! Wash day must be interminable." Madame de Renty patted Ghislaine on the wrist, then laughed. Ghislaine, tending to Christian's plate, gave no response or reaction. "Living here will be quite the holiday, then."

"Absolutely, and I can't thank you enough—"

"Now, I must warn you not to romanticize Paris, as Americans so often do. The war has left its mark. Everything is still covered in soot—and you must remember to keep scraps of paper in your pockets. Most public restrooms have no toilet paper! But"—she held up a finger—"life is returning to normal. Museums are open—with most of their artwork recovered, and I have yet to see an American soldier who isn't handsome."

"Mother!" Ghislaine protested, though barely above a whisper.

Madame de Renty continued, praising the French for their resilience and mentioning some sights she planned to take Jackie to see. Jackie wondered, as she sipped vichyssoise and nodded agreeably at the right moments, if her host mother preferred dominating the conversation or if it was a tick of nervous energy. Either way, she relished Madame's vivaciousness.

No direct mention of Monsieur de Renty occurred. However, when Madame spoke of her noble countrymen—such valiant men—her stare grew distant. Christian's squeal broke her from the heavy mood, and nothing more was said. All Jackie knew about Monsieur, again from Janet, was that he'd died in the war.

"May we be excused?" Claude had waited till the meal was over and Madame stood to brew a fresh pot of coffee. "I'd like to take Jackie for a quick jaunt, show her around a bit."

Ghislaine sent Jackie a disapproving glare.

"Shouldn't we take care of the dishes first?" Jackie had no intention of shirking her newly assigned duties, if that's what had Ghislaine riled.

Madame's hearty laugh returned. "Young people. Always so eager to explore. Yes, my dears, off with you."

"But—"

Madame shooed her. "Go, dear. I may not be so agreeable in the morning."

Claude took Jackie by the hand and led her down the stairs—wasting no time on the elevator—and out onto the streets of Montparnasse. They crossed over the Seine and hailed a cab, which they rode to Le Select, a café swollen with patrons and vibrating from the jazz music within. Over cigarettes and ginger ales, they discussed their favorite music and hobbies, and each shared a sample of what their day-to-day was like. Jackie told Claude about Danseuse and learned that Claude loved riding but wasn't very skilled. She offered to give Claude tips if they ever went riding, but guilt squeezed her chest as she remembered the promise to her father that she wouldn't ride.

After drinks, they walked to Reid Hall, where Jackie reconnected with a few classmates, including Bea, and introduced them to Claude. Together, the women walked the university grounds and found the buildings where their classes would be held. Then, with the evening set in and the late hour, Jackie suggested returning home.

Once the other girls had left for the dormitory, Claude turned to Jackie with a glint in her eyes. "Are you up for an adventure?"

"I think so." Jackie drew out her answer, curious but uncertain as to what Claude had in mind.

Taking Jackie's hand again, Claude led them down Rue Saint-Jacques to the Latin Quarter. They kept going until the liveliness and ample lighting had faded, and before long, the mouth-covering stench of refuse welcomed them into an area that unsettled Jackie.

"What are we doing here?" She asked, barely above a whisper.

Without a reply, Claude jerked Jackie into the covered doorway of a darkened building. They hung back in the shadows a few minutes, then Claude peeked around the corner and waved for Jackie to join her.

"Look."

About half a block away, three women ambled near a street corner.

She swallowed hard.

"You aren't planning to—"

"Heavens, no!" Claude said. "I just think it's strange and tragic and fascinating to watch. These same three girls are here every night, and they can't be much older than fifteen. You could say this is their territory. I've seen others, but they never last. It's always these three. Darla, Mila, and Fifi."

"You *know* them?"

"Of course not! I named them for fun. Darla's a runaway from Russia, she's saving up money to head to America. Mila, she's an orphan, lost all her family in the war, has nothing. And Fifi, she's here just to spite her mom, but she attends church regular. Isn't that a riot?"

Jackie thought of Lee, always frustrated with life and eager to flirt with rebellion. Though for Lee, rebellion meant forgetting to wear her gloves or making the family late to an engagement. A healthy fear of her mother kept her in line.

Though Jackie had no intention of mentioning it, she and Yusha occasionally snuck off to a bar in Newport's red-light district. Not that Newport's seedy side could compare to a Paris slum, but Jackie had tested her flirting with the intoxicated naval officers, even practiced using a sultry voice. At the moment, such brazenness escaped her.

"Do you do this often?" Standing on the step above Claude, she couldn't see her face.

"Depends on what you call often."

"You haven't ever...tried this, have you?"

"Lord sakes, no! There wouldn't be enough forgiveness in Our Lady of the Assumption. Not to mention what my mother would do to me." Claude stared at the girls, quite for a beat. "Still, I wonder what *really* makes them do it."

"Desperation, I would think."

"Probably. Would you ever?"

"Of course not!"

"Not even for one night? I mean, what if it was like a good thing-bad thing. Say you could earn one million dollars, the good thing. But you had to do it, be a prostitute for a whole night, the bad thing. Would you do it?"

Once again, Jackie wasn't sure what answer Claude wanted. Was she provoked by a genuine curiosity, or was she attempting to flush out a character flaw in Jackie? This was one reason why she found women friends difficult. She understood the art of give and take but had no desire to expose her raw emotional side so soon.

Jackie rested her cheek against the building's stone. "Maybe for a hundred million."

Claude's eyes boggled. "Expensive girl!"

"You'd want to be sure, wouldn't you? That you'd never have to worry about money again. Isn't that the point?"

Claude conceded with a tip of her head to the side. "We'd better scat then, before someone makes you that offer."

They crouched and clasped hands as they scurried back the direction they came. Near Le Select, they hopped into a cab for the short ride home.

Concern stewed in Jackie. Had she traded Lee's dramatics for Claude's reckless behavior? Was she expected to be responsible for Claude in some way, if things went awry? Or was she just overreacting?

Regardless, Jackie ached for Claude. While she had tended the Rhode Island Red hens and helped run Hammersmith Farm during the war, Claude and Ghislaine had been sent away from home and forced to wade in the tide of not-knowing. Not knowing what would become of their home, their country, their parents. Eventually welcomed home by devastation. Jackie surmised that surviving—like Alice's son and the de Rentys—came at its own price.

Perhaps Claude's antics, frazzled and misguided as they were, revealed an attempt to recover from the loss of her father. Jackie couldn't fault her for that, and it pained her she had no immediate comfort or solution to offer. She determined to be there for Claude, best she could. Simultaneously, trepidation breathed down Jackie's neck. Who knew how risky—or risqué—Claude would be?

She stared out the window of the cab. *Less than a day in and it's not the Paris I envisioned.*

FIVE

Though Jackie and Claude slipped inside the apartment noiselessly, the steady grind of the grandfather clock announced the unsightly hour. A pathetic notion of victory stirred in Jackie's chest—until a light flared from the parlor. The girls startled at the sight of Madame de Renty sitting near a window that faced the street, a pocket watch cradled in her palm.

She snapped the timepiece closed and raised her stare to the girls.

"The test of good manners is to be able to put up pleasantly with bad ones." Madame, wearing a rosy smirk, shrugged. "Or so the saying goes."

"Sorry, Mother," Claude piped. "It's all my fault."

"Claude, I think it's best for you to head to your room. I'd like to speak with Miss Bouvier alone."

Claude's shoulders hung like wet towels on a hook and she held her hands behind her back. She passed Jackie a look of sympathy, then disappeared into the unlit hallway.

Jackie maintained her posture without appearing defensive.

Madame remained silent until Claude was out of earshot. "Please, dear, join me." She gestured to a chair across from her. As Jackie sat, Madame poured a small glass of sherry.

Jackie passed on the offer to join her.

"That one is like her sister." Madame hooked a nod in Claude's direction. "Anxious to prove she's grown, yet she has no real idea what it means. And you see what state her sister's in."

She nipped her sherry while Jackie kept quiet.

"It was my father's." Madame caressed the pocket watch with her thumb.

"Oh." A weak pip, Jackie thought, but felt it was better than silence.

"That's a lie. It's a tawdry watch next to the one my father owned. His was made with real gold. This one," she palmed it like a small rock, ready to hurl, "is pewter. You see, when the Nazis came, they ravaged our belongings, took what they wanted. The girls, they were lucky. We got them out of the city in time." Madame sighed heavily. "Has Claude spoken of her father?"

"Not directly, ma'am." Jackie thought of the gloom that passed across Claude's face earlier when she glimpsed her father's portrait on the nightstand.

"Robert and I were deported. That was their word for it. Of course, the Jews were treated much worse. Inhumanely, really, like defective animals. I overheard one guard say they were only fit for extermination. Another word the invaders favored." She slipped the watch into a pocket of her housecoat. "Eventually, the *Boche* came for those of us working against them."

Jackie recognized the slang term for the Germans.

"It was only a matter of time, before we were found out. Robert and I were part of the Resistance, working as spies for the British government. When they deported us to Ravensbruck, I expected we'd both be killed upon arrival. Some days, I wished that had been the case." With her lips pressed and her eyes downcast, she reflected silently for a moment. "They separated us instead. Robert was moved to Dora, a slave labor camp and forced to work on an underground missile factory. He lasted four months. I think he lost hope of ever seeing us again—of ever seeing France free. I forgave him for that, for loving us too much."

She tilted her head back and finished the sherry. Perhaps it was also a means to roll back the tears in her eyes.

"Since the war, I've not been the disciplinarian I once was. Not without my Robert. I wouldn't want you to think I'm a poor mother, not scolding my girl for coming home in the dead of night." She paused, then twiddled her fingers as if she missed holding the watch. "Claude needs a gentle hand for now, and I hope, dear Jacqueline, you'll bear in mind what she's been through—Ghislaine, too—before you're apt to think harshly of them."

"I understand," Jackie said, though unsure if more of an answer was necessary.

With that, Madame de Renty told her she could turn in for the night. Jackie's first instinct was to head for her room and put the evening behind her, but she turned to her host.

"May I call you Countess?"

Even by the dim lamp light, Jackie could see the corners of Madame's lips curl.

"Whatever title you think fits best, my dear."

Madame had lost enough. No need for her title to be robbed from her as well. Jackie kept those thoughts to herself and instead—gave a slight curtsey. "Good night, Countess."

AS MUCH AS Jackie despised the poor impression she'd made on the countess that night, it dwindled—she hoped—in the flurry of activity that became her new Parisian life. With Claude resuming her classes at Sciences Po as well, academics became the life and breath of the apartment. Upon attending her first lecture, Jackie found Claude's assessment of the Sorbonne spot-on. The professor was formally introduced, then sat in a plush chair, center stage, and read from his notes for an hour. The only saving graces for Jackie were the rich architecture of the amphitheatre and the *polycopies*, full transcriptions of the lectures, available to students in the bookstore.

The other student-boarders the countess had rented Jackie's room to ended up changing their plans. Timidly, the countess queried Jackie as to whether or not she minded her arrangement with Claude, to which Jackie replied she was perfectly fine with. The countess relaxed and explained how much easier life would be if Ghislaine and Christian were to use the room instead of bunking with her. Jackie made no objections, and quietly hoped her agreeableness might garner her a bit of favor with Ghislaine.

Delight surged through Jackie on the evening of her first art class École des Beaux-Arts. As she settled on a stool and at an easel near the front of the room, the anticipation made her near-giddy. Painting had long been one of her passions, one of her strengths, even though she had yet to create a rendering of Danseuse that she treasured. Hope simmered within her. For what could elevate her talents more than an art class in Paris?

Samples of various mediums adorned the room—clay, charcoal sketches, acrylic paintings—making Jackie squeal inwardly that she'd soon be working with each of them. A hint of turpentine in the air made her forget she was in a classroom setting and gave her the feel of a genuine artisan studio.

When the instructor arrived, a navy wool beret snug and angled around his head, class began with two stiff claps of his hands. He sailed through his introduction with sharp, well-pronounced French and hands that never stopped moving. Jackie strained to keep up and thought he spoke of how he refused to adhere to traditional teaching methods, that he encouraged them to be quick studies, and to embrace his unconventional methods.

Another clap-clap resounded in the room like thunder. Jackie's fellow students readied their easels and supplies. She followed suit and enjoyed a warm rush, seeing no one else that she recognized. Convinced she would thrive and excel at each assignment, she welcomed a deep breath in.

But then her confidence drained, along with the rosy warmth that anticipation had brought to her face, when a familiar-looking man entered the room. It was him—the stranger who had played coy with her, teased her even, and left the tender bouquet of lavender on her chair at the restaurant in Sassenage.

Mere seconds lapsed before his eyes found Jackie. No obvious emotion played out on his face, but she felt certain she detected a hidden smirk. Heat flashed through her, and for an instant, because of his lack of reaction, she thought she was wrong. Was this the man her eyes had flirted with, though only for the briefest of moments? An intense gaze at his teal-gray eyes and recognition of his sharp, prominent nose assured Jackie this was indeed the man of her fleeting desire.

He perched on the pedestal in the middle of the room. It was at that moment Jackie realized the man was wearing a brown robe. Bare, stubby toes pointed her way. His hair hung as loose and free as his demeanor. With his gaze still locked on Jackie, he untied the robe and let it drop over the stool. He planted one foot on the white tile floor and rested his other foot against a rung beneath his seat. Whether to taunt Jackie or simply for the sake of comfort, he opened his legs, probably farther than necessary, and placed a hand on each thigh. Then he tweaked a corner of his mouth upward to complete his pose.

The now-familiar clap-clap rang out again. The instructor advised the class to paint what they felt and assured them there was no wrong technique. His words became lost in the jumble of Jackie's mind as he instructed the students to begin.

Jackie had seen a man—men—nude before, not that she cared for the recollection or that it dulled the sensations currently roaring through her. But it lessened the shock. At least, that's what she told herself.

She relied on short, shallow breaths to maintain her focus and steady her hand. Two attempts and an inner scolding were required. Slowly, she committed brushstrokes to paper and tamped down the chorus of questions ringing through her head. How had he ended up in Paris—in her class? Had he followed her? She refused to allow the chance-circumstance—the absurdity of it all—to mar her efforts.

It meant nothing. She chanted it silently. Wished the mantra would sink in as she curved her brush to copy the man's muscular legs. She moved on to his perfect, perfect...Jackie dipped her brush into the jar of water at her easel. Stirred it too furiously but not enough for others to notice. The room seemed to tilt, and she fought back the ballooning feel of indignity—or was it lust?

She peeked around the side of her easel, determined to rein in her overreactions, and soaked up his naked form with her eyes. He parted his lips, which gave the impression he was blowing a kiss in slow motion. Jackie bit her bottom lip and urged her resolve to remain constant. Perspiration threatened—which was foreign to a debutant who'd been taught how to play badminton without producing a drop of sweat. She knew, even though a word had never passed between them, that he was caught up in the imagination of Jackie being naked. When she dared to imagine their flesh touching, lightening flashed before her, and she was grateful the gasp she felt didn't escape her mouth and into the room.

WHEN THE CLASS FINISHED, Jackie concentrated on cleaning and organizing her supplies. Furiously, again. By the time her attention returned to the room, she found no sign of the man.

The instructor congratulated everyone on work well-done and proclaimed the class dismissed. The hand claps followed.

Jackie huffed, an unladylike move for one of Miss Porter's caliber, but she couldn't shake being perturbed. That man, strikingly handsome as he was, had compromised her work. Appearing here and there, never speaking to her yet eager to bait her with meaningless flirtations. Now, she risked her talents being viewed as average, all because of her failed self-control.

If she ever saw that man again and spoke to him, she vowed to tell him that she was never speaking to him again.

Dear Yusha,

A few weeks in my Paris home and I have carved out two lives—flying from the de Rentys' to the Sorbonne and Reid Hall, in a lovely, quiet rainy world—or, like a maid on her day off, putting on a fur coat and going to town and being swanky at the Ritz. I like the first part best, as

I have an absolute mania now about speaking French perfectly. We never speak a word of English in the apartment, and I don't see many Americans apart from the university. Lectures on existentialism and French Communism are popular and never-ending.

Would you believe I'm taking a class on International Relations since 1870? The hour might drag if it weren't for our professor. He lost an arm in World War I and delivers his speeches the way I imagine Teddy Roosevelt might—with a passionate sternness. It comes as no surprise, but there are so many writers and artists here! I've shared coffee with a few. Such divine company! Please tell me you're looking after Danseuse and Lee. She doesn't write often, but I know that's her style.

Much love,
Jackie

SIX

Claude ran into the kitchen the next morning, waving an envelope the way an injured bird might flap its healthy wing, in a desperate attempt to escape a crouching cat.

"It's come, Mother! The invitation to the de Ganays' autumn ball!"

Ghislaine and Jackie, prepping vegetables, wiped their hands and joined Claude at the table as she handed the envelope to her mother. Christian, who'd been playing on the floor, stood and curiously peered over the tabletop at the women as the countess ripped into the correspondence.

"Did you say the de Ganay family?" Jackie asked. "I know them! One of their cousins is a dear friend back home. We've been sailing together and attend the same summer parties."

"How wonderful!" The countess withdrew the invite and read it aloud. "*Mon Dieu!* It's the day after tomorrow!"

"The post must be late in delivering again." Claude and her mother shared a moment of exasperation while Ghislaine, aside from a twitch of her brow, didn't bother with a reaction.

"Does that mean you won't have enough time to RSVP?" Jackie asked.

The countess laughed. "Everyone invited is *expected* to attend, my dear. Few circumstances exist that would keep one from the de Ganays' autumn ball. The challenge will be in finding a proper dress. There won't be time for alterations. Which reminds me, have you an outfit for such an occasion, dear?"

"Yes. I brought several formal dresses."

The countess traded glances with her daughters.

"That's fine, dear." She tucked the invite back into its ripped sheath.

Jackie sensed their doubt. "Should I try one on then, see if it's fitting for the ball?"

The ladies agreed. Jackie dashed to her room and soon returned in a satin navy gown that cascaded to her ankles. The de Rentys' silence gave her all the criticism she needed. Jackie sighed with disappointment.

"It's a lovely dress," the countess said, "but it's not grand enough for the party. The de Ganays are one of the most prominent families in France. Their autumn ball is the social equivalent of Bastille Day. This will be your debut into the highest castes of French society, my dear." She shot a mournful glance over Jackie's dress. "Are you certain you want to enter the Château de Courances wearing this?"

Doubt rarely clouded Jackie's mind when it came to her wardrobe. Though her confidence in her current ensemble wasn't entirely shaken, she was disappointed when the countess addressed her daughter.

"Claude, perhaps she could wear one of your old dresses."

"Of course! Let's see!" Claude led the charge to a hallway closet and plucked out a garment from deep within. She held up a rumpled peach chiffon frock and shook it out. "Want to try it?"

Jackie ignored the tightness in her throat as she eyed the dress. Had she ever worn peach? With no other recourse—or reason to outright reject the offer—she agreed to the change. In the bedroom, Jackie wiggled into the bodice while Claude pulled and tucked until every piece of material lay in place.

"There." Claude stepped back and examined Jackie head to toe.

"Do you think it will work?" Jackie could accept the color, for one night anyway.

Claude shook her head, smiling. "When the beaux get a look at you, another war might break out over who gets to fill your dance card. You're sure to capture the attention of every man in attendance."

Jackie checked herself in the bedroom mirror. Admiration for the floor-length gown didn't overcome her like she hoped, but Claude's bright eyes and smile sealed her commitment to the dress. Not that she shared Claude's prediction about capturing hearts and dance partners. Such thoughts made her insides tremble. Her desire to be part of the crowd, to learn from hanging back and observing, seemed to be slipping away.

She let it go. More importantly, she joined Claude in the joy of the moment—and the excitement of attending her first Parisian ball. Tomorrow, Jackie would wire her father and Grampy for more money, citing that funds were needed for a new dress. Chances were fair that they both might admonish her spending, but worse was the notion of wearing more of Claude's hand-me-downs. For all Jackie knew, Claude had a burlap evening dress that might be considered suitable stuffed in that closet.

COUNTESS DE RENTY had not exaggerated in describing the de Ganays' estate. Formally known as the Château de Courances, due to its location, a tree-lined roadway led visitors to the four-story Louis XIII-style structure. A horseshoe-shaped staircase at the home's entrance allowed for a smooth flow of the guests' arrival. Buildings flanked the main house and created the feel of an exaggerated courtyard. Water contributed much to the home's design with a moat, a large reflecting pool in the rear, fountains throughout the gardens, and a canal farther back on the property.

"Such an interesting history, the de Ganays," the countess said. "Thankfully, the château and the family survived the Nazis. They took over the château for several years, used it as a base for their *Luftwaffe*." She huffed. "The de Ganays have been an influential family for as long as anyone can remember. They belong to the Jockey Club and the country club in Saint-Cloud but are perhaps most noted for being counselors to kings." She nodded toward the château as their car approached it. "Shows, doesn't it?"

Once inside, they were soon greeted by their host, Paul de Ganay, and his family. Though Jackie could only recall meeting him two or three times in Newport, she recognized him immediately. A few years older than Jackie, his plump cheeks and boyish features enhanced when he smiled. He greeted Jackie warmly and asked after his cousin. The de Renty women held back and beamed proudly. Jackie suspected they were already envisioning the two as a couple—and taking small delight in bringing them together.

As Jackie and Paul spoke, another young man approached and cupped his hand onto Paul's shoulder.

"Smashing party as always, Ganay." Taller than Paul and with shimmer-white skin, he wore his blonde locks combed back. His ramrod posture suggested a military background, and his lantern jaw and jutting chin begged to be immortalized in a portrait. The young lady at his side kept her arm tightly looped around his and blinked her long, dark lashes bashfully.

Jackie tamped down the envy that threatened, mainly from the lady's sapphire-colored dress.

"I have yet to meet this divine creature." The man nudged in front of Paul and reached for Jackie's hand.

"Jacqueline Bouvier," Claude offered. "She's an exchange student from America, staying with us while she attends the Sorbonne." She turned her wide eyes to Jackie. "This is Philip Laurent. *Count* Philip." Her eyebrows shot up to emphasize the title.

"Ever so pleased to make your acquaintance." He kissed the top of Jackie's immaculate-white glove. The penetrating gaze from his cornflower-blue eyes made Jackie's insides flutter, and she would've guessed him to be Paul's age or older.

After introducing his escort as Adele, he ignored her sheepish grin. With Jackie's hand still in his, he said, "I trust you'll save a dance for me, Miss Bouvier."

"Perhaps, Mr. Laurent." She withdrew her hand as Claude's mouth fell open and Paul feigned a cough.

Philip, with Adele tucked even closer to his side, made his parting remarks. Before blending into the festive crowd, he glanced over his shoulder at Jackie. The linger of his stare conveying his intrigue.

"Better watch out for Philip," Paul said into Jackie's ear. "He's not used to being rebuked, and if he likes you, well, God help you."

Jackie reined in her coy grin. "Oh, I'm not worried."

ASIDE FROM HER DEBUTANTE BALL, Jackie couldn't recall a time she'd been paraded so. The evening melted into rounds of faces and introductions, as she was presented by Claude and the countess at every turn. The two had not overstated the popularity of the ball either, and Jackie soon lost hope of remembering names.

She danced with every man near her age and several quite a stroke older. Philip Laurent proved to be the swiftest on his feet, though his pinky and ring fingers rested a touch lower than Jackie's waist. Their conversation flowed, though it broached nothing of importance.

When Paul de Ganay found her later on, sitting among a small group of ladies and discussing the availability of hosiery, she was more than happy to accept his invite for a stroll in the garden. With only the rising crescent moon as their chaperone, they didn't saunter far from the main house.

"You'll have to come back and see the grounds in the daytime." Paul draped his tuxedo coat across Jackie's shoulders. "It's magnificent out here and so peaceful."

Jackie took in the crisp night air. "It already reminds me of my grandfather's estate. One of my favorite places to be alone."

"You prefer being alone?" Paul nodded over his shoulder. "Over this?"

She looked to the windows. Partygoers intoxicated from a mix of laughter and dull conversations filled the glass panes while a warm gaiety emitted from the château. Much of Jackie's life revolved around social events, when she wasn't at the stables or reading. What she disliked most was the pressure to be pretty rather than interesting. Not that she held any control over such a subjective variable. She wasn't Lee. But men were drawn to beauty, not necessarily intelligence. As she watched the crowd from outside, she liked the feel of being removed from the hub—and at the same time knowing she could return and easily assimilate.

"I prefer not to be bored." Jackie hoped her subtle grin served an adequate thanks to Paul for extracting her from the topic of hosiery. Another peeve of hers when it came to parties—ladies were expected to gather and converse with ladies, and never to linger too long with a gentleman. Oh, the things women could drone on about.

Paul removed a pack of cigarettes from his pants pocket and offered one to Jackie. She peeled the glove off her right hand and joined him in a smoke. He hopped on the stone ledge that surrounded the patio and pointed out various barons, artists, and wealthy landowners as they appeared in the château's windows. With each he included a bit of gossip.

She soaked it up and asked pointed questions that seemed to impress Paul. When Philip stepped into the glimmering frame, though, Paul's frisky humor dissipated.

"The irresistible Philip Laurent." Paul took a drag of his cigarette, then spewed the smoke in Philip's direction. "Prides himself as being one of France's most eligible bachelors. It's hard to argue against. He served in the war, protected his family's assets and business throughout the occupation, and earned the rank of Commandant in the Foreign Legion."

"What business is his family in?"

"They own a massive vineyard in Bordeaux, along with interests in a marina in Nice—where he keeps a yacht—and they dabble in the perfume industry. Some say he was even part of a plot to assassinate Hitler, though it never came to fruition."

"Mmm." Jackie sensed a note of jealousy in Paul's voice and made a point to sound indifferent.

"He's rarely seen with the same girl twice, and something tells me he'd love to work his charms on you. A fresh American girl, who's eager for the French experience."

Jackie met his half-squinting gaze. She could've spoiled it for Paul, mentioned what a gentleman Philip had been during their dance. Even give away that she had a spark of interest in the man. But she didn't.

"I'm only eager for the arts and the education. I couldn't care less about the men."

Paul laughed with her at the mild insult. "Then perhaps I'll do my best to dissuade him when he comes asking about you. He'll want to know what type of girl you are. Is there anything special I should share with him?"

Jackie puffed her cigarette. "Tell him I'm the type who gets a headache from wine. That I'm allergic to perfume and that I can't swim."

More laughter resounded between them. As Paul finished his smoke and discarded the butt, Jackie chanced a look toward Philip. She wondered if she was wrong about him, and if Paul's resentment only masked his own shortcomings. Would Paul pander her lies, perhaps in an attempt to keep her attentions for himself? Jackie belonged to no one. She was willing to play their games and test the flexibilities of convention. And why not? She wasn't one to turn away a wealthy pursuer without sampling the *French experience* on her own accord.

BACK AT THE DE RENTYS' apartment late that night, Claude all but salivated with curiosity.

"What did you think of Philip?"

Jackie, after expunging herself from the peach gown—and silently bidding it good riddance—knew to measure her responses carefully. More was at stake than simply exposing her whims.

"Well, he's something, isn't he?"

Claude's shoulders fell. "Oh, come on now. You must have felt something for him? He practically cornered me, you know. Wanted to know everything about you."

"Really?" Jackie's scalp prickled. In her mind their interactions hadn't been extraordinary. Pleasant, yes, but nothing that tilted the earth beneath her pumps or left her hungry for their next encounter. "So you know him well then?"

"Mmm, well enough. He and Ghislaine dated but it hardly lasted a month."

A shudder ran through Jackie. "Oh, I didn't know...."

"Of course you didn't." Claude shrugged. "That's been ages ago, before she was married. Mother remembers it better than I do and said they weren't a very good fit. I have a feeling he's smitten with you, though."

Jackie liked the idea, but her own emotions didn't flutter for the man and she couldn't pinpoint why. Perhaps she was more like her father—a lover of the chase but hesitant when expectations and commitment loomed.

Now, hearing that Philip and Ghislaine had been an item, however brief, tainted the man for Jackie. She would need to ask Ghislaine about it but the idea of broaching such a personal topic made Jackie uneasy. The last thing she needed in her new home was a greater chasm between her and Ghislaine.

"What's wrong with Paul anyway?"

Claude considered it a moment. "Nothing, I suppose. He's handsome and rich, but Philip..." She spun on the balls of her feet and landed on her bed. "He's ethereal almost. The kind of man you can imagine changing the world."

Jackie didn't share Claude's confidence. In fact, she suspected that both Claude and Paul had mistaken Philip's arrogance for charisma. Even so, as she nuzzled into the cool covers that night, drowsy and satisfied, she wasn't about to discount any man just yet.

AS JACKIE and her host family discussed the ball over breakfast the next morning, the bell rang. Ghislaine was quick to answer and returned to the kitchen a moment later with a robust, fragrant bouquet of lavender chrysanthemums.

"They're for Jackie." A smile curled the corner of her mouth as she handed Jackie the card.

With heat rouging her cheeks, Jackie tore into the correspondence and read it aloud. "Thank you for the dance. Looking forward to calling on you soon. Warm regards, Philip."

Claude squealed as the countess's eyes popped with excitement.

"See." Claude pinched Jackie's arm playfully. "I knew you made an impression."

"That's very kind of him." Breathlessness gripped Jackie. "But we hardly spoke, and we only shared one dance."

"Sometimes that's all it takes, my dear." The countess winked when Jackie looked her way.

The bell rang again.

"Could it be more flowers?" Claude bounded for the door. The others followed, a heightened anticipation stirring the apartment. Christian toddled at their heels. When Claude opened the door, Philip stood at the threshold, his gray trilby hat in one hand and a bouquet of white peonies in the other.

"Good morning, ladies." He bowed slightly and tipped a glance toward each of them as he was welcomed inside.

"What timing," Claude said. "Your flowers just arrived."

"Ah, splendid. I didn't want to arrive unprepared, though." His charming smirk appeared. "But these are for you, Countess de Renty."

The countess received them with a jovial laugh and thanked him. "Please come right in and join us for breakfast. You must."

"I would love to, but I didn't come to intrude." He reached inside his breast pocket and removed slips of paper. "If it pleases you ladies, I'd like you to accompany me tonight to the Palais Garnier." He handed the tickets to Jackie.

Balcony seats? The gesture left her speechless.

"You are too kind." The countess gave Jackie a gentle nudge from behind, as if to awaken her from a trance. "We would be delighted."

"Yes. This is so generous." While Jackie had been the object of pursuit before, it had never been at such a furious and luxurious pace. Such flattery seized her, made her breathless.

Philip beamed with satisfaction as he tousled Christian's hair. "I'll let you return to your meal, then, and look forward to seeing you tonight." His stare held on Jackie.

Cheerful goodbyes sent him off.

Claude leaned against the door in a dramatic fashion. "Can you believe it? One dance and he's infatuated."

Jackie tensed, fearing Claude's display might injure Ghislaine.

"He's wasted no time in making his interests known." The countess inhaled the aroma of her bouquet, eyes peering over the snow-white petals at her houseguest.

Jackie struggled inwardly for an appropriate response combined with genuine emotion. She'd discovered through her vast, yet respectable, experience with enamored beaux that discernment was her strength. Minutes into a conversation she could detect a spark or lack thereof. With Philip, her impressions had not solidified. Encouragement and approval from Claude and the countess only deepened her conflict—but she refused to be mesmerized by their influence.

"You could be making too much of this." Jackie kept her tone firm though not harsh.

The countess smiled. "Unlikely, my dear, but I'm eager to see how it plays out."

AFTER CLASSES, Jackie rushed back to the apartment to prepare for the ballet. She'd maintained her focus, absorbing what she could during the lecture on the works and methods of Edgar Degas. However, she welcomed the chance to escape an evening at home. Only a night at the Palais Garnier could dull the history and creation of Degas's *Little Dancer*. She intended to review her notes later.

Entering the apartment, Jackie found Ghislaine in the kitchen.

"Is Christian napping?" She took a dishtowel and joined Ghislaine in drying and putting away dishes.

"He's with Mother. She wanted to pick up a fresh cake from the bakery and fresh grounds for the coffee press."

A slight smile came to her lips. Jackie had given her ration card to the countess. Restrictions on coffee and sugar had eased, but she was pleased to contribute to the household, if only in a small way.

"She's thrilled to entertain company again," Ghislaine added, "even though hosting Philip makes her nervous."

"Oh?"

"I told her not to worry or go about making an extra fuss. Philip knows us, knows how we live. We're not likely to impress him." She slid a stack of dishes into a hutch. "But she wants to do it for you, I'm sure. Doesn't want to ruin your chances with him."

Jackie didn't know Ghislaine well enough to know if her grin was forced or not.

"I didn't mean to cause any trouble—"

"Oh, I didn't mean it that way. It's just that Mother thinks things will go back to the way they were before the war. That's not really possible now, is it?" Ghislaine's eyes grew dim.

"I'm so sorry for the things you've lost to the war. Your father most especially." Jackie didn't know what she'd do without her father in her life, difficult as he could be at times.

"Thank you." She dabbed the corners of her eyes. "I don't mean to burden you."

Jackie, in what she considered a bold move, reached for Ghislaine's hand. "It's a privilege for me to be here and to get to know you."

Ghislaine blinked back the glistening tears and met Jackie's gaze. It was the first time she'd regarded Jackie without a hint of disdain—and was the first meaningful conversation they'd shared since Jackie placed her satchel and travel case inside the apartment.

"I hope Philip coming by doesn't..." Jackie rummaged through her mind for the right word, but then settled for, "upset you too much."

Ghislaine sighed. "Of course not. Philip and I were never all that serious. Claude and Mother make it out to be more than it was." She squeezed Jackie's hand affectionately before letting go. "He never showed up at the crack of dawn with flowers and ballet tickets for me."

Heat clawed up the back of Jackie's neck, though she didn't understand why.

"I suppose we should get ready." She stole a cleansing breath, hoping to loosen the sudden knot in her stomach.

"I don't plan on going this evening."

"Because of Christian? I'm sure we could find someone to sit with him."

"Ballet puts me to sleep. I'd much rather turn pottery."

Jackie grinned and made a mental note. She'd never dabbled with pottery but decided exploring the medium with Ghislaine would be the best time to try. As she headed for the bedroom, Jackie's cheeks tingled with a sense of pride. She suspected that Ghislaine didn't befriend women easily or share much of herself with others. So Jackie didn't take it lightly, gaining a morsel of knowledge about her housemate. Jackie knew those feelings—understood the need for emotional barriers and caution—and she purposed to nurture her friendship with Ghislaine with sincerity. A delicate balance was required, Jackie believed. One that didn't overwhelm Ghislaine with too much interest or too many questions. A laugh bubbled in Jackie's chest as she realized Ghislaine could be her ideal companion.

WHEN THE BELL rang later that evening, ten minutes earlier than expected, Jackie and her hosts stood ready. The hazelnut aroma of the freshly brewed coffee and the wafting scent of the crumb cake waltzed through the apartment, cut in only by the dash of perfume the ladies had sprayed. They gathered near the door in fervent expectation, their dresses pressed, their curls tight.

But when Paul de Ganay entered, the atmosphere shifted to mild befuddlement.

"Paul, lovely to see you again so soon." The countess stepped forward and encouraged him in. She checked the faces of the young ladies. "We weren't expecting you...or your friend."

Another man came in behind Paul.

"This is Renee," Paul said. "Family friend. I believe you met last night."

Greetings followed.

"I apologize for not calling beforehand." Paul's luster dimmed as he took in their baffled faces and noticed their formal attire. "Pardon me. Have I interrupted, come at a bad time?"

"Well, you see—" The bell drowned out the countess.

Renee, standing closest to the door, opened it.

Philip stepped forth, his navy silk cape swishing around him, his presence alighting the room. "Greetings, all." He removed his hat and surveyed the room with a swift glance. "Ganay, didn't expect to run into you this evening."

"Yes, just thought I'd pop in, surprise the ladies with a visit." Paul rubbed his hands together, noted the plated slices of cake. "Foolish of me, perhaps."

"Nonsense!" Philip's voice rose above the ladies' protest, and his gaze rested on Jackie. "Who could blame you?"

After a beat of silence, Paul said, "I should be going."

The countess stepped in front of him, blocking his attempted exit. "If you don't have any other plans this evening, why don't you and Renee accompany Philip and the ladies. Because if I'm not mistaken, Philip just happens to have two extra tickets for this evening?"

Philip's eyebrows shot up and words failed him.

"Yes," the countess continued, "you see, as we were about to explain, Ghislaine and I can't make it tonight. Christian had a touch of a fever earlier and she wants to stay with him, and I, well," the countess gave a pathetic, phony cough, "I may be coming down with something as well, so it's best if I'm not out in a chilly theater."

Mild snickers infected the room.

"In that case, she's right, Ganay. You and your friend should join us." Philip nodded toward Renee.

Paul looked to Jackie, as if it were her approval he preferred. "If you're sure..."

"Absolutely!" Philip stood beside her, as if they were already solidified as a couple. "No need to let these balcony seats go to waste."

The countess, exceedingly pleased with the outcome, insisted everyone sit and enjoy the refreshments.

As they settled and chatter ensued, Jackie detected the subtle way Philip and Paul regarded each other. Expressions fixed. Philip, his chin held high like a victory banner. Paul, aglow with pride that he'd prevented Philip from having Jackie to himself.

Sipping her coffee, she knew the cordial duel had commenced. But what would prevail? Did each man have a genuine interest in winning her affection, or were they driven more by the desire to out-do the other? Either way, Jackie wasn't anxious to be won.

SEVEN

October 1949

Although she attended mass regularly with the de Rentys at Our Lady of the Assumption, Jackie's primary religion was her devotion to correspondence. At least twice a week, after setting aside her books and studies, she penned letters home. Each note was tailored to its recipient, and she made a conscious effort not to share the same information twice. While she wrote to Lee about shopping and Parisian fashions, she told Yusha about the nightlife, the latest cafés she'd visited, and mutual acquaintances she happened to run into. With her parents and Grampy, she mentioned her studies and was always careful to include her longing for the things she missed most—her young siblings, Danseuse, and Narragansett Bay. She saved most of her gossip for Martha, finding comfort in the fact Martha would share the letters only with Charles.

A busy week unfolded for Jackie, with Philip and Paul visiting or ringing daily. She feared the relentless attention would exasperate the countess and irritate Ghislaine, but instead of complaining, they reveled in the gifts—a bottle of Château Lafite Rothschild among the most exquisite from Philip, while Paul limped along, bestowing a Bvlgari silk scarf.

Jackie secretly enjoyed the attention, but the gifts, thoughtful and expensive as they were, didn't reflect a personal touch. Too much wine gave Jackie a headache, so she often refrained, and rarely did she find scarves flattering.

By Wednesday evening, the courting competition had reached a fevered pitch. Paul showed up to apologize profusely for having missed lunch with Jackie at the Ritz, due to a previous, forgotten engagement he couldn't reschedule. He hoped, not-so-secretly, that Jackie might be free that evening. Philip arrived shortly thereafter, before Jackie could explain to Paul that they had secured tickets to the ballet again, with Claude joining them.

In her usual manner of rescuing one from disappointing circumstances, the countess intervened and insisted Paul stay for dinner. By the time Jackie, Philip, and Claude left, Paul's droopy shoulders and equally droopy mood had recovered.

However, their evening at the opera was thwarted when an electrical issue cancelled the production.

When the trio returned to the apartment, much earlier than anyone had expected, they joined Paul, Ghislaine, the countess, and Christian, who were already cozied up to bowls of the countess's garbure, with fresh loaves of baguettes that crackled when sliced into. The stew's aroma soothed the edges of the men's frustrations and drew the group together. Afterward, a game of charades ensued with Claude and Ghislaine emerging as victors.

"We've learned a valuable lesson tonight," Philip said, "to never pair sisters."

"So true," Jackie chimed in, her cheeks sore from laughter. "My sister and I seem to communicate without speaking. I think it only develops among close siblings." A pang of misery struck her, knowing months would pass before she'd see Lee again. She hadn't expected to miss her as intensely as she did. So many things happened daily that Jackie would never have enough time to write and share them all with her sister.

"Again! Again!" Christian demanded, popping up on his toes. He'd performed perfectly as a cat and a bird with guidance from his mother.

"It's bedtime for you, young man." Ghislaine slowly lifted him into her arms.

"I want to play," he whined, his body gone limp, which proved to be the best form of rebellion he could muster.

"Tomorrow, sweet boy." Ghislaine kissed his forehead and took him to their room after bidding everyone goodnight.

It wasn't unusual for the de Renty women to disperse, leaving Jackie alone in the parlor with her caller. Tonight, as the countess gathered dishes, and refused offers of help, Jackie was left with two gentlemen, one pouring apple brandy and one occupying the opposite end of the divan she was sitting on. Claude lingered, almost as if she couldn't relent her spectator status or decide if staying demonstrated poor manners. Jackie gave her nothing in the way of an expression that favored either choice.

"On the whole, I'd say none of us could've planned a better evening." Philip served the drinks to each of them, along with his winsome smile.

"It was splendid." Jackie meant it, for it was the first time she didn't feel like the object of the tug-of-war between the two men's egos.

"That little Christian, he's quite something." Philip settled in an armchair across from Jackie and spoke as if he were talking only to her. "Almost makes you hunger for one of your own...doesn't he?"

Paul slightly choked on his drink while Claude's eyebrows nearly leapt from her forehead.

Jackie understood what Philip was up to, tempting her to picture them as a happy couple, entertaining in their home, with children running about.

"Almost." She paired her response with a mild grin, proving she was neither startled nor embarrassed by the suggestion. Philip's ploy may have been genuine. Perhaps he was dreaming of that next phase of life, of what was surely expected of a man of his bearings and stature. But he wasn't the first to tease Jackie with such an ideal.

"Well," Paul cut in when the silence held too long, "what about tomorrow night? I'd love to take you to dinner, Jackie. There's a wonderful bistro right on the Seine—"

"I have an art class in the evening."

"We could meet after. Enjoy a nightcap together and a stroll home."

"That's kind of you, Paul." Jackie had no grounds to refuse him, though a mild sense of suffocation rose in her chest. She needed a way to quell the battle.

"YOU JUST HAVE to come right out and tell them, you know," Claude said after they'd settled into bed. The soft scents of soap and cold cream mixed in the dark as each of them released a sigh of exhaustion.

"Tell who what?" Jackie's asked.

"Paul and Philip. You're going to have to pick between them, sooner or later."

Jackie raked her fingers through her hair gently as she stared at the ceiling. "What if I want to pick me?"

A soft laugh came from Claude. "Sounds like something you'd say."

"I pick going back in time and untangling the whole thing. I want to get to know Paul and Philip apart from each other, and without the unnecessary pretense of marriage or commitment being involved."

"You're right, of course, but it might be too late. They're men, infamous in the department of poor decision making and unable to admit their mistakes." Claude exhaled heavily. "I'm worried for you. It seems as though the predicament is already wearing on you."

Jackie thought back to their last moments in the parlor, when Philip and Paul eagerly scarfed at filling up her every waking moment. Her expression must have given away her exasperation. Selfishly, though, she didn't want to create more of a stir between the men, because she truly enjoyed their company and soaking up as much of Paris as possible. Being on the arm of Philip or Paul meant the best seats in the house, meeting actors backstage or even dining with them after the show at a nearby club. Luxuries Jackie didn't want to render too hastily.

And then it suddenly struck her that she was in danger of being insensitive. Two men were grappling for her attention—right under Claude's nose and in her own home—while Claude herself hungered for romance.

"There's no need to worry, Claude. Men get bored and distracted easily." Naturally, Jackie's mind drifted to her father and his careless liaisons. The ways he showered women with attention until he'd had his carnal fill. Then, he turned dismissive. Jackie determined never to be so gullible. Or vulnerable. "We'll see which happens first."

Silence followed, long enough to convince Jackie that Claude had drifted to sleep. But then Claude said, "I don't want to stay a virgin forever."

"Oh?" The comment tumbled from Jackie's mouth and lacked any effort to disguise her shock.

"You don't intend to go to your wedding night inexperienced, do you?"

Jackie groped for the right words. "I—"

Thump. Thump. The broom handle resounded from the countess's room.

"Girls." The thin wall separating the spaces muffled her voice. "To bed with you both!"

They huddled under their quilts, both having no desire to ruffle her further. Jackie clutched her covers tightly, grateful for an escape from the conversation but once again burdened with worry for her dear Claude.

TREPIDATION PRODDED Jackie as she entered her art class at the École des Beaux-Arts the following evening. Since her instructor had proven his devotion to unconventional methods, what would tonight's session include? An in-depth exploration of Dali's sexuality through his work? Or would the class be encouraged to create their own erotic painting, inspired by Hokusai's sensual works?

But nothing burned on her mind more than the possibility of seeing her mysterious admirer again, which had its own quandaries. *Delusional!* She told herself. *I've gone delusional to think of that man as an admirer. He's hardly more than a phantom. For all I know he could be disturbed.*

The instructor had provided no name, no introduction for the man, and Jackie could only guess what his connection might be to the instructor or the school. She envied the man, or at least his talent for appearing and disappearing in various situations. Captivated by his mystique, more than she wanted to admit, she told herself—yet again—that it was absurd to devote so much thought to the man and that she needed to clog the fountains of her imaginations.

She failed, mostly, at convincing herself, but when her instructor entered and began the class with his sharp claps, she welcomed the change in focus. Fortunately, compared to last week, the class was tame in learning daubism, the technique of painting with palette knives and the backs of spoons.

At the end of class, she readied herself to leave, knowing that Paul might already be waiting for her. He wasn't though, and as she lingered near the exit, a realization struck that she and Paul hadn't agreed on a specific spot to meet. After several minutes, she started toward to Le Select, the closest and most likely place they'd end up for coffee anyway. A mild agitation threatened her mood as she remembered Paul's habit of being late.

Her head down and her pace certain, she stopped when she heard a voice from behind.

"You're quite the artist."

Jackie turned and saw him. The man—her *admirer*—sitting on a bench against the building with his legs outstretched and a cigarette smoldering between two fingers.

Other students filed past her as she took him in, waited for air to return to her lungs.

"Thank you." It was paltry, she knew. "But may I ask where you've seen my work?" Jackie had considered her art charming at its best and amateurish at its worst. She played to her strengths, such as when she created Frenzied Frieda, a cartoon character featured in the *Salmagundy*, the school newspaper at Miss Porter's. Jackie could hold her own when it came to watercolors, but her work certainly wasn't in danger of being confused with Winslow Homer paintings.

Her admirer hooked a nod toward the school as he stood and approached.

"Jean-Luke granted me a look-see at last week's paintings." He took a hit on his cigarette. "I must say that yours was my favorite."

"How could you know which sketch was mine?" She was helpless against the warmth flushing her cheeks. Helpless against the images of his nude body taking the forefront of her mind.

He shrugged a shoulder with a nonchalant flair, looking dapper in a charcoal pin-striped suit "I visited your easel, after you'd gone."

So you watched me leave? Then you went to my easel and indulged in critiquing my work? Heat crawled across her body as she imaged posing nude. The sheer terror and freedom that must come with such exposure. The excitement of sculpting his body with brushstrokes revisited, and she hoped, desperately, that her face didn't show it.

"You made for an interesting subject." Had she said that, *aloud*? Clearly the adrenaline pounding through her had fogged her brain.

He laughed. Then in one swift movement he finished his smoke and flicked the butt aside.

"Your French is excellent, for an American."

The tang dashed into his comment irked her, as it usually did when someone remarked, *I wouldn't have guessed you were American.* As if being an American fluent in French was impossible. In turn, she considered noting that he wasn't native but refrained, since she couldn't place his accent.

"And you're prolific, for a bohemian." She bit the inside of her bottom lip, agonizing that her comments weren't as sharp and clever as she liked. The intensity of his gaze—those gray-teal eyes—bound her like raw, newly braided ropes. Clouded her thinking and at the same time heightened her senses. She was convinced that if her fingertip even hovered near his skin, a static charge would pass between them.

"Is that what I am?" He stepped closer, the corner of his mouth curling.

"I wouldn't know." They were now alone, the light traffic of student bodies having thinned. It reminded her what a complete stranger the man was. She feared she'd been foolish, feasting on romantic notions the way her classmates sighed and swooned over their beaux—which bored her.

He glanced at the ground and slid his hands into his pants pockets, perhaps sensing Jackie's nerves.

"It might better to continue this conversation elsewhere." He squeezed his shoulders together, as if warding off a chill. "There's a café close by. Can I interest you in a coffee?"

"I'm not in the habit of gallivanting with strange men."

"Good. Neither am I."

She couldn't stifle her smirk but recovered quickly. As much as his wit intrigued her, propriety cautioned.

"You're only a bit confused," he continued. "I'm not strange, as you suggest, only a stranger to you. Believe me, there is quite a difference. I have a sure-fire remedy for that. An introduction, perhaps overdue." He withdrew his right hand from his pocket and extended it toward her. "Marceau van den Berg."

She shook his hand. "Jacqueline Bouvier, Jackie, if you please."

"Bouvier? How unexpected." He bowed slightly, then arched an eyebrow. "And if we're honest, Miss Bouvier, I'm the one at the disadvantage."

"How so?"

"Well, you were already privy to my underlings and the three scars I obtained as a young man."

Jackie recalled the marks. A raised white line on his right upper thigh. A jagged curvature on the left side of his mid-torso. A deep divot on his lower abdomen. Striking as they were curious. Of course, she could say that for most of his features. Even as he stood before her, fully clothed.

"Does that knowledge constitute an advantage?"

"*Touché*, my lady." He stared at her a moment, then asked, "What brings you to Paris?"

She launched into a full explanation about Vassar and the Smith program. Marceau, eyes alight, seemed to absorb her every rambling word. It was unlike her to dominate a conversation. How was it that this man made her deviate from her norm so effortlessly?

"It's fortunate that our paths crossed. First in Grenoble, now in Paris," he said.

"Is it?" Jackie despised every word from her mouth.

"You know I watched you, that night in Sassenage. There was something immediately special about you. At first, I thought it was in your eyes, and the way you reached across the patio to me without a word. Then I saw you dance with the ladies in your group. And there it was again. But it struck me the most when you returned to your seat and found the lavender I'd left for you. You searched for me only to assume I'd gone."

Delight prickled Jackie's skin with goosebumps. The way he described watching her should've bothered her, but instead, it made her feel desired.

"You kept the lavender in your lap," Marceau continued, "and said nothing of it to your friends. Touching it with your fingertips while something like regret seem to come over you. Not that the others noticed. You wouldn't let them or share the little secret we had going. It probably sounds trite, but I found you extraordinary."

His words wrapped around her like fine silk against bare, smooth skin. She couldn't let on how right he was, how he had managed to read her emotions so well. Then tucked away the memory of her, like a keepsake.

"So you followed me to Paris." She pressed her lips together and averted her eyes, hoping the tease of her sentiment wasn't lost on him.

"Naturally," he ribbed with a mild grin. "I had to find the young lady who mesmerized me at a cozy hamlet on a lonely night."

As they enjoyed a laugh, swift footfalls beat the pavement behind them, and a man called out, "Jackie! Oh, Jackie. Glad I caught up with you."

"Paul." His name came out as much as a revelation as it did a statement, Jackie having forgotten about their meeting.

"Sorry I'm a little late." He turned to Marceau. "Why, Marceau! What on earth are you doing here? How good to run into you!" Paul reached for his hand and shook it heartily.

Marceau responded in kind, his smug mystique exchanged for a more jovial expression. He glanced at Jackie as if trying to gauge the depth of her relationship with Paul.

"How long's it been?"

Marceau ran his hand over his loose curls. "Not since Rosenburg."

"Ages then." Paul straightened, and to Jackie's surprise, spoke to Marceau in a different language. Russian, if she had to venture a guess.

Marceau responded likewise. They continued their exchange, with bursts of chortles, for several minutes. Jackie's skin prickled again as she felt left out and wondered if they were talking about her.

"You're living in Paris now?" Paul switched back to French, after their cheer dwindled, and perhaps having also sensed Jackie's discomfort.

Marceau nodded, once again followed Paul's lead. "Nothing permanent though."

Paul seemed to expect more of an explanation but moved on when Marceau didn't elaborate. "And you know Jackie?"

Their gazes connected, though they restrained any traces of their mutual interest in one another.

"Only recently," Marceau offered.

"Yes." Jackie wished she could bite back the word, letting it slip so anxiously.

Paul darted a glance between them. "You should join us. We're heading for a cocktail."

"I appreciate that, but I need to be going."

Jackie's heart quickened at the thought of their encounter coming to an end. "Oh, please do." A lump of guilt lodged in her throat.

"That's kind of you both." Marceau tilted his head slightly, looking at her. A hint of his smugness returned. "But we have an early day tomorrow. I'll see you first thing in the morning. Sunrise, in fact. That special lecture on light and color for oil painting, remember?"

Jackie replied with a dazed nod.

"The Trocadéro, then, at dawn?" A pleased yet hopeful grin stretched across his face.

"Dawn." Jackie didn't relish the thought of rising so early, but who was to say she could sleep anyway, knowing that she would see Marceau again. Elation spiraled through her.

Marceau and Paul shook hands again before they parted. As she watched Marceau go, a strange admiration rose within her. What a clever man he was. She wanted to bask in his craftiness, thoughtfully arranging a rendezvous for them in a split-second. And right under Paul's nose.

"A fellow classmate?" Paul asked.

Jackie tugged her stare from Marceau's stride. "We were in art class together." No need to pestle and mortar the details, not that there were many to share.

"Still feeling up for a coffee?" Paul's eyes narrowed, as if he sensed Jackie was off-kilter.

"Yes, of course." She put forth her cheerful disposition, not wanting his suspicions aroused. After all, Paul had been a good friend from the start. If nothing else, he deserved Jackie's full attention and charms. But it occurred to her, quite acutely as they set a brisk pace toward Le Select, that neither Paul nor Philip had stoked Jackie's sensitivities the way Marceau had, and with strikingly less efforts.

Aside from a handful of flirtations that never led anywhere serious, Jackie had little to compare against her budding interest in Marceau. Letting her imaginations run like an untamed stallion across a sun-kissed meadow was useless. She still knew nothing about the man—where he came from, where he belonged, and what on earth he was up to, popping up on the edges of Jackie's life.

Such questions, along with dozens more, deafened Paul's well-meaning chatter while they walked. Marceau's words—that promise of seeing him tomorrow—consumed Jackie's focus, as did the curiosity of whether or not he truly intended for them to paint.

ONCE THEY SETTLED at Le Select, wine in hand instead of coffee, Jackie determined to concentrate on Paul—and what he could tell her about Marceau. Guilt nibbled at her insides but was trumped by the possibility of plumbing secrets from Paul.

"How is it you know Marceau?"

He dipped his nose into his wine glass before taking a sip. "The

Rosenburg. It's a boarding school in Switzerland. Only the finest for Europe's rich and royal. A small group of us spent six years there, Marceau included."

"And you both speak Russian?"

Paul quipped a laugh. "Yes. Rosenburg had a grueling schedule. Rigorous academics and athletics. Probably what helped keep all of us in line. Mostly. Along with fencing, skiing, swimming, and boxing, we had to study six languages. You could say Marceau and I mastered Russian. We were the only ones among our group who could make much of it, so we devised a routine, if you will. A sort of patchwork of phrases. 'The king likes hot biscuits with tea'. He might reply with 'The ostrich jumped over the fence.' On it would go, until we ran out of things to say. Our instructors were not amused, but our classmates were baffled. Thought we were geniuses. Yes, we were quite the duo."

She didn't know how to quell the excitement stirring inside her. Hearing that Marceau was well-educated, richly cultured—and not without a playful side—validated her budding infatuation. "In that case you both must have a feast of memories to revisit."

"You could say that, not that I've thought about school or Marceau for years." Paul's grin paired with a far-away look in his eyes. "He's... different, you know."

Jackie didn't, but wanted to. "How so?"

"For one thing, he's not French. Not entirely."

He said it in a way that implied a defect, which reminded Jackie of the rub she felt each time she heard, *I never would've guessed you were American.* She considered reminding him that she wasn't French, either, but restrained herself. "Is that important?"

Paul broke from his thoughts. "No, I suppose not. What I meant was, Marceau was one for staging pranks and breaking the rules. He always got away with it. Harmless antics for the most part, but a few of us would get reprimanded for his mischief. Nothing too serious, mind you, but at times we weren't sure how much we could trust him."

Recollections of the pranks and antics she'd commandeered at boarding school flooded her mind. Pilfering cookies from the kitchen pantry each week. Dropping a slice of chocolate cream pie into the lap of a crass teacher as they practiced the serving and hosting duties they were likely to perform as wives. Her apology, delivered so breathlessly and convincingly, saved her from punishment. The same couldn't be said for the time she covered the toilet seat in the head mistress's private bath with Vaseline. She'd been found out, after the fact, and reprimanded sharply.

"Why the piqued interest?" Paul asked, his tone once-again ripe with caution.

"You seemed so pleased to see him, I thought he was a dear friend."

"He was actually. Maybe I'm being too harsh." Paul seemed to reflect on his own memories for a moment.

"Paul, I have a wild idea." Jackie placed her hand on top of his and leaned in toward him. "Why don't we agree to being good friends?" She'd tired of the pain that sharpened in her chest each time Paul became defensive. "I want to go back to that night on the terrace, where we gossiped and didn't have a care in the world. That worked for us, much better than these strict roles neither of us are suited for."

He let her words sink in, then his features softened with relief. "I think you're right. We were devilish that night, and the only time since that compares is our night of charades." He put his other hand on top of hers. "Does this mean I'm out of the race, that I no longer have a chance at winning your heart and affections?"

Jackie wished she held more control over her emotions. That she could flip a switch and ignite her feelings. While Paul seemed like a suitable man, worthy of her affections, he didn't enflame her passions or curiosities. Not like Marceau had. And now that she'd experienced that flicker of arousal, she didn't want to settle—and she didn't want to hurt Paul as she grappled to make sense of it all.

"Let's not think of it like that," she told him. "I'd much rather enjoy your company and let fate run its course."

He nodded. "Fair enough, my dear."

Jackie withdrew her hand.

"But tell me, is something stirring between you and Marceau?"

"I've only just learned his name." But she couldn't deny how the very mention of that name now sent a jolt of excitement through her.

"Keep your eyes wide open with that one. Mind how far you trust him." Paul swirled his pinot noir before taking a drink. "I wonder what he's doing here, bothering with an art class."

Jackie's fascination ratcheted, much like Paul's, she surmised, but she couldn't press on with endless questions. Paul already proved too sensitive to her interest in Marceau. A change in tactics seemed necessary.

"Are there any men besides you that I can trust in this country?"

He didn't match her playfulness. "He's an entirely different animal from Philip. At least what I remember about him. Philip's arrogant and spoiled. With Marceau, you never knew what he was thinking. Often a master at keeping secrets. Some of us wondered how far he would take the pranks, or how much risk he'd take with our reputations. He's skillful at certain things and was never one to pass on a dare. You might say he's reckless, or even dangerous."

Jackie let no reaction escape. Hearing the word *dangerous* surged her need for answers—and sent a chill down her spine—but nothing would keep her from meeting Marceau first thing in the morning.

EIGHT

Burdened thoughts and wistful anticipation made for fitful sleep. Finally, Jackie abandoned her bed and fretted that every sleepless minute would show on her face. By now she knew the squeaks and groans of the floor in the apartment well enough to maneuver around them. Careful not to wake anyone, she dressed and readied in the water closet. Her nerves, she feared, would make her clumsy, but no incidents resulted.

She grabbed her satchel, stuffed with books and her notepad, since she would head directly to the Sorbonne after her rendezvous with Marceau. Leaving the apartment, with everyone still asleep, gave her a sense of accomplishment. No one would worry, finding her gone so early, since she'd had previous occasions of being the first one out of the house. Occasions that related to school. Occasions that the countess or Claude knew about beforehand.

Besides, Paul knew where she was, should anything happen.

Again, there was the word she couldn't rub from her conscious all night: *dangerous*. Paul had released it, like a wild, rabid animal. And here she was, trying to rationalize her actions, all to appease a burning attraction she felt. Though Paul had been vague, his reservations toward Marceau were clear. How far would this fascination drive her? Or blind her?

Arriving at the Trocadéro took little time, since it was located in the 16th arrondissement. Named after the Battle of Trocadéro that took place in southern Spain, where French troops squashed a rebellion against Ferdinand VII in 1823, the Trocadéro palace no longer existed. In its place the Palais de Chaillot now stood. Actually two separate buildings, the Palais de Chaillot was constructed in 1937 for the Universal Exhibition, and the spacious, surrounding area became known as Trocadéro Square. Its raised elevation provided a platform-like view of the Eiffel Tower. Although Jackie couldn't say how much area was represented, she did know finding Marceau would prove challenging, once the crowds thickened.

Huddled in her tweed coat, Jackie's body pulsed with expectancy. The Eiffel Tower, roughly a quarter mile away and skirted in the fog of early dawn, stood majestic and imposing on the other side of the Seine. People scuttled about and taxi horns punctuated the air, though not as enticingly as the fresh-baked pastries and the aroma of just-percolated coffee from street vendors' carts.

Ordinarily, Jackie would've appreciated this glimpse of Parisian life, how it mirrored life at home as a new day began. Concern pricked her. How would she ever spot Marceau? But then she noticed a man in front of two easels. She watched him for a moment, then made her way toward him. When he saw her, he waved and greeted her with that charming grin. Her confidence elevated.

Surely a man with an interest in painting the sunrise wasn't dangerous.

"I'm pleased you made it so early," he said.

"Did you think I wouldn't come?"

He eyed her. "You had reason enough not to come, but I was hopeful."

"What reason might that be?"

"I imagine our friend Paul had a great deal to share." He shrugged. "I wondered if he might change your mind about me."

Jackie liked seeing Marceau uncertain, unsure of what she now knew about him. Not that she'd gained any true insights from Paul, but Marceau didn't need to be made aware.

"Paul's a good friend."

Marceau's eyes narrowed. "*Just* a good friend?"

Jackie responded with only a grin.

Undaunted, he went on, "He's an upstanding man, or he was when I knew him, anyway. Always quick to do the right thing, but he had a fondness for cigars, which were forbidden on school grounds. Every man has his vice."

"And what was yours?"

Her boldness seemed to please him. "I'm partial to a Finnish sauna, followed by a massage and a stout beer. A fire-cooked sausage would make it perfect, but why be greedy?"

"Hardly a sin, but you seem to have a preference for nudity in some of your actions. That may be concerning."

He laughed. "A valid point." With a dry brush, he wiped his canvas. "Shall we paint then?"

Jackie took her place at the easel and glanced over the supplies. Six glass jars of paint, white to amber to scarlet with shades in between. Three brushes. A gray rag stained with paint dabs. She shed her coat. The fog had scattered while the sun was beginning to peek over the horizon.

Marceau's techniques and his gentle way of instruction fascinated her immediately. The way he expertly dabbed and mixed colors on the palette with a palette knife proved his skill. She never would have dared to add a pinprick of cobalt to deepen the shade of orange needed to mimic the morning's sky, as he did. He quickly educated her on how to thin the paints with water and the importance of keeping the tips of the brushes wet during a session. Then, he cautioned her against impatience.

"Capture the color, not the scenery," he encouraged.

When finished, they stepped back to admire one another's renderings. She couldn't say how long they'd painted, only that she'd been consumed with setting herself to the task and doing well. The yearning to be with Marceau—that had sustained her through a sleepless night and delivered her to his side so early—had shifted. She'd willingly become a student, and learned more than she'd anticipated, even becoming driven and intent to impress him, if that were possible.

But her breath caught when she viewed Marceau's creation. Any hope she had of dazzling him faded as she realized he had managed a rough pencil sketch of her, gazing at the glorious sunrise. His use of color, much more intense than Jackie's, drew her in, while the sketch of her profile made her feel as if she were looking at a photograph.

"Now, the colors will dry darker," Marceau said, "but I can seal these with a resin varnish. It'll make the paints glossy and bright."

"You learned this from Jean-Luke?" Calling her instructor by his first name tasted strange in Jackie's mouth, even though Jean-Luke wasn't a great deal older than her. Not like Professor Plum.

"No. I studied at an art school in Berlin for a short while. My mother insisted. She loved the arts and instilled it in me."

"And your father?"

"Dutch. Well, some might say. He's from the Netherlands."

"That explains your accent, and why Paul said you weren't entirely French."

"Neither is Paul. His mother is from Argentina, but yes, ancestry is important. It can open doors, win the approval of certain society groups." He gave a half-shrug as he rubbed a brush between the folds of the paint rag. "It also causes disputes."

"Such as?"

He waited a moment, then sighed. "There are things I can't tell you, Jackie. It has nothing to do with you, but it's best that you don't know too much about me. If the time comes and I can explain, believe me, I will. Gladly. But for now, I can't behave in conventional ways. Not like Paul or anyone else for that matter. I can't share the ballet with you or escort you to my favorite little place for chocolate croissants. I'd like to. In fact, there's not much I care about these days, besides getting to know you."

Jackie swore her chest had filled with a hot air balloon. "But I don't understand—"

"I know, and it's best you don't." He took her hand and gently rubbed away a drop of goldenrod on the cusp of her knuckle. The pad of his thumb against her skin made her pulse pound in her ears. "It's a lot to ask, I realize, and maybe it's too much to ask." His eyes met hers. "We can steal away together, share moments like this, but my life is uncertain. You'll have to trust me—recklessly. If that's impossible to accept, I wouldn't blame you."

Her insides warred, made her feel torn. Why would she consider seeing this man under such unusual circumstances? And why the extremes? Was he wanted by the police? She could only imagine, and she knew he wouldn't tell her if she asked. Was she being gullible for this handsome stranger? And to what end? What could come of their fragmented encounters?

On the other hand, his heightened mystique elevated her curiosities. What woman would go to such lengths to trust a man she barely knew? The impropriety of it all made her feel alive like never before.

"I'm not one for making grand promises." Jackie didn't know what else to say. How did one agree to a sort of non-arrangement?

"Then I won't ask for any." He kissed the spot on her hand he'd polished clean, then proceeded to pack up the art supplies.

Jackie donned her coat and took up her satchel. "I need to go."

Marceau locked his gray-teal gaze with hers as he stepped close to her. She lifted her chin, imperceptibly she hoped, but unbelievably hungry and ready, should he kiss her. Carefully, she drew in a deep breath. Marceau caressed the side of her cheek delicately, sending shivers of delight through her body. He spoke her name in a whisper and tucked strands of her hair behind her ear. Then he withdrew his hand.

"When might I see you again?" She fisted her hands inside her pockets. Could she sound more desperate? More eager for this wicked blend of mystery and brazen desire?

"There's always a chance I may walk away and never see you again."

Jackie swallowed hard, nodded. *He keeps making it worse. How could he say that or do that to me? After...* But in truth, she had no grounds to deserve better from him. Perhaps he was even lying to her. Using her. Though for what purpose, she couldn't say. Nevertheless, a sliver of anger tugged at her, and she took a step back.

"I'm being too harsh, too honest. I just don't want you taken by surprise."

She turned from him, feeling more foolish by the minute. A surge of instinct—or was it a return of common sense—told her to simply leave. Forget Marceau and the jumble of complications that came with him.

"I'll come to you, Jackie," Marceau called after her. Timidity laced his voice. "I'll find you."

Jackie didn't look back as she swiped teardrops from her eyes.

A DULL RESOLVE came over her. She set a pace for Reid Hall, certain she could catch Bea before lectures started. Not that she could tell Bea anything, but she wanted to feel grounded again. Bea had a way of making her feel solid on her feet.

She slipped into the dormitory. Sleepy-eyed girls, a few with rollers in their hair, passed by. Upon reaching the room Bea shared with three other girls, Jackie tapped on the door before letting herself in. The other girls, all of whom she knew, milled about in the tight space, brushing their hair and yanking on woolen sweaters. Chit-chat flowed since Jackie's visits to the dorm had been sporadic but not uncommon. No sense of alarm arose from anyone at her early, unexpected arrival. Precisely the way she wanted it.

Bea provided the rich distraction Jackie craved. Groaning, as usual, about her early class, Bea roused at Jackie's nudging and encouragement. Jackie found solace in being mildly useful. Here among a throng of friends, casual as they were, she felt reconnected, anchored to reality. Where she belonged.

After class they indulged in cigarettes and coffee and talked about nothing important. Jackie envied Bea and suspected that she would never tolerate a man being secretive with her, no matter how handsome and alluring he was. Yet here she was, similar to Bea in several regards, but submitting herself for soft torture.

BACK AT THE DE RENTYS' apartment that afternoon, feeling more like her studious, clear-headed self, Jackie took Christian onto her lap as the countess handed her a stack of newly delivered letters.

"You may want to open that one first." The countess, an eyebrow sharply arched, tapped the note on top of the stack.

Jackie slid the pad of her thumb over the stationary, taking in the wax seal—a family crest—and the *P L* monogram. Christian held the other letters but was more interested in watching Jackie open the envelope in her hand. Her jaw fell slack when she read the invitation.

"Nothing bad, I hope," the countess said, eyeing her.

"No, the contrary in fact. Philip has arranged for us to lunch at the Palace of Versailles tomorrow afternoon. A private lunch and tour."

The countess put a hand to her cheek. "My word, Jackie dear! You've certainly captured his attention. Securing the palace for a private tour...well, I've hardly heard of such a thing!"

Neither had Jackie. She and her traveling companions had visited the palace last summer. Versailles had been a highlight for her. She and the other girls spent a whole day exploring the castle and its grounds. Its majesty and historical significance compared only to meeting and shaking hands with Winston Churchill at a garden party in London that summer.

The countess clasped her hands together lightly. "But I do feel for Paul. I worry that his integrity gets overshadowed by Philip's outrageous displays." She loudly whispered the last two words as if she were hesitant to say them.

"I value Paul's friendship very much," Jackie admitted, though she wasn't anxious to let the countess know how mixed and jumbled her emotions had become for each man.

"I'm glad to hear it." She shook her head. "My! The lengths a man must go to these days for a woman's heart."

Perhaps Jackie should have protested, but she kept mum when the countess delivered that side-eye stare. Not eager to admit it, she was thrilled that Philip was trying too hard—especially with a private tour of Versailles. Such a stark contrast to Marceau's actions, and Jackie believed she deserved being treated like royalty. Though she couldn't ensure that her feelings toward Philip would change because of it.

Harboring such a notion made Jackie feel like a vamp. She had no intention of hurting Philip, but how she wished she could make Marceau ache for her company. Just a little.

She considered asking the countess about Ghislaine and Philip's short-lived relationship but decided against it. The best recourse was to speak with Ghislaine. She sighed, fully aware that her impish side just wanted to stir up a bit of trouble.

NATURALLY, Claude's reaction to the news of Jackie and Philip's impending rendezvous sent her to near-hysterics of glee.

"Let's celebrate tonight! We could go to that jazz club you like, Le Tabou. Ghislaine, will you come?"

Ghislaine offered a drole smile, as if her sister should know better than to suggest such a thing. "I'll leave the reveling up to you, Claude." She lifted Christian into her arms. "It sounds wonderful, though, Jackie. You're very fortunate to have such an experience."

Jackie flashed a smile for Ghislaine, and gratefulness swelled in her as she gauged her remark was genuine. Ghislaine's feelings mattered to her, and she didn't want to make a show of her emotions or Philip's generosity. "Thank you. Yes, I'm delighted to go."

That evening, Jackie and Claude took a taxi to Saint-Germain and walked down Rue Dauphine to the club. When they entered Le Tabou, Jackie's tepid mood went cold the moment she spotted Renee across the smoke-filled room.

"What's Renee doing here?" Jackie asked in Claude's ear.

She laughed. "Well, that's a surprise. I only telephoned and invited ladies to join us, but I spoke to Renee earlier and mentioned that we'd made plans to come here. I didn't think he'd show up."

Although Claude may not have expected Renee to join their intimate party, she wasted no time in making a beeline for him at the bar and throwing her arms around him.

With Claude still clinging to him, Renee held up a hand, acknowledging Jackie and the other ladies. She returned the gesture, but her stomach wanted to lurch at the sight of him.

"What is it?" Bea seemed to sense Jackie's change in demeanor.

"There's something I don't like about him."

Bea glimpsed the happy couple, then returned her attention to Jackie. "Glad I'm not on the other end of that."

Jackie shooed her away with a paltry smile as Claude and Renee joined them.

Despite the vivacious thump of the music, the rhythmic hiss of the cymbals, and the serenade of the saxophone, Jackie could only focus on Renee. He made no apologies for his intrusion and mainly spoke to Claude, with his lips tickling her ear. He made sure her glass was never empty and sat closer to her than Jackie liked. Though the lounge was warm, he kept an arm around Claude, and sometimes Jackie lost sight of his hand. Claude basked in the attention.

Jackie traded more than one perturbed side glance with Bea and the other girls, who also seemed bothered by him. At least she wasn't the only one who picked up on his oily ways. Though, for the life of her, she couldn't understand how Claude managed to be oblivious to Renee's nauseating allure.

As the night stretched, so did Jackie's discontent. Bea caught the eye of a uniformed American soldier and abandoned their table for a dimly lit corner and the soldier's lap. The other girls, with their drinks kicking in, preferred the dance floor over the front seats to the Claude and Renee spectacle.

Jackie stuck to seltzer water, which did little to quench her growing fury. As the cocktails dulled Claude's senses, Renee's hands seemed to enjoy more freedom around her waist. When Renee nestled into Claude's neck, Jackie reached across the table for her friend and firmly nabbed her wrist.

"We could use a trip to the powder room." But flustered, Jackie had forgotten her surroundings. The bar, like most public places in Paris, perhaps most of Europe, had deplorable bathrooms. Small platforms where a lady could place her feet and squat over a hole, while holding her skirt in a gather and her panties overstretched at her knees. Toilet paper was in rare supply, which subjected newspapers like *France-Soir* to being torn into handy scraps.

Claude laughed, lobbed her head sideways at the suggestion.

"Then let's get some air and have a smoke," Jackie persisted.

Renee, his smarmy stare slinking over Jackie, seemed attuned to her tactics but not discouraged. Claude clumsily made her way over Renee and Jackie took her by the arm.

When they stepped outside, Jackie helped her lean against the building as she struck a match for their cigarettes.

"You might want to ease up on the drinks." She handed Claude the lit cigarette and hoped she wouldn't burn herself.

"Funny. You don't seem worried about Bea."

Claude's sudden coherence stunned Jackie. Not that she could argue the point. Bea had a talent for attracting attention, when she wanted and when it served a purpose for her. Jackie admired—no, envied—that ability to swirl in and out of roles, though she worried that Bea took her flirtations too far and didn't bother with subtlety. Consequences didn't seem to plague Bea, which puzzled Jackie. Regardless, she sensed that Bea knew how to take care of herself. Unlike Claude.

"Is that where you're drawing inspiration from? Bea?" Jackie's tone had more bite than she intended.

Claude, the back of her head propped against the building's stone exterior, didn't answer.

"I can't speak to Bea the same way I can to you. She's a different girl than you. Not one who cares for her reputation at times." Jackie flushed. Was she betraying Bea by letting such a remark fly so loosely? Not that she meant to sound offensive—or had a desire to tamper with losing Bea's friendship. "I know that's not you, Claude, and to be very frank, I don't trust Renee. His intentions are unctuous at best."

"Unctuous? Sakes alive, where'd you get that word?" Claude rolled her eyes and took a drag of her cigarette.

"You know what I mean, Claude. You hardly know the man, and he seems to be having fun at your expense."

Claude straightened, furrowed her brow. "Maybe he can't afford to show up in a gold chariot and take me riding across the French countryside that his family owns."

Jackie absorbed the jab. "He seems to be doing fine, flooding you with cocktails."

"It's not for you to worry about." She tugged at her dress and shook out her hair. "Renee likes me, and that's all I care about tonight." Claude walked heavily to the door and let herself back in.

Jackie huffed. Words had failed her, and she feared the night was far from over. Claude was beyond the point of being reasonable and apparently simmering with resentment. Jackie finished her smoke, wishing she could inhale the strength she would need for getting them out of the bar and safely home.

SEVERAL HOURS and several drinks for Claude later, the group left Le Tabou and dispersed in different directions. Bea, tucked under the arm of her soldier, bid Jackie and the others farewell, stating that she was in good hands and that her escort would get her back to Reid Hall. Jackie shouldered Claude, who could barely stand. Renee, bored with Claude's drunkenness, bid goodnights to everyone and made no offer to see the ladies home in a taxi.

Jackie found her anger and disgust purposeful, giving her the needed momentum to drag and hoist Claude along. Available taxis proved sparse. They slogged in the direction of home, but she knew it would take them the rest of the night to cover the four miles with Claude's current condition. Claude protested and claimed she couldn't go on. Jackie helped her to a bench, deciding it was easier to give her a minute than to fuss. She appreciated that decision even more when Claude hurled into the grass.

Night caved in and the chilled air seeped through their cocktail dresses and shawls. When Jackie was confident Claude was empty and spent, she managed to flag down a taxi. She encouraged Claude to pull herself together and summon the strength to make it home, but Claude drifted between varied stages of consciousness. Jackie, acting as a crutch, flour-sacked her into the taxi.

Once their feet hit Mozart Avenue, Jackie led Claude on a wobble-walk to the second floor apartment. When they crossed the threshold, she gave no thought to waking the household and cared only about landing Claude in her bed, which she managed. Although she expected the countess or Ghislaine to pop into their room, complaining about the late hour, the noise, or both, no one stirred.

Finally, after slipping off Claude's shoes and folding the covers over her, Jackie plopped onto her own bed. Her disdain for Renee deepened as exhaustion catapulted her into a desperate sleep.

JACKIE CRANKED the coffee mill steadily the next morning and packed the percolator's basket, wondering if she had enough grounds for the strength of coffee she needed. Claude, too. As the countess and Ghislaine, with Christian at her heels, trickled into the kitchen, only morning greetings were exchanged. Neither of the women looked rested and avoiding eye contact with Jackie seemed to be a priority.

Misery marred Claude when she shuffled to the table.

Jackie gave up grinding the coffee beans, worried the sound might exacerbate Claude's hangover. She gave her already poured mug to Claude, who massaged her forehead and kept her eyes closed. Christian proved to be the only one interested in food.

Jackie sat and began picking at her nails under the table, aching for someone to speak about last night. Was the countess angry they had violated curfew and Claude had stumbled in drunk? Was Ghislaine angry that her mother wasn't reprimanding her sister for her deplorable behavior? Surely, they both must have heard Claude's heavy footfalls and groans as they made their way to bed.

"Have you decided what you're wearing today, dear?" the countess asked Jackie, though her voice lacked the joy today's occasion deserved.

"My red pleated skirt and white blouse."

"Oh, you'll look so lovely." She stirred her coffee until she sensed Claude's sensitivity to the scraping of the spoon against the ceramic cup.

So that's how it's going to be.

Jackie couldn't blame them. Perhaps now wasn't the best time to accost Claude.

On the other hand, she thought of her mother. Janet was an expert when it came to petty torments. She preferred pinpricking those who'd wronged her or disobeyed with passive aggressive treatments rather than being straightforward and unleashing her irritation. *A lady must meter her anger*, she was fond of saying. For Jackie, not talking about a matter felt worse than facing the argument, the fallout, or the lecture likely to result.

"I should get ready." Jackie excused herself.

Perhaps the countess was waiting until she had her family alone. Correcting Claude in front of their guest wasn't ideal. Jackie wished she had a way to make things easier on Claude—and mostly, a way to make her see what a fiend Renee was.

BY THE TIME Philip arrived with his driver and his father's secretary, who would also serve as the day's chaperone, Jackie had readied and hoped to trade the knots in her stomach for butterflies. Leaving the apartment released her from the somberness within, and the sun-drenched morning and mild temperatures promised a picturesque setting.

She knew, or at the very least suspected, that having the Palace of Versailles all to themselves would be impossible. The grounds, the château, and everything associated with the historic property and its buildings covered over two thousand acres. However, Jackie imagined that Philip's idea of a private tour meant venturing into rooms and areas—possibly having access to sculptures or paintings—not currently available for public display. Excitement teemed within her as she wondered how much access Philip's reputation, or that of his family, would lend.

And she was right. Though clusters of visitors dotted the vast landscape, Jackie and Philip had their own tour guide, and each room or section they came to, from the breathtaking Hall of Mirrors to the Royal Apartments to the Royal Chapel and Opera, they had to themselves. Other guests were temporarily prohibited from entering, which made Jackie feel terribly selfish and regal both at the same time.

Their guide overwhelmed them with the history of the grand

salons, the half-barreled ceilings, and the stories behind the frescoes, paintings, and sculptures.

Jackie declined to visit the Temple of Love, a twelve-column, dome-topped structure that housed a statue of Cupid. During last summer's visit to the palace, she and her friends had been told that young women who touched either Cupid or the columns became cursed in childbearing. Usually, she put little stock in superstitions but wasn't willing to test this particular notion. Her apprehension and explanation amused Philip—and whether he'd heard of the legend or not, he didn't say.

Jackie felt foolish after mentioning it, and warmth sizzled her cheeks. She didn't intend to sound flighty or naïve and feared Philip was mentally plunking her into the category of *flighty, like so many others*. But her insecurities dissipated when their guide triggered a lever, disguised as a wall sconce, and a bookcase cracked open into another room.

"A secret passage?" Jackie asked.

Philip said nothing and held out his hand, indicating she could enter first.

She stepped into a small library—once Marie Antoinette's private library, according to their guide—and found a bistro-style table with a plated lunch for two awaiting.

"Oh, Philip, it's lovely." She took her seat, awed by the room and its bounty. An open window allowed for the autumn breeze to join them, along with a view of the grounds.

"I had a feeling you'd like being surrounded by books in a private little alcove."

The recess, composed of three walls of nearly-floor-to-ceiling books, had enough room to accommodate the table and chairs but little else.

They talked of the palace, with Jackie stating how thrilling it was to enjoy such a tour, especially so close to the anniversary of the treaty's signing. Philip dove into his wary views of Communism but remained confident France would grow ever stronger in the new decade. She admired his patriotism and said as much.

After lunch, the tour of the palace continued and drew to an end in the gardens. Their tour guide encouraged them to roam about and enjoy the seasonal foliage and flowers, then parted. Although the breath, width, and depth of the outdoor spaces were too expansive for them to cover it all, Jackie and Philip strolled through the groves and along the canal before returning to the château. They sat on a bench near the reflecting pool. Satiated from the long day, they took in the scenery of boxwoods, shorn into various swirls and shapes, and the chipmunks scurrying along the pebbled ground in search of food.

"It's been a wonderful afternoon." Jackie meant it, and she had enjoyed being with Philip more than she'd expected. His knowledge of the Marie Antoinette portrait by Lebrun and the history of the silver furniture had enthralled her. As they sat together, silent for the first time that day, she knew this was the kind of life she wanted—with a man who could surprise her and entertain her and be still with her. Not one who was wrapped in secrets.

She caught her breath when she realized it was the first time her thoughts had wandered to Marceau that day. How could that be? Because there she was, surrounded by history, splendor, adored...and yet, it wasn't enough to erase the man who couldn't give her nearly as much. Part of her dared to imagine sharing the outing with Marceau, though she couldn't understand her own obsession. For all she knew, the man was dirt poor, displaced somehow by the war, aimless, and with no means to care for himself, let alone someone else.

No. She couldn't tolerate such imaginations. Not when Philip had been perfect in manners and deed.

"If you're agreeable, Jackie, I'd like for my family to host a party. For us."

His emphasis on the last two words didn't go unnoticed.

"For us?" She didn't mean to sound coy or ungrateful. Repeating the phrase helped it sink in. "What are we celebrating, Philip?"

The corners of his lips curled. "The fact we've found each other, and that we make a good fit."

"One full day together and you know that we're a match?" Her comment was part tease, part inquiry.

"A wealth of opportunities await me. There's a chance, when the government has become more settled, here and across Europe, that I could become a head of state. Or I could assume a new role in the military, an officer's rank, of course. Talk is also brewing about a partnership with Monaco, where we could expand our family's business in Nice. At any rate, the choosing will be mine. My parents have hinted that it's time I settle down. I don't disagree."

"Philip, you know I'm here for school and my studies. When classes end in the spring..." She didn't want to say it. Didn't want to sound as though she meant to hurt him. Not after the day had been so flawless.

His face displayed a self-satisfied expression, one that looked well-worn and etched into his shimmering skin. "I'm not worried."

Her flesh prickled at hearing the same words she'd uttered to Paul after first meeting Philip. Had he overheard her that night, or was he truly convinced that he'd wooed her in one fell swoop? As much as she liked his confidence, along with the enticement of an extraordinary lifestyle, she didn't feel the rush of jubilation—the certainty—that she hoped would flood her soul.

She refused to press her point. If Philip wanted to throw a party, she wouldn't hold him back. Perhaps it was wrong, or encouraged him unduly, but being pursued and heralded in front of crowds with a château as a backdrop, was exactly what she wanted.

ARRIVING BACK at the apartment near ten o'clock that evening, Jackie made a quieter entrance than the night before. She welcomed the silence, assuming everyone was asleep, but wondered how the de Rentys had spent the day—and how Claude was feeling. With too much buzzing in her head to sleep, she went to the kitchen and opened the door to the Juliet balcony and leaned against the wrought iron railing that came up to her waist. Stars glistened across the sapphire-tinted sky. She closed her eyes a moment and savored the stillness and calm of the city.

"How incredible was it?" Claude asked softly. She joined Jackie at the railing and took in a deep breath of the night air.

"I think everything Philip planned went off without a hitch."

Jackie ran her hands along her sleeves, not that she was chilled. Caution prodded her as she recalled Claude's words from last night: *Maybe he can't afford to show up in a gold chariot....* Naturally, Jackie understood the effects of alcohol, but she sensed the truth in Claude's tipsy sentiment. That Claude wanted her own Prince Charming. Did she really want to hear how wonderful Jackie's day had been? Or that Philip might be throwing a party, commemorating them as a couple?

"I figured as much." She gave an easy yet weathered grin. Her hair hung loose and soft, like she'd just bathed. "I'm sorry about last night. I know I owe you for taking care of me. Can't say I remember a great deal, but it was good of you to get me home safe. Mother said so."

Several thoughts tumbled through Jackie's mind, including her hunch that the countess preferred to confront Claude after Jackie had left. Relief oozed over her, believing the countess had been firm but gentle in her reprimand. At the very least, they'd discussed last night. She wouldn't comb for details. Claude's admission of not remembering much complicated matters, though. Was she resentful of Jackie's relationship with Philip, or had she only been trying to get Jackie to back down her concerns over Claude's condition? Jackie wouldn't venture into that minefield either.

Instead, she wanted to rage against Renee, harp on about how he kept Claude drinking and was quick to abandon her when she became too drunk to handle. Worse, he'd shown no concern for getting her home safely. But Jackie thought it was too soon, that a degree of humiliation had wrapped itself around Claude like a wet cloak. She had no desire to make her suffer more.

"We all get carried away sometimes." It was the best thing she could come up with, though she hoped last night provided a lasting lesson all its own. On the other hand, she vowed to become a stalwart watchdog over Lee, whether her little sister liked it or not. "I'd never just leave you. I hope you know that."

Claude blushed. "I do. Leastways now I do."

"Can you make me a promise?"

"Maybe."

"Promise me you'll take better care of yourself. There's nothing wrong with waiting for the right guy to come along. You really deserve a man who will be good to you."

Claude slinked back against the door frame and said nothing.

"You're the most up-beat person I know," Jackie went on. "No one tells jokes as well as you, and seeing you with Christian, I know you'll be a wonderful mother someday. You better set your standards high, right here and now, Claude de Renty, because I'm not sure there's a man out there who really deserves you."

She smiled. "Thanks. You know, I never really thought about what I wanted when it came to men and relationships. Not until you came along."

Inwardly, Jackie beamed a little.

I'm still figuring out what I want too.

NINE

November 1949

If nothing else, Jackie and the rest of the girls from the Smith program admired Miss Langley for her tiresome efforts to expose them to Paris's history and culture. Although attending plays, touring museums, and visiting cathedrals also served to keep them occupied outside of their studies, they all knew it was also a means to keep them out of trouble. Jackie had missed and been excused from certain events due to the busy tug-of-war between Philip and Paul, but one excursion she refused to miss was their private tour of Nôtre Dame Cathedral.

Their outing, heralded by nuns in full habit from the Sisters of the Sacred, oozed reverence. Out of respect, Jackie and the girls donned chapel veils, even though the tradition didn't still hold and they weren't taking Eucharist. The Sisters, three of them, were hard to differentiate, as they each reflected the same mannerisms, had parchment-paper-like skin, and spoke with a quiet tenderness that forced the girls to listen intently.

Though Jackie knew from her studies that Napoleon's coronation was held at Nôtre Dame, she hadn't realized that Joan of Arc had been beatified there. The gothic architecture, the famous stained-glass rose window that had been removed and stored during the wars, and the seventeenth century organ awed Jackie and her companions.

She had hoped they would be granted a peek at the relics from the Crucifixion, namely, the Crown of Thorns. The church also held a piece of wood from the Cross and a nail. The Sisters mentioned the relics, with constrained delight, but said the crown, preserved in a gilded, crystalline reliquary, was only taken out for Mass on Good Friday.

When the tour ended, Jackie and the girls were allowed to explore the nave, or if they were so inclined, to pray at the altar. After a brief prayer, she rose to stroll the nave, her fingertips brushing the pews as she walked by. She hadn't noticed at first, but Bea was at her side.

"How was it?" she asked, keeping her voice down.

Jackie gave her a quizzical glance.

"Versailles. Spending the day with Philip?" Bea clarified.

Jackie smiled. "It was as wonderful as you might imagine. Philip is so thoughtful and attentive."

Bea stopped walking. "Thoughtful and attentive. Doesn't sound romantic. Or fiery."

Frustration and embarrassment flared, not realizing there were right and wrong answers. "Am I supposed to say something other than the truth?"

"Well," Bea tilted her head and sashayed several steps before spinning around, "I expected to hear how swept away you felt, how dreadfully in love you've fallen with Philip. Instead, you label him like a good servant."

Jackie restrained from clenching her jaw, even though Bea's words delivered a pinch of hurt. "Falling in love takes time." The lack of conviction in her own remark deepened her embarrassment. She slid into a pew and sat, grateful that Miss Langley, the other girls, and the Sisters couldn't hear their conversation—or read the distress surely mounting on her face.

Bea sat next to her and gazed up at the flying buttresses.

Jackie welcomed the reprieve and basked in the majesty of the church while she regrouped on the inside.

She couldn't deny the truth in Bea's observation, but the accuracy of it struck her sharply. If she wasn't fooling Bea, then what on earth did Philip think?

"France certainly has its share of tragic love affairs," Bea said.

Jackie nodded.

"You've heard what happen here, haven't you?" Bea pointed forward. "Right there on the altar?"

"No."

She reared back. "I can't believe it. There's actually a historical event I've read about that you haven't?"

Not knowing what to say, Jackie forced a half-hearted grin.

"Then you're going to love this. About twenty years ago, a woman burst in here and shot herself with a pistol. She died on the altar."

"That's terrible." Jackie's gaze locked on the altar, where she'd just said a humble prayer for her family. Now, she envisioned a young woman, sprawled and dying on the same spot. A shiver ran through her as she tried to imagine the woman's despair and anguish. "What possessed her to take her own life?"

"Her lover. She'd been having an affair with a married man. When she pushed him, wanted more than just being the other woman, he refused. Cast her away and would have nothing else to do with her. She despaired, because it was the second time she'd fallen for a man she couldn't have. The rejection became too much."

"But to shoot yourself...in a church...." Jackie couldn't comprehend the desperation. "How awful for her, not to have the love she needed."

They sat in silence but noticed several people setting up chairs and music stands on the choir platform. Men carrying cased instruments began arriving and taking seats.

"How's Claude?"

"Well enough." Images of Claude's drunken condition reeled through Jackie's mind. "Hopefully she's wiser too."

Bea nodded her agreement. "It might suit her to be more careful next time."

Hearing the words *next time* landed a pit in Jackie's stomach. She didn't want there to be a next time of Claude losing herself and getting swallowed by the repercussions. But maybe Bea had a point. Not every girl learned her lesson after a misstep.

"I spoke to her about it. More than anything I hope she's through with that Renee."

Bea snickered. "Yes, he's a snake, and he's not too good at hiding it."

After a moment, Jackie looked at her, "How did you fare that night, getting home?"

"With my soldier friend? What was his name?" She cocked her head. "Gilbert, I think. Nice enough. He walked me back to the dorm."

"And?"

"Wasn't as though I could invite him in. Besides, Jackie, what kind of girl do you take me for?" Her tone was playful enough.

"You spent most of the night sitting in Gilbert's lap. I suppose you'll have to tell me what kind of girl does that." Jackie did her best impersonation of Lauren Bacall's attitude from *To Have and To Have Not*, where she'd delivered her famous line: *You know how to whistle, don't you, Steve?* Fitting, for the moment, Jackie thought.

Bea laughed, but not loud enough to disturb anyone. "Men are lured so easily. Tell them what they want to hear, when they want to hear it, and they go weak in the knees as if they don't know any better. Let them peek at your cleavage and give them kisses that they feel everywhere, they turn to putty."

Jealousy speared Jackie. She didn't have enough cleavage worth peeking at. Not like Bea, whose buxom curves shaped every blouse and dress she wore. *Flat* and *boxy* were the terms Jackie used to describe her figure.

But Jackie knew Bea was right. Women shamelessly fawned and strutted themselves in front of her father, and he reciprocated with his own flirtations and teases. Even Yusha had his moments of weakness when a pretty girl caught his eye.

"I only let him kiss me after he walked me back." Bea shrugged and puckered her cherry-colored lips. "He wants to see me when he gets back home. Says his family runs a dairy farm in Minnesota. Hmph. Can you imagine anything more boring than living on a dairy farm?"

Jackie's adoration for Hammersmith Farm rose up, but she kept her thoughts to herself. "What does appeal to you then?"

Bea sighed. "I want a big house with lots of fireplaces and hot water every time I turn on the faucet. I want a shiny new Cadillac and trips to the seaside in summer. A minimum of three servants and a vegetable garden." For a moment her face beamed. "But it's not that easy when you don't have the proper background."

"What do you mean?"

"I watch you, Jackie, and the way these men chase after you with their tongues wagging. It would be revolting if it weren't so hilarious and true. You know how to make them eat out of your hand without even trying. They love that you're from Vassar and that your family's rooted in the social register. Whether they know it or not doesn't matter. It's reflected in your mannerisms and perfect style. You'll have your pick of any wealthy man you want, which you already do."

"We're hardly that different, Bea. You grew up in Connecticut and spent summers at the Larchmont Yacht Club."

Bea looked away. "That's what I told you. I grew up in government housing in Baltimore. My mother had her way with every sailor and recruit that passed through Annapolis. She never knew who my father was and didn't have time to be a mother." She looked at Jackie, waited for her revelation to take hold. "I put a few embellishments on my application for Smith. It was my only hope of getting out of there. I didn't want to end up like my mother."

Jackie couldn't mask her astonishment, both at Bea's subterfuge and at hearing her true history. Her adoration for Bea wasn't tarnished, but Jackie wondered if she herself could've mustered such a scheme.

"Some of us have to bend the rules to get what we want," Bea said. "We used what we've got to our advantage. But you already know that, don't you?" She winked. "That's one of the things I like about you, Jackie. Despite that pretty little pedigree, you're not too good to slum a little."

Miss Langley, her voice audible but metered in reverence, called for the girls' attention.

"Girls, we are in for a special treat! The Montmartre Orchestra is setting up for practice and we're invited to stay. Come."

Jackie, Bea, and the remaining girls filed into the pews while instruments were tuned. Moments later, the conductor rapped his baton atop his music stand. The members eased into "Amazing Grace". Jackie's breath caught when she spotted Marceau playing the violin.

"You know him?" Bea whispered.

"I believe so."

Marceau's gaze found Jackie, but he never broke his concentration. Four pieces later, Miss Langley led the girls in a soft clap and standing ovation.

"Bravo! Simply wonderful!"

The musicians also stood and bowed. Marceau's impish yet delicious stare lent special attention to Jackie. As the girls were dismissed, the orchestra members were released for a reprieve. Marceau joined Jackie and Bea. Introductions followed.

"You're very talented." Bea said it as she shook his hand, holding on to him longer than necessary as she made a little side-to-side twist.

"Thank you, although you must have a distinct knack for being able to hear a single instrument through that ensemble."

Marceau's attempt at sarcasm seemed to bounce off Bea. She flashed her salacious grin and batted her charcoal lashes as if she fed off the attention. Jackie, a bit on edge after learning of Bea's deception, tamped down her annoyance at Bea's flirtation. At the same time, she couldn't let her unbridled infatuation for Marceau show. Seeing another woman tempt Marceau made Jackie forget how frustrated she'd been with him the last time they'd parted, after painting the sunrise at the Trocadéro.

"Quite the surprise, seeing you here." Marceau turned his attention to Jackie. His eyes lit for her in a way they hadn't for Bea. Buxom curves be damned.

"We're on an educational tour," Jackie explained.

Marceau's eyes drifted over her lips as she spoke, and his lips parted ever so slightly.

Then he looked to Bea. "Forgive me, please, but would you mind if I stole her aside for a minute?"

Cheerfulness fell from Bea's face like a lead balloon from the sky. She turned sharply on her heels and left them. Jackie knew she'd have work to do, both in repairing her status with Bea and soothing the scorn that surely simmered under Bea's skin.

Possibly standing too close and with his head nearly touching Jackie's, Marceau's gaze traced the contours of her face with his eyes. "You're lovelier every time I see you."

Jackie's senses prickled, being so close to him. His appearance—a crisp-white shirt under a vest, hair trimmed and clean-shaven cheeks, with the scent of Clubman aftershave—made Jackie ache for answers. *Where have you been, Marceau? Why the change? Is it for the orchestra only...or something—someone—else? Is there someone else?*

"And I must apologize for the way I left things between us." Regret flashed in his eyes. "You were right to turn your back on me. Honestly, I wouldn't blame you if you never wanted to see me or speak to me again."

Jackie swallowed. He could ask her to run away with him, right now—right out those old doors in front of her classmates and God—and she just might.

"I only wish you would trust me more and let me understand." She didn't want to push. Didn't want the moment to melt into an argument. After the Trocadéro, she had no idea if she would see him again. Now, making him feel guilty didn't interest her. "You say you can't call on me, as though you're hiding from something, but here you are, playing in an orchestra."

"Filling in for a friend. He's hoping to return before their big performance at Malmaison. You could say I'm holding his spot. Fortunate that I love the music and know how to play."

Jackie's grin began to fail as confusion budded within her.

Marceau must have sensed her need for more substantial answers. He stepped even closer to her. "I know. My actions contradict themselves. Believe me, I hope to tell you everything as soon as I can." He lowered his voice. "But not here, or in present company."

Neither of them risked a glance at Bea, who stood on the fringes of the Smith group, her arms crossed in front of her chest.

"Then when?" Would she ever not sound like an anxious fool?

"Are you free tonight? We could meet at the catacombs."

Jackie stalled, though there was no possibility she would pass on a chance to see him. When she agreed, they parted ways.

"Another man under your spell." Bea said it with noticeable disdain in her voice when Jackie joined the group.

"Oh, don't be silly. He's a friend of Paul's." A statement that held enough truth, Jackie hoped, though her voice wavered.

"Play it however you like, Jackie, but that man is practically diseased with love for you. It's plain to see."

Jackie peeked in Marceau's direction. Walking back to rejoin the orchestra, he turned his head and looked her way. His smile appeared when their stares met, and she had to breathe through the flutter in her chest.

Diseased with love for her? How she hoped that to be true.

GRAY CLOUDS SHROUDED the moonlight when the Denfert-Rochereau metro stop delivered Jackie to the catacombs that evening. She had yet to tour the underground labyrinth built from the bones of millions of Parisians, though the site was located a little over a mile from the Sorbonne.

There she found Marceau waiting, leaning against a lamppost with his woolen newsboy cap pulled down tight.

"You made it."

Although she couldn't say for sure, a hint of relief tinged his voice. Had he worried she would change her mind?

He embraced her and lovingly pecked her cheek. "Are you sure you want to go down?" Delight glistened in his eyes.

Jackie had her reservations. She'd fibbed to the countess, claiming she was going to a late-evening lecture and meeting friends after. Once again, meeting Marceau meant skimping on details of her whereabouts, which both thrilled and concerned her.

"I've never been. Why wouldn't I want to see it?" She refrained from adding how she wanted her first time exploring underground to be alone with him.

Marceau led her to the entrance. Although they were there past regular hours for visitors, he managed to open each door they encountered. Soon they came to a spiral staircase that wound down into the dark. Not naturally squeamish, Jackie put her hand to her chest when she peered into the darkened abyss.

"Don't worry." Marceau squeezed her hand. "I came prepared." He clicked on a flashlight and aimed the beam at the stairs.

She hoped her mild grin reassured him as she prayed for stiff courage so she wouldn't dissolve into a scared, cringy girl.

As they descended, they grasped the railing, rather than each other. Slow but steady, they made their way down.

"Are you familiar with the history here?"

"A little. Only that cemeteries became too full and bodies were moved underground."

"That's right. Back in the 1700s, the cemetery at Saints-Innocents became full. Not surprising, since it had provided a resting place for bodies for ten centuries. The tipping point came when the spring rains kept unearthing those souls."

Jackie shuddered at the thought.

"Another problem reached its brink as well," Marceau continued. "The city had lost much of its foundation to the underground quarries, where limestone was extracted and used to construct many buildings, including Nôtre Dame. A portion of Rue Denfert-Rochereau even collapsed. Louis XVI came to the rescue, though. Old bones found a new purpose, you might say. An architect was hired, and he arranged the bones to provide a support system for the city. At the same time, I think you'll find it was a clever way to commemorate those who've passed before us. Fallen from wars, disease, plague, and even old age."

They reached a hallway. Jackie glimpsed the stone walls and could touch both sides if she stretched out her arms. The ceiling wasn't as high as she would've liked, but neither she nor Marceau were in danger of scraping their heads. Occasional drops of groundwater pecked the tops of their heads as they walked.

"This is a network created from men working the quarries. It's an elaborate system really. Covers the entire city. A web of about three hundred kilometers."

A doorway met them with the banner *Stop, this is The Empire of the Dead* carved into the stone molding.

"This is where the catacombs begin."

Marceau swept the light back and forth slowly so Jackie could take in the walls, lined with skulls and femurs. As they walked, chipped and broken skulls stared back at them with their empty sockets and dull amber tint, and Jackie took in how the skulls were arranged in straight lines, scallop designs, and the formation of the cross. Femur bones, stacked with their socket-end out, completed the simple design.

"Most of the quarry tunnels aren't accessible for visitors, and it's no wonder. Wouldn't take long to get lost."

The galleries they entered featured placards noting the cemeteries where the remains came from.

"Some say Louis XVI and Marie Antoinette ended up down here. Their bodies were disposed of in a mass grave, but others claim their bones were recovered and placed in the tombs at Saint-Denis." He turned to Jackie, who stared at him with wide-eyed wonder. "Depends on what you prefer, I suppose."

They moved on and entered the gallery containing the ossuary, which Jackie found to be as close to a sanctuary as one could hope to find in such a setting. A white cross contrasted against the ash-matte of the bones while the scalloped arrangement of skulls created a less somber tone for the area.

Marceau ran the beam of light along the walls. "But if you're not one for rumors, don't worry. The remains of Robespierre and Charles Perrault, among others, are down here."

"Who's Charles Perrault?"

"He penned Cinderella. Not what I think of as a fairytale ending." Drips of water tapped stagnant puddles and created an echoing symphony. "Did you know the Nazis used parts of this as a bunker? Rumor has it that the Resistance was headquartered here as well. And within that four-year span they never ran into each other. Another testament to the vastness of these tunnels."

"You seem so familiar with this place."

"It's proven useful for me. There are all sorts of access points around the city."

"Please don't tell me you've slept down here."

"No. Too damp and chilly for me."

"Are you some sort of tour guide? That is, when you're not substituting for the Montmartre Orchestra." Contrariness curled the corner of her mouth.

He folded his arms across his chest, the flashlight tucked in the crook of his elbow and shining upward. "You're never going to let up on me, are you?"

"Paul said you could be dangerous." Jackie regretted her bluntness but gauged his reaction, which turned out to be pure amusement. It bothered her, both his ease at her random quips and the uncontrollability of her random quips. But how could she form a sensible agenda in her head when it came to Marceau, since he thrived on the unpredictable. She'd readily admit, though, questioning his dangerousness now proved ill-timed.

Marceau stepped closer, light from the flashlight creating deep shadows across his face. "What do you think?"

"I keep changing my mind about you." A truth she hadn't intended to share.

He focused on her lips, and she feared he'd glimpsed them quiver. Despite that her every nerve sizzled with excitement, Jackie would draw back, if he moved any closer. She wouldn't kiss him. Not while they were surrounded by the remains of six million Parisians, in the mildew-scented bowels of the city.

As if he'd read her mind, Marceau stepped back. He shone the light around the space, then turned the light toward her.

"Come on. I think the tour has ended. Let's get some fresh air and a drink."

He led them out of the catacombs and back to the lamp-lighted streets of Paris. Jackie breathed deep. Absent of a breeze, the warm autumn night embraced her while the sky had cleared, allowing the moon's brilliance to dominate.

As they walked, it struck Jackie what a fraud she was. She tolerated Marceau's eccentric ways with little resistance. Yet she would've instantly lost interest in Philip if his pursuits hadn't been so bold and valiant. It made no sense to her, especially now, wrapped in the glow of him. Bea—perhaps Claude, too—would call her out on her hypocrisy. Deservedly so, but she couldn't care less. And what about the risk to her reputation? Sneaking around in the dark with a man her friend had described as dangerous—was it worth it? She glanced at him as they walked, her hand comfortably in his, and checked her racing heart.

It was worth the risk. But what would become of her if Marceau pushed their relationship forward the way Philip did?

They arrived at a café that resembled Hopper's *Nighthawks* painting. A thin crowd of patrons dispersed around the counter and within the space. At his suggestion, Jackie tried the Turkish coffee. It was thicker and stronger than she liked, so he ordered her a more traditional serving, along with a slice of carrot cake for them to share.

"It'll be a wonder if I get any sleep tonight," she said, "drinking two cups of coffee at this hour."

"That may work in our favor, then, because I wasn't eager to escort you home. Not yet." Coyness teased the corner of his mouth.

"Another underground site?" Her arched brow showed her mild amusement.

Marceau squinted. "You might consider this a more expected spot, but I have something I want to ask of you."

Jackie felt her body blush. "Oh?"

"Not here."

As if to exacerbate her curiosity, Marceau took his time finishing the cake. When they finally left the café, Jackie was buzzing with caffeine and a touch of nervous anticipation. He led them to the Square du Vert-Galant, a small garden honoring Henry IV, located on the pear-shaped peninsula of Île de la Cité with Sainte-Chapelle in the background and Nôtre Dame cathedral only a few steps farther away. Even at night, the lemon-colored leaves of the chestnut and the blazing red leaves of the maple trees couldn't be denied.

Her hand in Marceau's, Jackie followed him to the edge of the park. The Seine's waters lapped the rim, and a rowboat, tied to a stake, waffled in the gentle current.

He held out his hand toward the boat. "Will you join me?"

"This is what you wanted to ask me?"

"Partly." He moved his gaze to the inside of the rowboat, and she glimpsed what looked to be a leather-bound journal and pencils, lolling in the hull.

"That morning at the Trocadéro," Marceau said, "I drew your profile. It was hurried and coarse, but you were more captivating than Paris at the break of dawn. I wanted a moment when I could take my time, lavish in the contours of your face." He caressed her jawline with the backs of his fingers. "I thought nothing could be better than sketching you in the moonlight while we drifted on the Seine."

Words abandoned her as she became lost in his fantasy.

"I've never known a woman like you, Jackie, with such beauty and grace. You inspire me, and you've breathed new life into me. I didn't know it was possible to feel this way." He took both of her hands in his and brought them to his lips. "Will you join me?"

Breathless, light-headed, she nodded. With his help, she stepped carefully into the rowboat and sat.

After he made sure she was comfortable, Marceau got in, untied the rope, and pushed off with the paddle. He rowed only a few strokes, setting a slow course, then he tapped the excess water off the paddles and laid them inside the boat, mindful not to touch Jackie. After picking up his sketchbook, he flipped to an empty page.

"Just relax."

Jackie leaned against the bow and glanced at the sky. Constellations twinkled and the fortress-height walls of the Louvre began to crawl by.

"Something's not right." She sat upright.

Marceau's pencil paused and worry creased his face. "Have you changed your mind?"

She ran her hand along the back of her neck and nodded. "But it's not what you think. If we're going to do this, I want it to be a night we'll always remember." A brazenness surged through Jackie with an intensity she'd never felt before. She straightened herself and began unbuttoning her dress.

"Jackie!" He put his hand on hers to stop her. "No." Though weaker than an admonishment, his tone held firm.

"I'm not undressing to make love with you, Marceau. Only to make this portrait...unique. I want it to reflect how you make me feel."

His lips parted and eyes unblinking, Marceau let his hand fall away.

Jackie resumed undressing. Still seated in the boat, she slipped from her dress and under garments, folded them quickly, and set them neatly beside her. Every inch of her nude body tingled, as if she'd been brushed with static. She reclined again, as best she could, in the bow of the boat and placed her right arm over her head. With her left hand resting on her thigh, she bent her other leg slightly while her eyes never left Marceau's face.

His pencil went to work. He said nothing. No expression betrayed him. The water sloshing against the boat and the gentle scrape of charcoal across the paper were the only sounds to fill the charged air.

Posing nude had only played through Jackie's mind like an unfulfilled fantasy. She never believed for a moment that she'd have the courage or fortitude or gall to shed her clothes for someone—and certainly not in public. But it wasn't just about the sketch or being vulnerable for Marceau. She wanted him to know—to feel in his soul—the lengths she would go to for them to grow closer. Her clothes weren't the only thing discarded. Her inhibitions, fears, and faith in propriety lay there too.

Jackie paid little attention to the city's scenery as they floated. The moonlight held steady as they passed under bridges, affording no attention to the details of Pont Alexandre III, and later, the splendor of the Iron Lady herself—

"You two, in the boat! What are you doing out there?"

"The Sûreté!" Marceau whipped the sketchbook closed.

"Police?" Startled, Jackie snatched her clothes and held them over her bare flesh. Marceau turned, careful not to rock the boat any more than she already had, and to act as a shield for her. Frantically, she dressed as quickly as her nervous hands would allow.

"I asked what you're doing out there? You have no business being out there this late. Bring that boat in this minute."

Against the faint light of a streetlamp, Jackie could see two men, both dressed in Sûreté Nationale uniforms. Marceau paddled the rowboat back to the edge of Port de Genelle. He'd rowed slowly yet deliberately enough that Jackie was ruffled but dressed when the officers helped them out and onto the street.

"We were just enjoying the evening, sirs," Marceau said cordially. "No harm in that, is there?"

"Do you know what time it is?" barked the barrel-shaped officer.

"Late." He said it matter-of-factly, though without an undertone of rebellion.

The officer's face rumpled with disapproval. "Late enough that respectable citizens know better than to be out." His gaze dropped to the sketchpad. "What's that?" He took it from Marceau's hand before he could answer, then flipped through the pages while the other officer looked over his shoulder. When he came to Jackie's picture, he stopped and stared. Jackie sank back behind Marceau as much as she could and avoided his gawking.

"As I suspected." The hefty officer slapped the book shut. "You two were up to mischief. Looks like we'll need to take you in to headquarters."

The slender officer shook his head. "We don't take kindly to such vulgarities."

"Are you arresting us?"

"Have to teach you young people a lesson." Hefty officer, with his hands at their backs, started nudging them.

"But Officer, this is unnecessary," Marceau protested. "I can assure you we meant no harm—"

"Save it, Romeo!"

"But I'm an exchange student." Jackie whirled on her heels and faced the officer. "I can't go to jail!"

"You can if you break the law. Indecent exposure is frowned upon here."

"Sir, please!"

Jackie's words didn't move him. He shook his head and forced her to turn back around.

"You should've thought of the consequences before you took off your clothes."

TEN

The last time Jackie could recall being wracked with such terror was when she was sixteen and taking a seat—between her parents—in the headmistress's office. She'd been caught —ratted out actually—for squeezing green food coloring onto the headmistress's toothbrush, which tainted her teeth for days. Naturally, the headmistress said it was the last straw and held nothing back. She told Jackie's parents the litany of pranks Jackie had masterminded, including taping down items in the headmistress's top desk drawer, hiding an alarm clock in her office that went off during a disciplinary meeting, and greasing her private toilet seat with petroleum jelly, Jackie's most infamous prank.

Perturbed expressions from the headmistress and her mother assaulted her as the words *incorrigible, insolent, and willful* filled the stifled air. Janet had been miffed, sat stiff as a newly starched collar, though being near Jack Bouvier had a little something to do with it, Jackie suspected. Her father, with his legs crossed and posture reclined against the chair, puffed leisurely on his cigarette and showed no concern.

Now, as Jackie sat in a jail cell in Paris, that same terror returned. Amplified, though, when she practiced explaining the situation to her mother over the telephone—*God, I pray it doesn't come to that!* But how could she keep it from her? Jackie had been informed that she'd be released in twenty-four to forty-eight hours, depending on the charges. In the meantime, she was permitted to phone her loved ones.

As she'd entered police headquarters, her hand tightly laced with Marceau's, he'd whispered into her ear, "Don't worry. Say as little as possible. I'll work to get us out of here."

She nodded but found no comfort in his words. They were separated and planted into cells with iron bars and real criminals, from what Jackie could discern. The only humiliation she'd escaped was being in handcuffs.

She thumped the back of her head into the concrete block, wishing she could dull the racing thoughts. Despite the fear consuming her, she refused to cry. By now she had no idea what time it was. She closed her eyes. *This is what I deserve for trusting Marceau too much.* But an instant rebuke, coupled with shame, chased the thought away. *No, Marceau didn't suggest I take my clothes off. It's my own doing that we're both here, plunked into dank cells and on the brink of ruin. It's completely my fault.*

"Miss, you're free to leave." An officer unlocked the cell door, keys rattling. Marceau slipped passed him when the gap was wide enough and draped Jackie with his arm, like a shield ready to protect her.

"Are you all right, Jackie?"

"What's happening?"

After holding an index finger to his lips, he clasped her hand and eased her sudden anxieties with a lilt of a smile. Questions bombarded her, but she fell in behind him as he led them out of the containment area. All Jackie craved was the freedom waiting on the other side of the imposing doors that opened to the street outside, but various officers kept approaching Marceau and hindering their exit.

"We're so sorry for the inconvenience, sir."

"May we give you an escort home?"

"Is there anything we can do to make up for this misunderstanding, sir?"

"Thank you for your patience. We just didn't realize..."

"You have our assurance that no report will be filed of the incident."

Along with the cordial, apologetic remarks came handshakes and officers tipping their hats to Jackie. She nodded her thanks and kept her gaze moving. Confusion overwhelmed her. She wanted to shake her head, certain that her mastery of the language was slipping. The entrance doors were held open by two officers bidding them well and waving. Marceau reciprocated their waves and attention until they were on the sidewalk and setting a steady pace for Mozart Avenue.

Scarfing the night air to rid her nostrils of the urine-refuse stench lingering from the cell, she noticed the sketchbook tucked under Marceau's arm. How she hoped the nude outline of her body was still tucked inside and not being passed around at the police station. A petty distraction for what really plagued her mind: Why the lavish display of regret from the police officers? What lie—or truth—had he told them?

She darted a side glance his way and sensed he had his guard up. Tight shoulders and no eye contact giving him away. Most likely he was ready to defend himself against her questions. Disappointment stirred within her. *Why does he forsake every opportunity to draw us closer together? To draw me closer to him?*

"What did you do, Marceau?" Jackie couldn't take the silence any longer. "How did you get us out of there?"

He didn't hesitate. "I told them who I was."

She stopped in her tracks, causing him to stumble. "What is that supposed to mean?"

"It's complicated, but I couldn't let you sit in there all night. I had to do something, so I did."

"Then why don't you tell me what you shared with them?"

He slid his hands along her arms. "I will tell you. When the time is right." He kissed her forehead.

She pulled away from him, exasperated.

"Don't do this, Jackie, please. Don't make this an all-or-nothing moment. Not after tonight." His words trailed off as their eyes met. The ease of his stare suggested he was thinking about the rowboat and her nude body under the starlit night. She couldn't abandon her frustrations as easily. When he reached for her, as if he meant to tuck her hair behind her ear, she turned away and discouraged his touch.

"Marceau, I hope you destroy that picture of me."

JACKIE TREMBLED with exasperation as she walked on without him. Her efforts to disconnect herself from a show of emotion failed. Tears welled in her eyes and a sob built in her throat.

Why is nothing I do good enough for him? What does it take for that man to trust someone?

She was tired of never moving forward with him. Tired of only backward leaps.

Jackie dabbed and dried her eyes with her sleeve. The task of facing the countess took the forefront in her mind. Lying held no appeal. She would face her hostess and simply tell her the truth about tonight... sans the detail about being nude on the rowboat.

When she arrived at the apartment, no lights and no countess awaited. She thought it odd. Considering the night's events, she hadn't expected her return home to be anticlimactic. But as she headed to her room, gratefulness eased over her. She closed the bedroom door and counted it as a feat of accomplishment, having made little noise.

But then the relief drained away. Claude's bed was empty.

Jackie grabbed the bedside clock and held it close to her eyes in the dim light. Past three a.m. Jackie pawed Claude's bedding in disbelief.

Where on earth could she be?

Jackie went to the window, unlatched the doors, and peered down the alley for any signs of her friend. Panic swelled when the search proved fruitless. She bit her nails as she paced and tossed around the idea of waking the countess. Her breath caught when the knob to her room turned. Claude's silhouette slipped around the door and into the bedroom. She closed the door quietly and leaned against it.

"Gracious, Claude, where have you been?" Jackie's whisper came out desperate.

When the moonlight streaked Claude's face, Jackie glimpsed the bloodied and swollen lip.

"What happened?" She led Claude's to her bed, and they sat. Jackie reached to turn on the lamp, but Claude touched her with a trembling hand. Jackie waited as Claude drew ragged breaths and an outburst of tears seemed certain.

"I went out with Renee," she began, a thick croak in her voice. "He wanted to see me, and I thought it would be the most appropriate way for me to end the relationship. We went to a café near the Dome Church. He wanted to hold hands and kiss me, but I nudged him away, said we had something serious to discuss. By the time we made it to the café, I wanted to get it over with. I'll have you know I didn't have a thing to drink. He had a whiskey, and maybe he'd been drinking earlier. I don't know, but I was kind and straightforward and eager to get away from him. I told him we weren't compatible and that I wouldn't be seeing him anymore. He seemed surprised, upset even. Then he asked if we could stroll through the garden. I felt so bad for him I agreed. Almost had second thoughts about whether or not I was doing the right thing. But once we were there, walking alone, night caving in, he grabbed me."

Claude choked on her words. In the dim light, Jackie saw her eyes fill with tears. "He said such vile things and tried tearing at my clothes. I slapped him. He couldn't believe it, then he struck me so hard I fell to my knees. I didn't know what was going to happen to me." Her glistening eyes found Jackie's. "He could've killed me. I was praying to God that I wouldn't die there. Renee was about to reach for me again but heard something. I don't know what it was, but he leaned into me and said I wasn't worth it. Then he left me there. I curled up on the ground and cried. I must have passed out." She broke down, as if reliving the memory delivered the pain all over again.

Jackie drew her in and held her close.

"I was so afraid, Jackie. I never thought he would hurt me like that."

"I'm so sorry, Claude. You never should've been left alone with him. Thank God you're all right."

She realized how trivial her problems were considering the real danger Claude had endured. She squeezed her hard, and a part of her wished that Janet was there. Yes, Jackie ached for the security and reassurances only her mother could give.

ELEVEN

Jackie and Claude drifted into a slumber of exhaustion, with Claude still wrapped in Jackie's arms. Stiffness and aches, from their awkward sleeping positions, woke them early. Stretching and mild massages melted the discomforts, and Jackie wished last night's aftermath could be gone as easily. Her stomach knotted when she considered what awaited: telling the countess everything about Renee. There was no chance of hiding the bruises or Claude's busted lip.

The two dressed quietly, even though they heard the morning rustles, a sure sign the countess was up. Claude ran her brush through her hair so many times that Jackie worried she would irritate her scalp.

Stilling Claude's hand, she said gently, "You did nothing wrong last night."

Claude sighed and nodded. They squeezed hands before walking into the kitchen.

Upon seeing her daughter, the countess froze.

"Claude, what in God's great name—"

"It was Renee." Her tears erupted as she went to her mother's arms. Pieces of the story came out as Claude sobbed. The countess, taking in the injuries, lovingly stroked her daughter's face as tears brimmed her eyes. Words poured from both of them as the countess tried to make sense of the matter.

Jackie warmed a brioche loaf and set out peach preserves while the coffee brewed. After Claude took a moment to wipe her face, they gathered at the table. She calmly repeated the details of last night as Jackie set steaming mugs of coffee in front of each of them. A range of emotions battered the countess, from fury toward Renee to regret for not being more active in the girls' lives. The countess wanted to head to Sûreté headquarters right away and file charges against Renee, but Claude adamantly refused.

Jackie stiffened at the mention of Sûreté headquarters and fought to keep the repugnant smells from reviving in her mind. Her head spun when she considered last night's tumultuous events, how life changing they had been. The weight and finality of losing any hope she'd had for a relationship with Marceau; the rampant thoughts of what could've happened to Claude at the hand of Renee. The combination made her head throb and her stomach clench.

"No, Mother," Claude said. "We can't...do anything."

"But look at you. They'll clearly see that you've been attacked. Why, he'd be arrested, straight away."

"I'm too afraid, Mother." Fresh tears welled. "And it won't matter if charges are brought against him or not. It won't undo what happened."

Jackie pictured Claude, bleeding and unconscious on the church grounds. A shiver ran through her, knowing the night could've gone so much worse. A wave of nausea followed, knowing Renee would suffer no consequence.

Worry creased the countess's brow as she reached for Claude's hands. "We'll handle it the way you want." She pressed her lips tight as if to keep her true words from flowing.

Silence infected the air. Jackie wanted better for Claude but could do nothing. But as she munched on her warm bread, the sweetness of the peaches rolling in her mouth, an idea started to form along with a tinge of satisfaction.

Surely those years of pranking the headmistress could be drawn upon for certain...inspirations.

Dear Mummy,

I miss you. Forgive me please for beginning a letter on such a somber-sounding note, but I really do miss you. Perhaps this time away has made me realize how well you have taken care of me. I cannot imagine being a mother yet, but maybe now I understand why you've always put forth high expectations for me and Lee—it's for our own good. So we would know worth within ourselves and have a reasonable expectation of how others should treat us. Men in particular. I see that now, how important it is to be mindful of behaviors—and to carefully surround yourself with trustworthy people. For an unsoiled reputation matters deeply. Oh, how hard it must have been for you that day I boarded the SS De Grasse. Now I understand! I will confess that I was curious to see what rebellions I could muster, but only briefly. Being on my own means being my own person, and I want you to know I'm still your daughter in every sense, only now, I'm truly grateful for it.

My love always,
Jackie

JACKIE NEVER DREAMED she'd become a conspirator in a plot for vengeance, yet there she was, sneaking from the de Rentys' apartment to meet with her collaborators a couple of days after Claude's attack. Naturally, Philip and Paul were enraged when they learned that Claude had been hurt. Paul's anger reached a boiling point, as he felt responsible, since he'd brought Renee into their group. He nearly stormed off, intent on dealing with Renee on his own. It took some doing, but Jackie convinced Paul that the three of them could exact a thoughtful revenge. When Jackie shared that Claude refused to involve the Sûreté, it was easy to sway both men that a retaliation was needed. After much discussion, they crafted a simple plan.

Paul got word to Renee that several young men were headed to

Fontainebleau, a city about an hour's drive south of Paris and not far from Paul's home in Courances—specifically, to an abandoned church where a risqué cabaret show would take place, one where the girls would flirt and mingle with the crowd while cheap drinks flowed. Renee was cautioned not to tell anyone about the venue, that it would be attended by invite-only patrons, since this show was in its very early, experimental stage.

Ripe with interest, Renee met Henri, a mutual friend of Paul and Philip's, for drinks before they headed to Fontainebleau. Over a tall, cloudy glass of pastis, Henri ratcheted the tease, telling Renee the girls were as sultry as those depicted in *La Vie Parisienne* and were friendly to boot. Eager, despite the pastis kicking in hard, Renee hopped into Henri's car.

"I wouldn't mind an evening with a dame fawning over me." Renee slurred as he slumped in his seat. He batted his eyelids slowly, as if they'd suddenly become too heavy.

Henri grinned as he watched him from the corner of his eye. They had just passed Orly when Renee's snoring began. Henri loosed a loud cackle, but Renee didn't stir.

When Henri pulled up to the old church, which sat on a sliver of property owned by the de Ganays, the sweep of his headlights illuminated Paul, Philip, and Jackie.

"Did he suspect?" Paul asked as Henri got out of the car.

"Not a thing! Those two tablets of Nytol did the trick!"

"Keep your voice down," Philip warned.

They all looked toward the parsonage. Even in the night, the house, not much more than a shanty, showed its age. The sharpness of the moonlight created deep shadows and bathed the cottage in an eerie glow.

"It's all right," Paul said. "The old priest is well over eighty and hard of hearing. But still, we should get moving."

Paul and Henri moved Renee from the car and carried him into the old church. Jackie, flashlight in hand, lit the way and toted a bag of bird seed while Philip stayed at the car and to keep watch. Although it was a laborious task, Paul and Henri managed to lug Renee's limp body to the top of the modest bell tower. Startled pigeons fluttered from peaceful sleep. Feathers and dust showered the air like confetti. Jackie kept a gloved hand over her nose and mouth, but her efforts were no match for the putrid aroma of wood rot and bird droppings.

They laid Renee face down on the splintered floorboards. Pigeons cooed while Renee slumbered undisturbed.

Jackie stood over him, anger roiling inside her. She wanted justice for Claude, though what that truly meant, she couldn't say. A public flogging? The guillotine? For now, she settled for the humiliations he'd soon endure.

Henri removed Renee's jacket and tossed it aside. Paul took an empty bottle of cognac and placed it near Renee's hand. Jackie slipped a lacy pair of underwear from her coat pocket. Paul and Henri stared.

"They're not mine," she said, a touch of scolding in her quiet voice. "I bought them just for Renee." Her coy grin appeared as she knelt to stuff the panties into the pocket of Renee's jacket. She left part of the lace detail out and welcomed the scent of rosewater she'd sprayed on the garment. "Just one more thing." She stood and opened the bag of bird seed.

They stood in a tight circle, their eyes finding each other's in the pale darkness. It reminded her of a secret society. After tonight, if their plan went off without a hitch, their secret would bond them for life.

They took turns, each scooping out a generous handful of seed and sprinkling it over Renee.

The pigeons again stirred, prompting the three to make a hasty retreat. Paul then bolted and barricaded the door to the belfry, ensuring that Renee would have a long night with the roosting birds. The trio scrambled back to the car.

"Well?" Philip asked as they piled into Henri's Hotchkiss and the engine cranked to life.

Paul took the backseat with Jackie, a half-grin curling the side of his mouth. "He won't know what hit him."

"You're sure the priest will find him in the morning?" Jackie asked.

"Not absolutely, but Father Simon loves those dreadful birds." Paul shrugged. "Says that's what keeps him on at the parsonage, knowing those filthy things still need him. My family doesn't argue with him.

We let him be. He's earned the right to live out his days as he pleases, which revolves around sweeping a church no one attends and feeding birds in a crumbling bell tower."

"What if Renee wakes up and starts ringing that bell?" Worry clinched Philip's voice.

"Ha! He won't. Between the Nytol and the alcohol, he might sleep for two days."

Boisterous laughter ensued from Paul and Henri, and they took turns enacting Renee's reaction when he finally did wake.

Jackie leaned against the seat back, having no interest in their sport. She wondered how many women Renee had mistreated. She wasn't deceived into believing the stunt they'd concocted tonight would cure the malice that infected him. However, she fervently hoped that he might think twice and remember this the next time he went to strike a woman.

She grinned slightly. *What I wouldn't give to be there when he rouses with birds pecking his head and excrement covering his fine suit. Someday, I'll have to tell Claude what we've done.*

AS CLAUDE HEALED from her trauma, Jackie and the de Rentys kept close to home the next few days. Aside from telling Ghislaine, they didn't recount the details of the attack to anyone else. Christian was told that Claude fell. His little face scrunched with worry, Claude let him touch her bruised cheek and assured him she would be fine.

Claude consented to let Jackie privately tell their intimate circle of friends what had happened, not knowing that Philip and Paul already knew. Jackie told their friends at the university, including Bea, to ensure that word got around to other girls about Renee's volatile behavior.

In the days that followed, Bea shared a bit of gossip she'd picked up from another girl who'd once dated Renee.

"It's just the wildest thing," Bea whispered as she and Jackie settled at a table in the university library. "Renee was kidnapped."

"What?"

"Didn't you hear? Three men ambushed him. Knocked him out cold and took him to some wretched dungeon. They said they knew he was famous and worth a hefty ransom. The kidnappers took turns holding a knife to his throat and made him write letters to his family, telling them how they'd better pay up or Renee would wind up dead. And somehow, Renee found the strength to eventually overpower them. He escaped, but by the time he led authorities back to where he'd been held captive, the men were gone. It was quite the ordeal. My friend said Renee's face was all scratched up, almost like he'd wrestled a feral cat. Since the Sûreté had no leads, he was so shaken that he moved to Belgium. Or maybe it was Brussels."

As Jackie imagined Renee sharing the tall tale, her anger flared at the idea of him being pitied by some poor, naïve girl foolish enough to accept a word of his story. On the other hand, glee tickled her stomach when she pictured him being pecked and scraped by the pigeons.

"Was the story in the newspapers?" Jackie asked.

"That's exactly what I asked my friend. She said no. Renee preferred to keep the whole thing quiet."

"Really? Seems to me—if I were Renee—I'd want to warn others who are equally *famous*"—she gave the word emphasis but not too much—"and at the very least I'd want to get a description of the kidnappers out there...in case they try to nab someone else."

"I thought so too, but my friend said Renee was paranoid about the whole thing and didn't make a lot of sense." Bea leaned across the table. "But then I heard a completely different story from *another* friend."

"Oh?"

"*She* said that Renee ran out to the countryside with a prostitute. They found an abandoned house somewhere, downed a bottle of bourbon between them and went at it like jack rabbits."

Jackie squirmed in her wooden chair as her neck and face flushed.

"Once it was over, Renee refused to pay her, so she attacked him. Nicked up his face with her fingernails and clobbered him with a bottle of bourbon. Come to find out, an old man who's nearly deaf lives in the house but didn't hear a thing. He found Renee the next morning, battered and covered in scratches, and came close to having a heart attack. Renee's clothes were wrecked, he could hardly speak or walk, and he had the girl's panty." Bea eased back against her chair, shaking her head. "Now which do you believe?"

Jackie collected her thoughts. "I supposed there could be truth in each story. You know how tales get muddled when they pass from person to person. It's just like a game of telephone."

"One thing was certain, his face was thrashed. Whether by angry kidnappers or a scorned prostitute..." Bea shrugged dramatically.

Mindful of their surroundings, Jackie laughed softly—both at the distortion of tales and because of her insight to the truth. She enjoyed the shock and bewilderment—and pain and embarrassment—Renee had woken to.

Bea eyed her. "Do you think it had anything to do with Claude?"

Jackie composed herself, picked her words carefully. "I don't know Renee well, but from the experiences we've shared, I have a feeling Claude isn't the only woman he's wronged. With that in mind, it's impossible to say who might want to harm him. Or kidnap him."

They covered their mouths as they snickered, but Jackie wasn't the least bit fooled. She knew Bea was probing, looking for a reaction. Testing to see if Jackie knew anything more. An impish part of her considered telling Bea the truth, but she'd never do that to Philip or Paul. She couldn't let Bea in on the secret, mainly because the truth could reach the wrong ears—and severe repercussions could befall them. Jackie understood fierce loyalty, which added to her frustrations when she thought of Marceau never extending the boundaries of his trust.

WHEN JACKIE WASN'T ATTENDING classes or studying, she found herself entertaining Philip at the apartment, though they were never alone. Ghislaine spoiled them with chocolate soufflés while Christian never tired of climbing into Philip's lap with his well-worn copy of *The Little Prince*.

Bea, having forged her own friendship with Claude, also frequented the apartment, much to Jackie's relief. She had worried that Bea's admission about her phony background might destroy their bond, but after working through her mixed feelings about the ruse, she concluded that Bea's honesty was endearing. After all, Jackie had been raised with the mantra of *marry well*, drilled into her psyche by Janet, and had no intention of settling for an ordinary life.

Nothing changed for Bea, their conversation at the library about Renee being proof. She joined their gatherings, as usual, and no further mention was made of her situation. As always, she provided a good audience for Philip, laughing boisterously in the right places and taking an interest in the mundane, such as when he launched into his review of a current article he'd read on existentialism. During her evenings at Mozart Avenue, Bea also perfected two behaviors: snatching a swig of the malt whiskey when the countess was preoccupied with hosting duties and shooing away Christian any time he showed an interest in her attention.

Despite the growing affection Jackie had for her friends, a melancholy weighed on her. No messages, cryptic or otherwise, came to the apartment from Marceau. At times, when the apartment and even the company felt suffocating, she escaped in her mind with Marceau. Back to the catacombs or the rowboat. Sometimes to the restaurant at Sassenage.

The diversion of basking in those memories allowed her to relax, but only briefly. Feelings of betrayal surfaced, along with a burning shame for falling so completely for a man who clearly cared little for her. When longings arose in her—such as the dire need to find Marceau, to see his cheeky grin and the glint of his gray-teal eyes—Jackie forced a smile and refocused on whatever tale Philip was sharing with his usual zeal and dramatics.

The de Rentys hosted a modest version of Thanksgiving dinner in honor of Jackie, since the holiday held no true meaning for the French. Philip, Paul, and Bea joined them, making Jackie's ache for her family less acute. Their presence delighted her more than the food. The duck, because there were no turkeys, was too dry, while the chestnut soup with chives wasn't as satisfying as hearty helpings of corn pudding and stuffing. She missed the aromas that filled Hammersmith Farm in the week of baking that led up to dinner, and the array of pies that stretched the length and breadth of their own table. Because Hughdie loved pie.

Despite the generous hospitality the de Rentys constantly embraced her with, Jackie looked forward to getting away. Most of her classmates were planning European excursions or even a trip to the newly founded nation of Israel for the holiday break, but Jackie had plans for a solo trip.

December 1949

AUTUMN DWINDLED as an early winter ushered in. Frosty temperatures and gloomy skies that cried with sleet became the norm. As did Jackie's state of anxiety. She'd made no mention of her upcoming travel dates and had kept her train ticket hidden in her folded red skirt, tucked inside the dresser. Classes concluded for the semester, which revved her eagerness for the short escape to London.

In the days before she was due to leave, she basked in the holiday revelry of Paris. Lights and garland adorned every store. Carolers huddled in the streets and sang to their hearts' content. Mass at Sainte-Chapelle was ethereal with its sixteen stained-glass windows shimmering. Concerts were abundant in every church and venue the city had to offer.

Philip treated Jackie to a ride on the carousel near the Eiffel Tower and warm mugs of vin chaud afterward. The aromas of cinnamon and cardamom tickled her nostrils and invigorated her for shopping—perhaps to Philip's disappointment. Le Bon Marche, a massive department store that rivaled Bloomingdales both in wares and size, became a favorite of Jackie's with its holiday windows. She missed her younger siblings, knowing they would be awed by the displays.

Too many things plagued Jackie's mind. The reality of not being with her family during Christmas hit particularly hard. More so than she'd imagined. Guilt weighed on her for not matching Philip's gaiety—and for not showing him the appreciation he deserved for his thoughtful, romantic efforts. And when she thought about her upcoming travels, the guilt compounded, having made no mention of the trip to her hosts.

"Philip, I'm sorry, but would you mind taking me home now?"

Mild disbelief crossed his face as he looked at her.

"It's been a wonderful evening, but I have a light headache, and I can't seem to get my hands warm."

"Let's get you back then."

Jackie smiled and praised him for being such a gentleman. At the same time, she marveled at how she'd changed in only a few short months. She'd mastered the art of telling white lies and had become proficient at both sneaking around Paris at night and at guarding secrets. Would she become unrecognizable—in character and deed—to those she loved by springtime? A bone-chilling shudder ran through her as she did her best to focus on Philip and push the thought away.

ONE AFTERNOON, when the wind had kicked up along with the temperatures, Jackie ventured with Claude to La Maison du Chocolat, the de Rentys' preferred boutique for lemon and mint bonbons.

The warmth of the shop combined with the sweet scent of chocolate-tinged air greeted them when they entered.

"Mother loves coming here," Claude as they took their place in line. "It's one of her favorite things about Christmas, all the confections."

Jackie smiled. Merriment had infected the household in recent days. Not only did Claude and the countess hum incessantly, but they often remarked how wonderful it was to have Jackie with them to celebrate. Even Ghislaine and Christian danced in the kitchen while making dinner and singing "*Il Est Né, le Divin Enfant*." The constant cheer verbally paralyzed Jackie each time she attempted to tell one of them about her travel plans. So she smiled, joined in the liveliness—and lied to herself that a better moment would present itself for sharing her news. Part of her hesitation was also entwined with her desire to avoid the lengthy explanation of who Ann was—and why seeing her was so important.

When she had first arrived in Paris, Jackie had made a point of sending a telegram to Ann Plugge in London. Though it had been years since she'd seen or heard from Ann, she knew there would be no better time to reach out to her. In the cable, Jackie had expressed her desire to reconnect and to possibly visit her during the Christmas holiday. Even in black and white, Ann's enthusiasm was unmistakable. She relished the idea of Jackie's visit and had described herself as mad with preparation and counting down the days.

Now, standing shoulder-to-shoulder with Claude inside the store, regret churned in Jackie. Keeping secrets had served her well in the past, but this time, she knew her silence—and admission—would hurt Claude.

Sharing a room with Claude had proven thrilling and stifling. Jackie realized the depth of friendship she now shared with Claude wouldn't have developed so quickly if she'd had her own room, as originally intended. Although she'd spent the majority of her time with Claude and the countess, she managed to enjoy various tastes of Paris nightlife sans Claude, though she was careful not to get carried away with how good it felt to experience an evening apart from their group. Even when Jackie held back her enthusiasm, she still sensed that Claude's feelings were injured.

"We'll have to pop in at Stroher's too," Claude said, breaking Jackie from her thoughts.

"Won't that be a bit much?" Jackie wasn't keen on pastries.

"It's tradition. We always have their yule log. Silly, perhaps, but it helps Mother, the things we can still do the way we've always done them."

Jackie understood but said nothing.

"You're good for Mother. She says you have an old soul with the way you appreciate art and literature, and that your reserved demeanor is a rare quality in young people these days." Claude laughed. "Usually, the girls who Mother boards keep to themselves or the university. Not many have taken an interest in her the way you have. It's revived her a bit, I think."

They moved closer to the display counter, and Jackie considered her brief history with the de Rentys, some of which, in her mind, had not been worthy of the countess's praise.

"I'm grateful to share a home with you, and quite honestly, it's been more intimate than I expected." Of course, Philip's courtship and Paul's friendship had contributed to her being at the apartment more than she'd expected. "I only hope I haven't intruded or taken advantage of your mother's graciousness."

"Nonsense. It gives her a special pride. She needed to feel needed, and you've helped accomplish that." Claude beamed.

"Well, you know..." *I'll be off to London for a few days....* But the words didn't come. "That's nice to hear."

They traded grins. Somehow, Jackie managed to disguise her distress as guilt had its way with her.

JACKIE COULDN'T DO IT. She couldn't find a moment to preamble the countess or Claude about her trip. Now, with a bag packed and sitting at her feet, she checked herself in the mirror as Claude entered the room.

"What's this?" She glanced at the bag. "Off someplace?"

"Yes, to London for the weekend." Jackie's stomach clenched at the admission, but relief also came at finally having said something. "I'm visiting an old family friend."

"London? Seems sudden. I haven't heard you mention anything about going away."

"You're right. I have been remiss in bringing it up." No plausible excuses came to mind that Jackie could use to ease the delivery of her sudden leaving.

"Does Philip know?"

Jackie shook her head. "I didn't tell anyone. Silly of me."

"Oh."

"It's just a few days."

"Want some company then?" Claude pulled her suitcase from under her bed and tossed it on top. "I can throw some things together in a flash."

"That's so kind of you, but it's best if I go alone."

"Oh." The spike and thud of Claude's enthusiasm were nearly audible. She sank onto her bed.

Jackie hated the beat of silence that filled the room. This was precisely what she'd hoped to avoid. She pinched the fatty pad of her palm, a physical rebuke for not thinking the matter through.

"I'm sorry, Claude, but you wouldn't have any fun if you came." She bit her bottom lip, pained by the patronizing tone in her voice. "You know how Brits can be—stuffy, embarrassing, dull. And nothing to drink but tea?" She hoped her feeble attempt to make light of the situation would rescue them from the discomfort.

"Can't imagine why you'd want to go then." Claude made a quick, tight shrug.

"It's just one of those things I need to do. I'll tell you all about it when I get back, and you'll see that you didn't miss a thing. Philip will be happy to distract you, and you won't even notice I'm gone."

With a sigh, Claude relented. Jackie's farewells with the countess and Ghislaine went smoother than she expected, and despite their surprise at her leaving, both wished her safe travels. Claude accompanied her to the train and waved as the train left the station.

As she settled in for the long ride, Jackie didn't dwell on her promise to share everything with Claude when she returned. Instead, she reached into her coat pocket and withdrew the telegram she'd received days earlier.

JACKIE—LOOKING FORWARD TO YOUR ARRIVAL.
MUCH TO CATCH UP ON. AFFECTION, ANN

Her heart raced as she second-guessed her decision to see Ann. What would it accomplish? Wasn't it absurd, calling on her? Who was she to expect any kind of reception from Ann? Most of all, she couldn't escape thinking of her father and what he would say if he knew she was on her way to visit his former lover.

TWELVE

London, like much of Europe, was still resurrecting itself from the debris of the war. From the newspaper articles Jackie had read, she knew the city had endured the brunt of damage compared to other Allied countries. In particular, London had been subjected to the Blitz, a nine-month campaign of air raids and aerial bombings that included a fifty-seven day stretch of constant bombardment.

When Jackie arrived at the Hyde Park Corner tube station, she didn't have far to walk to the address Ann had supplied, 5 Hamilton Place. Hesitation crept up as she stood before the door of the Georgian-style mansion, not having expected such an elaborate, unscathed home. She cleared her throat, for the smog was heavy, and pressed the buzzer.

A portly and mostly hairless gentleman opened the door. Jackie suspected he was a butler—until his lively greeting rolled out.

"Ah, you must be Jackie." He embraced her, briefly, then welcomed her in. "Ann's spoken a great deal about you, including what a lovely young woman you are."

Speechlessness threatened, but when she noticed Ann waiting for her in the foyer, she cast her wonderment at the man aside, but not before uttering, "Thank you."

"It's wonderful to see you, Jackie." Ann held her warmly. Her porcelain skin and hands that reminded Jackie of butterfly lilies remained strong attributes. "This is Leonard, my husband."

"Lennie will do," he added, with congeniality.

Heat bombarded Jackie's face. The word *husband* echoed in her mind like the reverberating gong of a bronze church bell. She wished more than anything she hadn't come, and she hated that she'd given no thought to Ann's current love life. And why did it seem so insulting, to find out that she'd married?

Though she stumbled, Jackie recovered with the appropriate pleasantries.

"I've arranged brunch for you both in the lounge." Leonard grabbed his coat from a hook near the door. "Do enjoy, ladies." He kissed Ann and tipped his cap to Jackie before leaving.

His absence brought a mild relief, but Jackie was certain the embarrassment she felt had left a visible mark. She waited, in a beat of awkward silence, for Ann to pour forth an explanation, but Ann only fluffed the curls brushing the base of her neck. Perhaps her own way of working through embarrassment. Jackie couldn't tell for sure.

She also had not anticipated being in a position where they didn't fall into an easy, natural conversation. Worried the tension would eat her insides raw, she shoved out words.

"You're married now." She did her best to inject the joyfulness such a comment deserved.

"Yes." Ann took a deep breath, as if preparing to say more but sighed instead. "Lennie is such a dear, takes splendid care of me."

For Jackie, hearing Ann praise a man who wasn't her father felt as comfortable as trying on a jacket that was too small. Memories of Ann at Lasata during the summer flooded Jackie. The four of them—Ann, Jackie, Lee, and their father—had made a picturesque family. In Jackie's mind at least. Ann had been abundant with laughter and generous with affection. Her soft curls often caught the golden shimmer of the evening sun. Jackie and Lee both found Ann easy to be with and, strangely, worthy of their father. With striking features and lush brown hair, Ann matched John Bouvier in attractiveness. Her tender mannerisms and constant smile contrasted sharply against Janet's aversion to affection and her pursed lips.

"I'm happy for you," Jackie managed to say, though she feared her words sounded as forced and jagged as they felt coming out of her mouth. "Why wouldn't you marry?" At that, she decided to hush.

But just as she had been years before, Ann was good to her. Back at Lasata, when Jackie's father had first brought her around, Ann proved sensitive to Jackie and Lee's insecurity and discomfort of seeing their father with another woman. They picnicked on the grounds, did their best at tennis, and played with the dogs. Ann had enjoyed watching Jackie perform on her horse in the riding ring. Time with her had helped the girls heal, stabilizing them more than either of their parents had. Her gentle reassurances were often what they needed when wandering in the wilderness of divorce. When she broke the news that she was returning to London, Jackie feared she'd never stop crying.

Six years and an ocean had separated them.

Ann swept Jackie through several rooms, a modified tour of sorts, as she spoke about her home.

"It once belonged to the fourth Earl of Buckinghamshire, and it's so much easier to entertain here, compared to our old place. Mayfair's been a wonderful neighborhood for us."

Jackie smiled gently and nodded, unable to fully enjoy the history and details of the home as she normally would. It was simply a way for Ann to babble, Jackie knew, and she let her, since it was better than shoring up the conversation on her own.

They settled in the lounge and were tended to by servants. Eggs benedict with chorizo and bearnaise sauce, along with courgetti pancakes topped with caper dressing filled their plates, and they tackled the slow chore of getting to know each other anew. Although she'd telegraphed Ann weeks prior, Jackie had saved the details of her trip for now. She relayed the plans for her studies and hinted at leaving Vassar when she returned home. Naturally, Ann discouraged such a decision.

Ann then asked after Lee, a topic that cultivated ease for both of them. As Jackie unfolded stories about her sister, she was forced to separate herself from the girl she'd been that summer at Lasata to the young woman she was at present. Those memories, she realized with painful difficulty, belonged in the trunk of her mind, where they were safe. With them, she also tucked away that odd feeling of hopefulness that wanted to cling and pretend that Ann could still become her stepmother.

Ann spoke of the war and the damage their house had endured from the bombings. Every window on the first floor had been broken. Added to that was the loss of Lennie's seven cars they kept stored in the mews and their yacht in Cannes.

"How's your father?" she then asked.

"He's well." Had she said it with too much eagerness? Jackie prattled on about her father's work and active social life, when in reality she was needled by the fact her father had required several drying-out spells and had bounced around Manhattan apartments since Ann had seen him last.

Ann sighed and slouched back in her chair. "It never would've worked between us, Jackie. I loved that man—more than I should have, actually—but I'm glad to know he's all right."

Jackie twisted the linen napkin in her lap. "What makes you so sure it couldn't have worked?"

She fidgeted with her fingernails. "Your father's a very special sort. He's a prince, a rake, a dream, and a damn tramp, all before teatime. Sorry to say it, but he's not the sort who wants to settle down. I don't think he liked having the pressure of coming home every night. The expectations of structure just ate away at him. Dampened his spontaneity. And I don't think he'll ever be happy with just one woman."

Painful as it was to hear, Jackie knew the words were true. But she had relished Ann's ability to tame her father, to file the edges off his flaws. With Ann, Jack Bouvier had shown he could be a better man. To hear Ann speak of him, though, made Jackie wondered if she'd romanticized the notion. Maybe she'd hoped, too fiercely, that Ann could be her father's salvation. Not that it mattered now, with Ann being married.

"But it's more than that." Ann reached again for her curls and twiddled with the ends as she seemed to search for the right words.

"Maybe you deserve better, and I shouldn't tell you this, but," she sighed heavily, "I was already married when your father and I were together."

Jackie's breath caught, and she thought she might faint.

"Leonard knows everything, of course. We were in a bad spot back then. It took me flying off to America and falling in love with your father to restore my marriage, crazy as that sounds."

"And my father knew...about Leonard?"

Ann nodded.

That odd but undeniable hope that had encouraged Jackie to make this journey died an agonizing death inside her heart. Walking across the threshold and meeting Leonard had wounded Jackie beyond measure. Or so she thought.

"There's more."

Jackie's throat constricted. She didn't know if she could bear more news, more revelations that forever marred who Ann was to her and who she'd been.

"Leonard and I have children." She presented a photograph that showed three youngsters. "Frank is twelve. The twins, Greville and Gale just turned five. They're devilish at times but the absolute light of my world."

Jackie took in the photograph and absorbed the news. *Frank is twelve*. No mention had been made by Ann or Jackie's father, that Ann was a mother, and a sudden pang hit Jackie as she realized the boy had been cast aside—or at least unacknowledged—while Ann's affair with Black Jack had burned strong. Jackie batted away tears, hoping Ann didn't notice.

"They're lovely." She couldn't look at her for fear of breaking down.

Awkwardness now ripe between them, they each sipped their drinks, removed the napkins from their laps, and set aside their plates. Any action, aimless as it was, that masked their tension.

"I want you to know, Jackie, that no matter where we've ended up or who we've turned into, that I'll always cherish my time with you and your father."

"Thank you."

"You know, it's shocking to see how you've grown into a young lady.

Men must flock to you like bees around a hive. Your father must be going mad, chasing away the riff-raff."

Aggravation spiked in Jackie. She'd planned to share everything with Ann. To recount all of it—the autumn ball, her tangled feelings for Philip and Paul, and her intense desire for Marceau. A craving for Ann's advice had been building inside her, because talking to a grown woman who understood men and loss—a woman she herself respected—would mean so much. The closer the date came to her visit, the more Jackie had practiced in her head what she'd say, and she'd convinced herself that talking to Ann would calm the storm of her emotions.

Now, that anticipation lay at her feet like the charred ashes of a house fire.

"I want you to keep this in mind." Ann smiled. "Someday, when you fall in love, make sure he treats you well. Let your life be a majestic romance. Oh, how I do wish for you to find a man like Leonard."

BY THE TIME she left Ann's four-story mansion, Jackie was ready to cancel her stay and head back to Paris. But she didn't. She rushed across the street and registered at the bed and breakfast. Ann had invited her to stay in her home, but Jackie had feared the place would be too small and housing a guest too inconvenient, since she had no idea how wealthy Ann—or her husband—truly was. Clearly, there was enough room in the townhome for Jackie—and Ann's family, who Jackie knew nothing about—but escaping to her own private space now meant more than she could've imagined.

Alone in her suite, Jackie fell face forward onto the bed as tears let loose. She didn't understand the depth her sobs came from. *Did I really care that much about reuniting Ann and my father? Was such a thing even possible or within my control, just by coming here?* She suspected her grief resulted from discovering the truth about Ann—truths her father had already known. Not only was there no chance of Ann becoming her stepmother, but such a possibility had never existed. Lee's fantasy of their parents reconciling had more merit.

The phone in her room jingled. Jackie rolled over and sat up to answer it. Wiping her face, she did her best to keep her sorrow from leeching into her voice.

"Jackie, I know you just left, darling," Ann said, "but I wanted to make sure that you'll dine with us tonight. I'm anxious for you to get to know Leonard and to meet the children. I know you'll love them, given the chance...."

She couldn't refuse, even though the prospect of having Ann's family rubbed in her face equated to having salt poured on a wound. Seeing Ann and spending time with her was the only reason she'd come. She assured Ann she'd be there.

After hanging up the phone, Jackie lay back on the bed and stretched her arms over her head. *I can't do this.* The thought tormented her, along with images of the happy family prancing around her. But she had no choice.

Later that evening, refreshed and having smoothed away traces of her tears, Jackie joined the Plugges. To her surprise, the evening played out delightfully. Leonard and the children lavished Jackie with curiosity and warm respect. Conversation flowed as easily as a tugboat beneath the London Bridge, and the twins were more eager to hear about Danseuse than they were about scarfing dessert.

Their adventures continued the next day with sightseeing, which included stops at Big Ben and Buckingham Palace. Jackie marveled at how many landmarks and historic places had survived without damage. When the children grew tired, Ann suggested to Leonard that he take them home and she would enjoy lunch and shopping with Jackie. He agreed.

Ann whisked Jackie to Harrod's, though Jackie couldn't afford more than a pair of gloves. To Jackie's relief, Ann paid no attention and quickly selected several hats and dresses. After she arranged to have her purchases delivered, she claimed, "I'm desperate for a spot of tea. Shall we?"

Jackie didn't care for tea but accepting things she didn't like, without making a fuss or a display of her true emotions, became par for the holiday.

They found a restaurant and ordered a tea service. A piping-hot kettle arrived, flanked by two cups and saucers along with fresh crumpets and pickled salmon. Jackie adored the white China set adorned with red rose blooms.

"I hate that you're leaving tomorrow." Ann's teacup clinked against its saucer. "It's been marvelous, seeing you, hearing about your family. And the children adore you."

"They're a joy. You're really a wonderful mother. And wife." Jackie's irritation had subsided, but she still sipped the tea in a flimsy attempt to wash away any bitter taste that threatened. It took some getting used to, watching Ann and Leonard constantly exchange subtle affections, but Jackie couldn't begrudge her such happiness.

"I'm sorry for the way I treated you, told you everything without a warning or precursor. I feared you wouldn't come otherwise. Part of me felt I owed you an explanation, for being there for you and Lee for a short while and then disappearing. You'd both endured so much. Of course, I worried about telling you all this. You must think I'm little better than a harlot now." The corner of her lips curled.

"I would never think poorly of you!" Jackie meant it. Though exhausted from the torrent of letdowns she'd suffered since ringing Ann's doorbell, she couldn't undo the affection immortalized in her heart for Ann.

"He asked me to stay." Ann's gaze fell to her tea as she slightly twisted the cup on its saucer, making a soft grating sound. "He wanted me to divorce Leonard and marry him."

The disappointment Jackie had fought hard to subdue returned. As did her longings for Ann to be a permanent part of her life.

"Why didn't you?" Not that Jackie meant to suggest that her father was superior to Leonard, but...in her mind, he was. Leonard, as fine a man as he seemed, hardly fit with Ann's stunning beauty. Jackie guessed him to be quite a bit older than Ann. Jack Bouvier, though also a piece older than her, was still a sharply attractive man.

Then Jackie's heart sank. Her father couldn't afford the lifestyle Ann enjoyed—parties in Monte Carlo, shopping sprees at Harrod's, seeing the world on a yacht.

"My son. I saw what you and Lee were put through, and I didn't want that to become Frank's life. I couldn't imagine raising a child and watering him with the bitterness of my mistakes. I confessed, told my husband everything I'd done while we were separated." Ann gave a mild shrug. "He admitted to his own dalliances, which I suspected but didn't care about. I told him I wanted to save our marriage, if that were possible. He welcomed me home. It took time, for both of us, but we knew we'd made the right decision. Somehow, our love grew stronger."

Jealousy thrust a javelin into Jackie's chest. No one had given thought to saving her and Lee from such a fate. Her words didn't come easy. "That was...courageous...of you both."

"Thank you, Jackie." Ann reached for her hand and squeezed it. "You've been so dear and understanding. I don't know what I would've done if I'd lost your affections."

Bile roiled in her stomach. Horrific as she felt, Jackie wouldn't risk losing her friendship with Ann, no matter the pain that came with hearing her confessions.

"Take good care of your father, darling. He's not as strong as he presents."

She nodded. "Yes." Jackie had known that for some time.

ANN and her family delivered Jackie to the train station and bid her a hearty, tear-stained farewell. She returned the warm, unexpected sentiments. Her mood shifted, though, once she sat alone. Irascibility invaded and made for a poor traveling companion on the five-hour journey back to Paris. For added spite, the rocking and swaying of the car didn't agree with her. Sleet pelted the train's windows, and the gray clouds mirrored her gloom.

But when she departed the train at the Gare du Nord station, a spark of elation struck. Claude was there, grinning ear-to-ear as she waved and bounced on her toes. Being grasped into Claude's fierce embrace also lessened the vexation that plagued Jackie.

"What a welcome surprise."

"You were missed," Claude said. "Now lie to me and tell me you were miserable the whole time."

"Every minute." Guilt now joined the merry-go-round of Jackie's emotions. She couldn't burden Claude with the details of her misadventure—or expose what a fool she'd been to harbor the absurd fantasy of reconnecting her father with his former lover.

"Someone else missed you." Claude withdrew a pair of tickets from her handbag. "You'll have just enough time to drop off your bags and freshen up before Philip arrives to pick us up."

He's persistent. Perhaps too much so. Jackie squelched her immediate reaction of being irked. Really, it might be best. Instead of sitting in the apartment, dodging truthful answers to Claude's well-meaning questions about her trip, she would be enjoying *The Nutcracker*. Her plans for sulking inwardly had been thwarted, and what better gift could her friends have bestowed, even though they were unaware of her injured emotions.

"He's very thoughtful." She noticed they had balcony seating again. "I'm glad you're coming along."

"Philip said he arranged an escort for me." Claude cast her eyes downward as her face reddened. "Not sure I'm ready for that." She touched her healed lip, perhaps unconsciously.

"Oh, nonsense." Jackie put an arm around her. "It's good for you to meet new people and get on in life. You can't let what happened with Renee keep you from enjoying the ballet, of all things."

"Exactly what mother said."

The exuberance in their smiles matched. "We'll have a splendid time no matter what."

They boarded the metro for Mozart Avenue and sat. Claude rested her head on Jackie's shoulder. "I'm glad you're back."

"So am I."

CHRISTIAN THREW his arms around Jackie's legs when she walked into the apartment. Squealing her name, he rocked side to side and almost made Jackie lose her balance. Laughter ensued from everyone. Jackie tickled Christian's cheeks, then pulled him onto her hip. They exchanged fierce squeezes.

"Were there any messages for me?" Jackie had no shame in her greeting of the countess.

Taken aback and ruddy from the gaiety, the countess considered for a moment, then, "No, just your usual haul of mail, dear, which I left on your bed. I never know what Christian might tear into next."

Hope swelled in Jackie's chest. She took her bags and headed to her room, knowing full well that any expectation for a letter from Marceau was foolish. After dropping her bags, she sifted through the letters. Her zeal faded with each recognition. The bounty of letters, most likely containing Christmas cheer and perhaps money from her father and Grampy, couldn't lighten her despair.

She sighed. *What if I never see him again?*

Grave as it sounded in her head, she knew that was the most logical possibility. She had no real place in Marceau's life, nor he in hers. The depth of such truth cut into her heart—and explained why she preferred her delusions. As the anguish clawed at her, she remembered she had no time to wallow.

After a quick change, Jackie joined the de Rentys in the parlor and found Philip, and his friend, already waiting. She couldn't help noticing the twitch Philip's eyebrows made when she entered the room. Greetings followed.

"Lovely to see you again, Jaqueline." His gaze, intoxicated with charm, locked with hers as he kissed the top of her hand. "Allow me to introduce Martin."

Martin, with a wide, toothy grin and black framed glasses, reached out his hand but tripped on the edge of the rug as he approached Jackie. He recovered without falling. "Pleasure. Philip's told me a great deal about you and Claude."

"Nice to meet you, Martin, and I'm so happy you could join us." She glanced at Claude, who beamed with satisfaction.

The couples set off for the Theatre de la Ville against the dank cold. Though Jackie had attended many ballet performances throughout her lifetime, she was particularly mesmerized by the evening's show while Claude seemed more interested in her date. To Jackie's disbelief, she was able to shed the disappointment and sorrow that wanted to cling to her since leaving London. Philip deserved the credit for rescuing her from self-inflicted pity. When the curtain fell, she felt infected—finally—with Christmas cheer.

After the show, the couples headed to a café for separate tables. Once Jackie and Philip sat, she realized she wasn't hungry.

"Why don't we order hot chocolates and stroll the courtyard?"

Philip agreed.

Outside, with piping hot cups in mittened hands, they appreciated the holiday décor of the patio, and the drums of fire that took the edge off the chilly nighttime air.

"Thank you for this evening, Philip." Jackie welcomed the richness of her drink. "The ballet was amazing, and I'm flattered that you thought of sharing it with me." She was impressed, if not relieved, that he didn't punish her for not mentioning her trip.

"Really? Don't you know by now I aim to consume all of your attention?" His playful tone kept him from sounding too arrogant.

"I was under the impression that you preferred the company of various ladies, that you weren't the sort looking to get too bogged down."

His eyes narrowed as a keen expression appeared. "I'm the sort who can tell very quickly when a woman is right for him, and I must admit, Jaqueline, that you've nearly ruined me."

Her breath caught. "Oh?"

"Your appeal is, well, invigorating on every level. I've known few women who could match your beauty and wit. We enjoy the same interests, though your knowledge of history leaves me feeling inadequate."

They laughed.

He then arched his eyebrows. "But tell me, Jacqueline, am I the only one you're spending time with these days?"

It was one of her biggest concerns with Philip, that lavish gifts would come with expectations—such as the right to fill her social calendar. Was his hope for a commitment—or more—close at hand?

Jackie considered how seriously to take the matter. Perhaps she was overreacting, and Philip was more interested in knowing that he'd edged out Paul rather than won Jackie's heart.

"I'm not sure I should answer that. It could make me less appealing." She went with whimsy, trying to keep the mood light.

"Impossible." His tone, a mix of passion and tenderness, seized her.

Philip moved in close and ever so gently, pressed his lips to hers.

Jackie let him, allowed her body to respond. Their kiss endured, much like Cary Grant and Ingrid Bergman's in *Notorious*, and if she wasn't already blushing deeply, the idea of comparing herself to Ingrid Bergman certainly did her in.

Goosebumps plumped on her flesh. Warmth spread over her body.

When their lips finally parted, Philip, his eyes still closed, tilted his head back, as if drinking in her affection. Jackie herself felt dizzy with exhilaration.

"I've dreamed of kissing you since we met at the ball," he said, his eyes now meeting hers. "If I'm honest, most of my thoughts have been about you since that night. You've mesmerized me."

"I...I don't know what to say." Jackie's breaths came in small gasps as her heart verged on explosion. "You've been so wonderful to me, and I never expected to meet someone like you...or to feel this way."

The corner of his mouth ticked up, and he drew her close for another kiss.

PHILIP'S AFFECTION ignited a blaze of emotions in Jackie. The small taste of intimacy had sparked her imagination, and she dared to picture their wedding, hosting elaborate balls at the family estate, and vacationing together on the Riviera. Responses she hadn't expected. In her mind, thoughts of Philip had been limited to a man who was vying too hard for her attention, who's interest was bound to fizzle. She hadn't entertained fantasies of building a life with him—or fully explored whether she could love him enough to become his wife one day. Thoughts of Marceau had always interrupted.

Now, his declaration of love, the feel of his lips, played in her mind like a movie reel. Advancing their relationship seemed logical and imminent, though what that would entail, Jackie didn't know. What she did know was to keep it to herself.

Back at the apartment, she and Claude bid their beaux goodnight, with lingering stares, on the sidewalk. They headed inside, and the countess, bundled and sipping sherry, welcomed the recap of their evening. She apologized profusely for the dwindling heat, due to "that cantankerous furnace", and said the girls might want to consider sharing a bed for the night.

After bidding the countess goodnight, they headed to their room, still giddy from their evening, and dressed quickly for bed. Jackie placed the covers from her bed atop Claude's and the two of them snuggled in tight.

"What did you think of Martin?" Rather than basking in her bliss and rousing Claude's suspicions, Jackie thought it best to focus on the newcomer.

"I liked him." Claude went on about how they shared a mutual affinity and interest in Maurice Chevalier, both in his work and personal conflicts. They marveled at how they'd never met before, considering they'd attended many of the same shows at the Bobino music hall.

"What about you and Philip?" Claude asked, turning her head sideways. "He seemed happy as we walked home." She waited. "I saw you were holding hands. Was that the first time?"

Jackie shrank against the covers. Had it been the first time they'd done so? "I'm not sure."

"You two are certainly getting close. I think you're good for each other." She took in a deep breath and sighed. "You know if you get married, you'll belong to France permanently."

A swell of pride bloomed in Jackie, though she hoped it didn't show. Not that she'd admit it, but all she had thought about since her kiss with Philip was being his wife. She didn't know if that meant she was falling in love or if she was tipping into a realm of insanity, since she didn't know how either happened.

Laying back-to-back with Claude, Jackie drew up her legs and pulled the blankets up to her chin. It was the first moment that evening she let her mind drift to Marceau. A mistake, she knew. She ached for a way to exchange the longing she felt for Marceau with the budding ecstasy she'd found with Philip.

Why can't I be completely content with Philip's adoration? Why is this pining for Marceau so entwined around my heart?

Most painful wasn't the way they'd left things or the fact he'd made no contact. No, worse was not being able to tell someone, having no way to purge the build-up of her emotions.

She concluded it would do her no good, sharing her complex misery. If she told Claude or even Bea about her heartache over Marceau, Jackie believed it would tarnish her friends' perception of her. Once she spilled the details about how she met Marceau, as well as their ensuring encounters, neither Claude nor Bea would look at Jackie the same. Rumors and inuendo would flourish. Her reputation would be in tatters.

—Why, she practically threw herself at some vagabond! A Gypsy, I believe.

—Yes, she's beautiful and looks so poised, but I heard this story where she got naked with some strange man on a rowboat!

They'd talk about her the way they talked about Renee.

And when the gossip reached her social circles in New York—as salacious gossip obeyed no boundaries set by oceans or continents—Jackie would never know a peaceful moment at the Maidstone Club or any horse show on the East Coast. Judging eyes and whispers would follow her everywhere.

Jackie decided she could never trust another person with her innermost thoughts and secrets. She'd simply have to internalize her emotions and deal with them in private.

She couldn't afford to appear foolish or become a woman rumored to have loose morals. Feelings, as gigantic and cavernous and jarring as they could be, proved fickle and had no lasting strength. Outward displays of emotion also fed the notion that women were weak and had no self-control.

I won't let that be me. No matter what befalls.

JACKIE and the de Rentys accepted the invite to spend Christmas Eve and Christmas Day at Philip's countryside château, located slightly south of Chartres. Jackie was thrilled, not only because she'd meet

Philip's family and visit the estate, but also because of the promise of regular heat and a visit to the Chartres Cathedral.

Christian, on the other hand, had protested—with tears—at the news of hearing they would be spending the holiday away from home.

"Father Christmas won't bring me presents there." The childish twang in his small voice was tight and tense.

"Of course he will," Ghislaine reassured him as she ran her fingers through his hair. "He knows all about little children."

"That's right, dearest," the countess said. "He's always got an eye on you."

Once they arrived at the Laurents' château, Philip and his parents, Albert and Eustacia, greeted them, as did the aromas of pine and fresh baking. Philip mirrored his father in both stature and mannerisms. Eustacia, with her striking features and regal poise, reminded Jackie of Cayetana, the Duchess of Alba. As the Laurents promised that their daughters would make an appearance at dinner that evening, Jackie struggled to keep from staring at Eustacia's jaw-dropping diamond and ruby necklace.

Philip led Christian to one of their decorated trees and showed the boy that a few presents—with his name on them—already awaited. Awestruck, Christian sank to the rug, his bottom landing on his heels, and held and shook the wrapped gift as his questions poured forth. Jackie warmed, as she always did when Philip was attentive and playful with Christian.

Jackie and the de Rentys placed their bags in their respective rooms, then were treated to a tour by Philip. Ghislaine decided, after walking the grounds, which included a stable full of Arabian horses, to put Christian down for a nap. An earful of Laurent family history and conquests followed as they toured the château. Imposing family portraits, sculptures, and glassworks aided Philip's storytelling.

Afterward, the ladies were given time to refresh before dinner. Paul, Bea, and a variety of other friends joined them, along with Philip's sisters, who seemed to resent the festivities and preferred brooding over making acquaintances. Jackie couldn't say that Eustacia fared much better as a conversationalist, but the tiara she wore, similar to the Greville Emerald Tiara in shape and just as awe-inspiring, impressed everyone.

Aside from Philip, the Laurents excused themselves from joining in on the tree decorating after dinner. *'Twas the Night Before Christmas* was read, to Christian's delight, by a crackling fire and followed by sonnets from Shakespeare. Ghislaine, Christian, and the countess, weary from the day, decided to turn in. Others did the same.

"Our party is dwindling," Philip observed without discouragement.

"Well, I'm not tired," Bea said.

"Let's play cards!" Claude chimed in.

Set-up was required, but rousing games of Skat commenced and lasted beyond midnight. By then, the exhaustion of a good day had set in. Plans were discussed and settled upon for Christmas Day, which would include taking Christian on a ride in the cutter, if the predicted snowfall happened. Claude asked about ice skating on the pond, but Philip said temperatures hadn't been consistently cold enough to ensure a deep freeze of the water.

"Jackie, would you mind sitting with me for a bit?" Philip asked after the others had trailed out.

"Of course." She joined him at the hearth.

"I have a gift." Philip reached into a side table drawer and withdrew a present. Rectangular in shape and wrapped in plain brown paper, it was topped with a vivid red bow.

"Philip, you've been so generous already. You shouldn't have." Usually not one to shy away from presents, she meant it, and worried how easily she could be swayed by such tokens of affection. Upon ripping the paper, she found herself holding a copy of *Les Misérables* and sighed with delight.

"It's a first edition," Philip said, leaning in, "and signed."

Jackie opened the cover, and her jaw fell at the sight of Victor Hugo's inked scrawl on the page.

"How?" She regretted such an obvious reaction.

Philip answered with his winsome grin.

"Oh, it's too much, Philip. I can't imagine what it must be worth."

"Anything that brings such pleasure to your beautiful face is priceless in my view."

Questions edged at her. Would it always be this way, Philip going overboard with gifts? When would it be her turn to spoil him—and how on earth could she compete? Was that what it would take, eventually, to prove her love for him? She couldn't discern if such extravagant gifts were genuinely for her benefit and surprise, or if he really enjoyed showing off his wealth and resourcefulness.

Will it always be this way? Me, doubting his motives.

No. Because since their kiss, Philip had been different. Perhaps not even different, but a man who'd shed the arrogance he'd exuded from when Jackie first met him. She believed that if he were separated from his family's wealth and notoriety, Philip would still accomplish great things and establish his own reputation—one that proved lasting and impressive.

Philip put his hand on her shoulder, stealing her from her thoughts, and leaned in for a kiss.

"Come to my room, Jackie." He ran his fingertips down her arm, along her forearm. "Stay with me tonight."

THIRTEEN

January 1950

Dear Martha,

What a way to welcome the new year! Yes, it's frightfully cold here, and I never imagined how unhinged such a discomfort could make me. However, the friendships that have blossomed here have nourished me in ways I never expected. I envisioned myself as a temporary charge for Countess de Renty, one of the many students who would benefit from her generosities and eventually shuffle along. Perhaps forgotten among the others who would come to know her home—but no! They have endeared themselves to me immeasurably! I feel it is mutual, that the countess, Claude, and Ghislaine and I have enjoyed a special time, adorned with a garland of never to be forgotten memories. New Year's Eve now being another! Philip, whom I've written to you about, once again lavished us and brought bottles of Moet and Piper-Heidsieck champagne for the celebration. Paul, not to be outdone, I suppose, brought caviar. We sipped and toasted the night away. I know you'll ask, so I'll readily confess that we shared a midnight kiss. Not as you may picture it, though. Not one with a passionate embrace where he dipped me toward the floor. No, Philip is sensitive to my need for decorum, especially amidst our close group. I can't be like other girls, flamboyant and thoughtless with her beau in front of others. Claude, Bea, and Ghislaine aren't currently infatuated with anyone, and I must consider how they feel each time he shamelessly brings me a gift. Of course, I realize this is more about him displaying his wealth the way a peacock parades his handsome feathers. It can be wonderful, but I'm not certain the kind of life we would build. Philip loves owning expensive horses and doesn't care about riding them while I relish the kinship I have with Danseuse and can't fathom a life without riding. It may be immature, speaking of building a future with Philip. I feel so dreamy at the moment—too dreamy to believe such a carefree existence could endure, grounded only by camaraderie and our academic growth. Until real life wakes me, though, I will dream pleasantly.

Ever yours,
Jackie

Classes resumed at the Sorbonne and University of Paris in early January. A steady routine of attending lectures and pouring over her studies distracted her from the bitter cold that continued to infect the apartment.

One afternoon, while Ghislaine was out and Claude tended to Christian, the countess offered to take Jackie to the Louvre. Nothing could have pleased her more as steady rain had turned the previous snowfall into gray slush. Sustaining a cheerful mood proved nearly impossible. The invitation to submerge into art, Jackie believed, would be the perfect cure. She bundled into her coat and they rode the metro to the Rivoli stop.

Though she had visited the Louvre before, Jackie could never grow tired of the museum. Even if she were able to memorize the contents of every room and space, strolling its halls and galleries would never be dull. She imagined what it would be like, living close to such a collection of creativity, talent, and history. Her parents had taken her and Lee to Manhattan's museums, her favorite being the Metropolitan, but years had passed since she'd visited any.

"Let's pay our respects." The countess gave an eyebrow twitch before she led the way to the Denon wing, where the famed *Mona Lisa* awaited.

Although Jackie had viewed the half-portrait painting a few times, the reverenced awe she experienced, standing before the most famous piece of art in the world, had not dampened. The privilege of being there yet again wasn't lost on her. *If only there was a way to bring this painting home, for so many who may never visit Paris.*

"Have you seen *The Last Supper*?" the countess asked her, though their focus didn't waver from the painting.

"No."

"A masterpiece, in my opinion." Her head tilted sideways. "Years ago, Robert and I took a holiday to Italy with the girls. Such a merry time. Robert insisted we see everything. Rome, Verona, Pisa—oh, the places we went. Milan was special. As we stood there, admiring that impressive mural, Robert trembled. He was truly struck by what Christ was about to suffer. We held hands and prayed right there at the wall of that monastery. Claude was a bit frightened, seeing her father overcome with emotion, but I assured her he was fine. Then Robert looked to the Savior, and I'll never forget, he whispered, 'Greater love hath no man than this, that a man lay down his life for his friends'." The countess sighed and bowed her head.

Jackie felt the swell of a small crowd gathering behind them and gently ushered the countess away from the painting and into the hallway. Sorrow had gripped her, and Jackie shielded her as best she could from on-lookers.

The countess resumed her composure.

"Please forgive me, dear." She dabbed her eyes with a handkerchief she had plucked from her purse. "I should know better than to relay such fond moments in public."

"There's nothing to forgive. I admire the love you had for one another. Hearing his stories honors his memory, which you must keep alive for Christian. He needs to know what an incredible man his grandfather was."

"So kind of you, dear. Would you excuse me please? If you don't mind, I just need a few moments. Would it be all right if we congregated back at the entrance?"

The countess told Jackie to take her time, then excused herself and made for the latrine.

Jackie didn't mind continuing through the galleries on her own. She made a point of viewing *The Coronation of Emperor Napoleon*, a massive canvas of ten by six meters that captured Napoleon's historic, untraditional coronation at Nôtre Dame Cathedral. Other treasures she experienced included the Grand Salons of Napoleon III, which some say rivaled Versailles with its gold-adorned rooms accented with lush scarlet upholstery and Michelangelo's *Venus de Milo*.

Feeling renewed, Jackie decided it was time to find the countess. But when she turned to head toward the entrance, Marceau stood staring at her.

His face wore a sheen of white, as though he were staring at an apparition rather than a girl he'd shared an infatuation with.

A storm of emotions erupted inside her. "Marceau." His name slipped out anxiously, like a desert wanderer panting for water. But Jackie held her ground and made no move toward him, the most restraint she could demonstrate.

It didn't matter. He moved toward her.

He ran his fingers through his hair, freshly cut and styled, which paired nicely with the perfectly tailored suit he wore.

"How are you, Jackie?"

Words knotted in her throat. The last time she'd seen him, standing outside the apartment building, drenched in moonlight, she'd been so upset with him. They'd just left Sûreté headquarters. Jackie, still reeling with embarrassment and fear, wanted to know how he had arranged their release so effortlessly, but he'd offered no answers. Only his usual spiel of *I can't tell you why*.

"I'm so sorry, the way I left things between us," Marceau said. "It was never my intention that we wouldn't see each other—that I wouldn't have a chance to explain." He paused, as if he suspected he was rambling. Scarfing a deep breath, he tried again. "After all this time, your doubts about me must be like towering giants, and I can't blame you. There isn't time now for me to sort it out, but let me beg for your forgiveness and say that our night together meant everything to me and nearly changed my world—"

"Hello."

The interruption came from a young woman with blonde ringlets of hair framing her porcelain skin and cornflower-blue eyes that sparkled with innocence and curiosity. She shouldered up to Marceau, who shut his eyes for a moment and suddenly looked pale.

"I'm Sophie." She glanced at Marceau. Her half-grin indicated an amusement in Marceau's discomfort. "And you are?"

Jackie introduced herself, but dread bloomed in her chest and stunted her breathing. Watching how Sophie moved her shoulder against Marceau's and the way she flashed her eyes at him, Jackie prepared herself.

"I'm his wife."

Jackie had discretely puffed her chest, expectant of the verbal dagger.

Marceau forced a grin at Sophie.

"How do you two know each other?" Sophie slipped her hand into his.

"We shared an art class." Jackie picked her words carefully and forced her gaze away from their entwined hands.

"At the École des Beaux-Arts."

"Ah, yes, I remember you mentioning that." Sophie waved her free hand and delivered the remark sharply, as though the conversation bored her already. Then she snuggled against him. "You might say we're on our second honeymoon. After that dreadful war and being apart so long, we needed a chance to reconnect."

"Apart?" The word came out feebly.

Sophie looked at Jackie with confusion until the soft-spoken word registered. "Yes, not that he's probably told you, or anyone else for that matter. Marceau served in the war and was taken as a prisoner. He suffered a head injury and terrible amnesia. When he didn't return home for so long, I thought he was dead." She splayed her hand on her chest in a dramatic fashion.

Marceau pressed his lips together in an uncertain smile while avoiding eye contact with either woman.

"That must've been very trying for you." No emotion accompanied Jackie's sentiment, because she didn't know whether or not to believe Sophie.

"No one can imagine what I've been through. The waiting and wondering were pure agony. My life on hold. I suppose it's a miracle that we found each other again. And since he was here and I haven't been to Paris in so long, I thought, what a wonderful way for us to rediscover one another. Although I must say, it's dirty here. Not what I expected, but I suppose the most important thing is that we're together."

Sophie flashed a smile at Marceau that churned Jackie's insides. Her bewilderment aside, though, Jackie couldn't pinpoint why, but their interaction struck her as painful—as painful for her to watch as it was for them to endure.

"We should be going," Sophie said. "He's still not quite himself." She began pulling him away like a dog on a leash. "Come."

Marceau turned to Jackie, his wife on his opposite side, and paused for a moment. "It's good to see you again, Jackie." Sophie nudged him. "Take care."

Jackie inhaled to steady herself and to fight back the tears pricking her eyes.

JACKIE BECAME BEDRIDDEN the next two days, tormented, she told her hosts, by a horrific migraine, possibly complicated by the onset of the flu. Despite concerns from the countess and Claude, she repeatedly asked to be left alone, claiming she needed rest above all else. When she was shut up in the solitude, the calm and quiet of the apartment closing in on her as she missed lectures, she cried incessantly. So many questions tortured her concerning Marceau, the most persistent being *why*?

Why did he let me believe we were falling in love? That there was any kind of hope for us? Why didn't he tell me he'd been hurt in the war? And why didn't he tell me he was married?

Light rain pelted the windows the second evening of her self-imposed confinement, muffling the soft tap that sounded on the bedroom door. Claude poked her head in. "Paul's here. Is it okay if he comes in for a bit?"

Jackie had turned away visitors, especially Philip. Claude had tried verbally prodding her at night for answers, but to no avail. Jackie had not eaten for days and refused to be seen by the de Rentys' family doctor. But this was Paul. If she didn't make an effort, she could expect the countess to telephone her mother, the one thing that could add to Jackie's misery.

She nodded, and moments later Paul swooped around Claude, entering the room with a full tray.

"Heard you needed rescued from the doldrums." Paul set the tray on Jackie's nightstand and helped her into a sitting position.

She ran her hands over her face and hair, knowing she had to look a fright.

Claude left them as Paul placed a pillow across Jackie's lap, then positioned the tray atop the pillow. A bouquet of irises coaxed a grin from her as their aroma danced in the room. She glimpsed the bowl of hot soup and felt her insides quiver, an odd mix of starvation and hunger at work. Saltine crackers and slices of sourdough bread completed the meal.

"Oh, Paul. You shouldn't have gone to so much trouble."

"Chicken soup, isn't that it—the cure-all for you Americans?" Paul sat on the edge of her bed.

Though she wasn't sure if she could palate the soup, Jackie touched a spoonful of the broth to her lips and forced a sip. "It's delicious, Paul. Thank you. I do appreciate it, but I'm not very hungry just yet."

The pleased look on his face turned to mild defeat. He removed the tray from her lap and returned to sitting next to her on the bed.

"Maybe I'm being too bold." Paul rubbed his hands along his pants. "I could also be terribly wrong in my assumptions, but does this have anything to do with Marceau?"

Jackie's spine stiffened. "What makes you ask that?"

"Ever since that night, when I found you with him outside the art school, I've worried."

"You weren't very forthcoming when I asked about him."

"True." He shrugged. "I hoped there wasn't room for him in your life, that Philip and I were enough at the time. Looking back, I should've told you everything. Not simply teased you." He took her hand. "Before we get into this, might I ask, are you...in trouble, Jackie? Because if you are, I'd marry you." His cheeks colored. "I'd do anything to help you, and I hope you know that."

Jackie cupped the side of his face with her other hand. "I don't deserve your love and perfect friendship. No, I'm not in that kind of trouble, and I've never been intimate with Marceau." She couldn't believe she was confessing this to another man!

An easy smile stretched across his face but didn't last. "But you've been seeing him?" The words came gently and without accusation.

"I don't know how to describe my time with Marceau." She slouched against her pillows. "Sparse. Not the typical courtship."

"You had feelings for him, didn't you?"

Her chest swelled and tightened, thinking of the feelings he'd stirred in her. Jackie nodded. Then it poured out of her—how she met Marceau, the few outings they'd shared, even their episode on the rowboat and subsequent trip to police headquarters. She told him about running into Marceau and his wife at the Louvre and how she'd had no idea a wife existed. Tears dripped from her eyes and she let them. Because she didn't care anymore about controlling what Paul—or anyone else—might think of her. Not when her heart felt so broken.

Paul took her into his arms, and Jackie buried her face in the nook of his neck as her sorrow flowed. Minutes later, when she began to compose herself, Paul found a small box of tissues and handed it to her. She plucked several and wiped her face.

"I've met Sophie," Paul admitted. "She's quite beautiful, until you get to know her."

A sliver of vindication eased the rejection that had been coursing through Jackie.

"She's part of the Luxembourg royal family. Not in line for the throne but she comes with a hefty dowry." He sighed. "I'm getting ahead of myself. Like I told you months ago, many of us at Rosenburg thought Marceau was reckless to the point of being dangerous. Sophie would show up at social events and stare at Marceau. We used to tease him about it, because she was the most incredible girl we'd ever laid eyes on, but she was cold, maybe a little cruel, to everyone but him. It was no wonder, considering he belongs to branches of both the Dutch and Danish royalties. He told us their families had arranged for them to get married, and that he'd rather cut off his right arm than marry her."

Riveted, Jackie sat dumbstruck.

"Naturally, we were stunned." Paul continued. "Who wouldn't want to marry Sophie? But he knew things about her. He could see through her façade, as we all could, but it went deeper than that. He told us she was evil, said that she tried to kill him once, but he never gave us the details. Well," he slapped his thighs, "we didn't know whether to believe him or not. It was quite an accusation. We were all so young and different then, since the war hadn't scarred us yet." Another sigh seeped from him. "After school, most of us lost track of each other, except at social events here and there. I heard that he and Sophie had married. I'd forgotten about the two of them, with the war and rebuilding life after, that is—until that night he was with you. I suppose on one hand, I didn't want to say too much, fearful you might fall for him, and because I didn't know his situation. Asking him about Sophie didn't feel right, so I've wrestled with it ever since."

Hearing that Marceau was trapped in an unhappy marriage—and having seen the proof of it on his face—gave Jackie both a wicked satisfaction and pained her. Her longing for more answers hadn't dwindled, but she knew Paul couldn't expound on the information Sophie had shared about Marceau's capture and subsequent amnesia.

"You must think I'm laughable, crying and pining over a man who could never really mean anything to me. Someone I scarcely know." She gave a half-shrug. "He's barely more than a stranger to me."

"You, laughable? Never. It's impossible to control our emotions at times. They run away from us, chasing that one thing we can't have." He caressed the inside of her forearm. His soft fingertips glided along her skin and neared the crook in her arm but stopped abruptly. "If anything, I'm jealous of the rascal. He's earned your adoration, the one thing several of us have been clamoring for." He topped his comments with a disarming snicker.

"Now that you know how foolish I am I'll be less desirable." Jackie added her own jab of humor.

"Not a chance." Paul winked.

"I suppose hearing this explains a lot. At least now I know why he was always so coy and saying there were things he couldn't tell me." Putting pieces together about Marceau didn't make Jackie feel better though. She thought of their morning together at the Trocadéro, him teaching her how to capture the glory of a sunrise in paint colors. Inwardly, she chided herself for thinking there had been a deep connection between them.

"Well then," Paul said, "enough of this moping. I think it's time to abandon the gloom, and I know just the thing to cheer you up."

My Dear Little Sister,

You will be insanely envious of me now! I spent an entire afternoon at the design house of Coco Chanel! She wasn't there, of course, but she's just returned to Paris to restart her line. You won't believe the samples they let me have—a pair of shoes, a bottle of perfume—yes, yes—the perfume—along with a skirt and two blouses. They explained to me that her business relationships were still tender, as she was suspected of having some connection with the Nazis. The noble Mr. Churchill came to her defense, though, and that speaks to me more than rumors. I know you don't care a bit about politics (not that I do either), but I can't wait to show you these clothes...and perhaps share them with you. Today was another reminder of how much I miss you and the volumes of stories and whimsical tales I have to tell you. I hope my head can hold all the memories until then. Know how much I love you.

Always,

Jackie

JACKIE SPENT the rest of January wholly devoted to her studies, absorbing all her Nineteenth Century French Literature and History of French Architecture classes had to offer. Weekends allowed for social activities, including visits to Paul's and Philip's châteaux and dances hosted at Reid Hall where young men from the École Polytechnique happily waltzed with the Smith girls. Attending plays at the Athenee Theatre and salons continued, but for Jackie, a wariness hung on her shoulders as she wondered if she might see Marceau again. Paul, in-tune to her misery, never failed to reassure her when he sensed her contentment waning—and he seemed to relish having an insight into Jackie that Philip wasn't privy to.

Her feelings for Philip remained steady, though Jackie mentally noted a growing list of his quirks. For one, Philip lacked an intuitiveness and never seemed capable of discerning her moods. It seemed as if he expected his presence to always make her pleasant and gave little to no thought about her life apart from him. He opened doors for her but always managed a swift, effortless move that put him a step or two in front of her. He preferred speaking about topics he knew well, which included wine, the perils of France leaning toward Communism, and how superior Flaubert was to Proust. He described jazz as *screechy noise* and made snide remarks about Americans—especially the American soldiers in the city—that Jackie was, apparently, supposed to agree with or dismiss.

As winter dug in, Jackie was convinced she could live in Paris. Her love for the city ran deep and genuine, well beyond the adorations of a mere tourist. She could accept most of the downsides: the criticism of being an American and her abysmal finances. Harder to palate was the idea of life without her family, even though issues persisted and probably always would, and access to the ocean, or at least a substantial view of water, was harder to come by. A permanent arrangement—such as marrying Philip—would solidify her stay, but Jackie couldn't deny a niggling hesitation that rose in her chest whenever she deeply considered the matter.

February 1950

AS JACKIE and Claude returned home from an evening at the Grand Palais, they spoke of how they'd enjoyed touring the grounds and marveled at the creations for the Ice Sculpture Festival. They walked to the metro, warmed by their camaraderie and discussion of favorite pieces. Claude mentioned that Martin had telephoned, and they had made plans for dinner together later that week.

"Sounds like he's being quite the gentleman. Exactly what you deserve." Jackie grinned, wondering if Philip had told Martin about Renee and his appalling behavior. Not that she would ever ask.

"Yes, he's been thoughtful and fun to be around," she sighed, "but I think we both know we're not in love."

"It's still so soon. Maybe it needs more time."

"I suppose you could make yourself fall for someone, if you had enough reasons." Claude stole a glance at Jackie. "But the chemistry isn't there."

"Maybe that takes time too."

"Maybe, but I want to feel it from the start. You know, like in *Sense and Sensibility*, how Marianne falls for John Willoughby? How she's caught up in the excitement of how she feels when they're together? How attracted she is to him, all before she realizes their love could never be?"

For once, Jackie appreciated the cold and how it disguised her now-flaming cheeks. "Yes," she muttered.

"But eventually she falls in love with Colonel Brandon. It's not that she really *loves* him. I think she comes to love the way he loves her. She loves the security he can give her, and she knows that she's quite a catch for him. I want that John Willoughby kind of love, with the happily ever after, of course." She looked at Jackie. "Do you know what I mean?"

"Yes, I think I do." Since she'd never mentioned Marceau, she knew Claude's musings were genuine and not coming from a place of maliciousness. Still, the uncanniness of the comparison struck her.

"It's funny, though," Claude said. "I've never really cared much for Jane Austen."

Jackie's mind bobbled and raced as the train zipped toward Mozart Avenue. Did her life—her feelings for Marceau and Philip, at least—offer such a sharp comparison to Marianne's? She hadn't considered it, or the fact that Marianne had settled for a wealthy man who showered her with adulation. Was Jackie potentially settling when it came to Philip? She compartmentalized the thought. Now wasn't the time for a solid answer.

When they entered the apartment, flushed and fatigued, Jackie and Claude were greeted by a hearty, "Surprise!"

Janet stood in the middle of the parlor, arms open wide. Hughdie was closer to them, near the door while the countess, bent over a serving cart, poured hot water from the kettle into teacups.

Jackie, realizing her mouth was hanging open, made a point to remove the bewildered expression from her face. "Mummy! Hughdie! What on earth are you doing here?" She embraced Hughdie, who, eyes shining, planted a kiss on her cheek. They briefly traded endearments.

"I wanted to come after Christmas," Janet said, "but when I contacted the school, they said classes are suspended in February for a three-week break. Hearing that, I thought to myself, what a perfect time to visit, especially since you wouldn't have any plans and nothing to do. I convinced Hughdie we should go and"—she held out her hands—"here we are."

"I can't believe you're really here." Jackie clasped her hands together and squeezed tightly. "What a surprise."

"Yes, it's a lot for you to take in, I'm sure. We won't be staying here." Janet glanced over her shoulder at the countess. "Obviously."

The countess matched Janet's thin smile.

"But you'll want to join us at the Ritz, won't you, dear?"

It took Jackie a moment to realize Janet was speaking to her. "Of course, Mummy. How long will you be visiting?"

"The whole three weeks." Elation tinged Janet's voice.

Jackie swallowed hard.

"Don't worry, though. We plan to see more than just Paris."

"Oh?" Jackie traded glances with the countess and Claude.

"Yes, we've arranged for a road tour of Germany. Isn't that right, Hughdie?"

Still standing by the door, Hughdie straightened at the mention of his name. "Yes, dear. But the tour takes us through Germany and Austria, dear."

"Ah. I suppose the war has moved things around a bit. It will be thrilling, seeing all the changes."

Jackie focused on the linoleum floor and metered her breathing as a way to sooth her mild fury. Though Janet most likely had no idea how callous and thoughtless her remark was in the presence of two women who'd lost a family member to the war, it teetered on the edge of unforgiveable for Jackie.

"Can I help you get settled at the Ritz?" Not knowing how far Janet's oblivious insensitivities might stretch, she wanted her mother as far from her host family as possible.

"You might as well get your things, Jacqueline. You're coming with us."

Jackie looked at her. "Until your tour begins?"

"You're coming with us, dear. I knew you wouldn't want to miss out on such a grand adventure."

Silence pounded the room as Janet beamed, undeniably proud of herself for swooping in and whisking her daughter away on an unexpected excursion. For Jackie, though, it felt dreadfully similar to being taken hostage.

WITH JANET WAITING, and making small talk with the de Rentys over tea, Jackie packed and fretted about whether or not she had time to write a letter to Marceau. Not that she knew where to send it or if she could gather her thoughts clearly under such restraints. Even so, propelled by her emotions, she drew out a piece of paper and began in a rushed hand...

Dear Marceau,

I hope this finds you well. By now, I realize that I've been harboring a fantasy about us. Ever since that night in Sassenage, when you left those sprigs of lavender on my chair, I've thought about you. From that unusual beginning—if I dare call it that—up until I saw you at the Louvre, my heart has known every high and low. I don't know why I'm writing this. You may never read it. But if you do, I wanted you to know how much you've meant to me, and that the depths of my feelings for you have stunned me. I never imagined such emotions—and such despair were possible. I know we can't be together. A part of me aches, knowing our time together will last longer in my memories than it ever had a chance of existing in reality. Perhaps I'm making too much of this. Of us! Because there never was an us, only dreamy possibilities—or so I thought. I can't explain myself. Not like this. Not fully. Please know that you will always have a place in my heart.

Yours,
Jackie

HER BAGS IN HAND, Jackie returned to the parlor and pulled Claude aside without drawing attention from the others.

"Do me a favor and give this to Paul." She handed Claude the envelope. "Tell him it's for our mutual friend, in case he sees him."

Confusion scrunched Claude's features. "So it's not for Paul?"

"No, but I think he'll understand." Boldness mixed with brazenness in Jackie. She knew Claude would read the letter, and she couldn't blame her. Once Janet and Hughdie returned home, and Jackie returned to Paris, she expected a bombardment of questions from Claude, especially about the letter, but she would worry about that later. For now, she didn't want to leave Paris without a note to Marceau, ridiculous as it seemed. She would have given anything to stay behind and leave the traveling to Janet and Hughdie.

Claude tucked the envelope into her cardigan and nodded. Jackie loved her for it and embraced her. Why such a compulsion to leave a note had gripped her, she couldn't say. Perhaps she realized, achingly, that she still wanted to see Marceau again. There were so many things she wanted to hear him say, even though, like Marianne, she'd slowly come to accept that their love could never be.

FOURTEEN

By the time Jackie and her parents settled in at the Ritz, she longed to escape to the bar and down a few icy martinis. Boredom already gripped her to the point that she considered faking an illness or injury—anything that would save her from the next three weeks with her parents. Her love for them was unquestionable, but Janet showing up during what was supposed to be Jackie's lone year abroad felt like a betrayal of trust. As though Janet had to see that Jackie wasn't making a mockery of herself. The truth tucked in that notion rattled her, but Jackie would do her best to conceal the missteps she'd made while in Paris.

A knocked sounded on the door of their suite.

"Jackie, would you get that, please," Janet said.

When Jackie opened the door, a slight gasp escaped her. "Philip! What are you doing here?"

"I stopped by the apartment. We were supposed to attend the organ recital at Nôtre Dame."

In the melee of shock and awe that had struck her since seeing Janet and Hughdie, Jackie had forgotten about Philip. Her genuine apology easily won Philip's forgiveness.

"Claude gave me a recap of what happened, with your parents

showing up. She told me I'd find you here but that you were set to travel soon."

"Yes, I'm sorry I didn't get a note to you." The letter she'd left for Marceau ran through her mind. Claude would surely notice that Jackie had thought of Marceau, a stranger she'd never mentioned, before leaving, but not Philip. Oh, the explaining she would owe Claude.

"Do I need to sign for something?" Janet joined them at the door.

"Mummy, this is Philip." Introductions unfolded while Jackie's stomach knotted.

She hadn't talked about Philip in her letters home and wasn't prepared to fill her parents in on her social life. Yet there she was, informing them. "Philip is...quite a special friend." She finished with an awkward, uncertain smile as she watched her mother absorb the news.

"Jacqueline, where *are* your manners?" Janet bypassed her daughter and took Philip by the hand. "It's a delight to meet you. Please, please come in. Hughdie, why don't you call down and order up hors d'oeuvres and insist they hurry."

Hughdie reached for the telephone as Janet led Philip to the divan and offered him a seat. Jackie, left in the lurch and subtly pulling at her fingers, drew in a deep breath and took a seat across from them.

Amusement danced across Philip's face as Janet assaulted him with questions. The more she learned about Philip's family and background, the more she lit up with approval. Hughdie joined them when the *charcuterie* arrived, packed edge to edge with a variety of meats, cheeses, and nuts. Jackie plucked a smoke salmon canapé and chilled pâté Lorrain from the confection, just so she could have something to plate and sit upon her lap. More mind-numbing conversation followed. Jackie nibbled her appetizers and said little. Janet and Philip proved most adept at steering the chatter.

When he asked about their upcoming travel plans Janet filled him in.

"I admit," he said, taking the last canapé, "it's disappointing to hear you'll be gone so long, but a tour of Europe is always called for when you make such a journey."

"Well, if we'd known that Jacqueline had formed such an attachment..." Janet and Philip shared a light-hearted chuckle while Jackie and Hughdie traded glances. "Perhaps I shouldn't be surprised. Jacqueline's always had an affinity for France and her heritage. Maybe it's only fitting she's smitten by such an impressive gentleman as you, Philip."

He basked in the compliment, even dared to give Jackie a *Your mother loves me* smirk. "I have an idea. What if we have a party? A sort of celebration to welcome you all back. I could take care of everything, make all the arrangements. I'll need to discuss the details with my family, of course, but I know they'd love to host you at our estate. What do you think? Might even help the time apart go by faster." He took Jackie's hand into his.

She smiled, her head swimming with too much turmoil to form a reply.

"I know!" Philip squeezed her hand in his excitement. "Let's make it a masquerade ball! We'll invite everyone. The whole of France and more."

Janet clapped her hands together. "How exciting! It sounds splendid, Philip, but are you sure? That would be an enormous undertaking in only a matter of weeks."

"My family's prestige is rooted in their ability to host a smashing party. Wouldn't you say so, Jackie?"

Janet broke in before Jackie could speak. "Philip, why don't you plan to join us? You could meet up with us, say when we arrive in Munich? That should give you plenty of time to arrange your affairs. Plus, you could give us an update on the party. What do you say, Jackie?"

"Yes, Mummy." She loathed how the words came out like a conditioned response. Under the circumstances, it was the best she could do. Her body felt stretched at both ends and trampled upon. Now she had to work at pleasing her mother and Philip simultaneously with no opinion of her own mixed in.

She sighed. *Could this be a glimpse of my future if I marry Philip? The two of them in a constant state of complimenting one another while using and ignoring me?*

"This is splendid. Just splendid!" Janet said. "Can you imagine if we hadn't come?"

AS HESITANT AS Jackie was to leave Paris and her social activities, Vienna—and her parents—surprised her. Skiing suited the daytime chill while they spent their evenings waltzing or attending opera at Wiener Staatsopera. Jackie marveled, not only upon learning it was ball season for Vienna—of which Janet was eager to point out that she'd secured invites at several—but also at the ornate gothic architecture the city was known for. Janet showed no interest in touring St. Stephen's Cathedral, claiming it held no appeal, which disappointed Jackie greatly.

Hughdie, always eager to please everyone, took Jackie on a private tour of the church one morning while Janet recovered from a headache. Afterwards, they dashed, best they could in the brisk winds, to a nearby café. Steaming coffees and warm apple strudels helped them shrug off the cold.

"So tell me about this young man of yours," Hughdie said, after savoring a bite of the strudel.

Knowing she couldn't fib to her stepfather the way she could to her mother, Jackie tensed. Outside, snow began to fall with the same beauty as the carnation petals that had showered the crowd during last night's ball.

Inspired by the snow and the previous night, she started with the story of how she met Philip. How one dance had piqued his interest and prompted him to bring her dozens of flowers.

"Is it any wonder?" Hughdie said, a loving smile stretched on his face. "I knew the young men would come calling, but this Philip, he seems...rather intense in his pursuit." He let the remark sink in. "Is that what you want?"

A long sigh seeped from her parted lips. "He's been wonderful." She paused, fearful the truth would stumble out. *I prefer Paul's company over Philip's, but I'm not attracted to Paul romantically. I actually fell in love with another man, the first moment I saw him, but he's married.* She tugged at her fingers under the table.

"Wonderful. Hmm. That says something about him, but has he captured your heart? Are you thinking this is more than a fun fancy?"

She sipped her coffee and picked at the pastry. "What does Mummy think?"

"Your mother's been mesmerized. Money and the display of prim manners have a way of doing that to her. I caught her staring at you last night at the ball. I think it was as you were dancing with the young man who said he works as a guard at the Hofburg. I thought she'd taken ill. Her face had gone white. When I asked her if she was all right, she didn't look at me. Then she said, 'What will I do if I lose my Jacqueline to Europe?'"

Jackie tried to speak, tried to conjure up a verbal bandage that might heal her mother's premature wounds, but nothing formulated. She was deeply struck by her mother's sentiment. Because for the first time, Jackie believed her mother would truly miss their relationship, that Janet would be grieved by having her daughter living on the other side of the ocean and practically a world away—because Jackie felt the same.

Tears blurred her vision. She dabbed them away, frightfully embarrassed and hoping in vain that Hughdie hadn't noticed.

"She's worried. Worried that you may not be thinking clearly, and worried that you'll fall for the wrong man. She doesn't want your life to fall apart one day because you've mistaken fantasy and romance for lasting love."

Jackie arched an eyebrow. "Mummy said that?"

Hughdie conceded with a loving grin. "More or less."

She took a small bite of the strudel and put her frustrations into chewing. Was it really so hard for her mother to share this side of herself with her own daughter?

"I'll support you," Hughdie said, possibly noting Jackie's mild agitation, "whatever endeavor you choose, dear one, but I wanted to hear from you, what you were thinking about all this."

Minutes passed before Jackie quietly composed herself and her thoughts enough to respond.

"Thank you. You've always loved me perfectly. Better than I've deserved at times." Memories of her early days as a stepdaughter skidded through her mind. Though she'd approved of Hughdie when he and Janet began dating, she kicked off their married life with mild pranks and laziness when it came to her chores. Both were cured by the combination of Hughdie's light-heartedness towards her and news of the war.

"What if...I think I know what I want, but I don't know if it's right. Not completely."

"Then you don't let anyone pressure you, either way. Not your mother and certainly not this Philip."

The abrasive touch he added to Philip's name caused the corner of Jackie's mouth to curl.

"You don't seem to like him."

"I don't know the man. He charmed you mother easily enough, but he still has to go through me." He winked.

WHEN JACKIE TELEPHONED Claude late one afternoon, she could hardly stomach Claude's boisterous glee over the news and development of the masquerade ball.

"I do believe the whole city is buzzing!" Claude said. "Philip's doing, of course."

The crackling static made it easy for Jackie's attention to wane and gave her a plausible excuse as to why she wasn't responding with equal jubilation.

"Philip told us invitations were even being sent to President Auriol, Mireille Balin, and Colette! Could you imagine if even one of them came?" Claude went on to explain that Mireille Balin was one of her favorite actresses since *Lady Killer* and that she had read Colette's *Gigi* twice already. "And Paul stopped in for a visit."

"Oh?" Jackie perked up.

"I gave him your letter, told him what you said. He was intrigued and said he knew exactly who it was meant for." A pause followed, as if Claude hoped Jackie might let her in on the mystery recipient.

"Thank you for taking good care of the matter." Guilt needled her, knowing she sounded like a secretary. "I hope to explain when I get back."

"I'll be ready. Paul didn't seem as excited when we talked about the ball. He's convinced that Philip will propose to you that night. I think he was still hoping there might be a chance for you two."

Jackie wasn't fully persuaded that Paul clung to such hope, though she'd be the last to claim expertise when it came to a man's heart.

"I told him there was no hope," Claude continued. "Teasingly, of course, but isn't it dear, the way he cares for you? If you were to ask me, I would say that you make a better match with Paul, but that's just me."

Jackie sighed quietly, so Claude wouldn't hear. She didn't need the aggravation inspired by her friend's implication. Certainly not now. For all she knew, it could be a ploy by Paul to amplify any doubts she had simmering.

"I have to run now, Claude, but I do hope we can discuss this at length when I get back."

Jackie aimed to sound in control, unrattled, because too much already weighed on her heart to sort out, and bursting into tears, with Janet nearby simply wouldn't do.

WHEN JACKIE and Hughdie returned to their hotel room one crisp morning, the remains of a Sacher torte wedge wrapped and tucked in Jackie's coat, their feet were damp from tromping through the fresh-fallen snow. Janet had remained in their suite to write letters to Lee and several friends. She asked about their early morning outing as they dried and warmed their toes.

Though disappointed in the café's coffee, Hughdie praised the cake as he held up the bag containing a slice for Janet.

"I'm going to ring down for some slivovitz," he said, "and I don't feel a speck of guilt, warming up with a spirit. Would you care for a serving, dear? Jackie?"

Both declined, and Jackie thought about last night's ball, where they'd tasted the plum brandy for the first time. Her lips and chest had warmed immediately, and she couldn't blame Hughdie for craving a shot.

The tray arrived, along with a side order of tafelspitz, which Hughdie offered to share.

Janet grimaced and shook her head, as did Jackie.

They discussed their plans for the day, which Janet said included shopping.

"We must prepare for Jacqueline's ball."

Hughdie darted a glance at Jackie, who nodded absentmindedly while Janet ticked off items they needed to find.

"Ladies, if you'll excuse me, please, I'm going to go sit in the sauna and get a scrub." He laid a robe and towel, from the hotel, over his forearm. "Enjoy some time together."

Jackie and her mother bundled up before leaving the hotel, a list of recommended shops in Janet's purse. Outside, the sky was overcast but the snow had stopped. With their steps crunching as they ventured from shop to shop, the afternoon was deemed a success as they purchased several dresses and stoles Janet considered acceptable for the ball.

When they returned to their room, Janet had the bellhop lay out the dresses while she and Jackie sipped hot chocolate.

"Have you telephoned Philip since we arrived?" Janet asked, as they settled in two tufted chairs. A window, frosted on the edges of the glass, framed the city below.

"No." *You know I haven't.*

"That was eight days ago, dear. Don't you think you should check on him, make sure that he's not too miserable without you?" Janet batted her eyes bashfully.

Jackie wasn't sorry that she'd missed out on her mother's relentless tips on how to play coquettish with a man.

"Maybe I want him to be miserable."

Janet shot her daughter a look of confused appalment.

Jackie laughed. "I'm only teasing, Mummy."

"I don't think you realize what a rare find you have in Philip. A wealthy nobleman with his sights set on becoming a diplomat."

"Not that you've forgotten, but Philp lives in France."

"Yes." A somberness tinged her voice.

Part of Jackie believed Hughdie had exaggerated Janet's remark about losing Jackie to Europe. A stab of hurt flared in her chest. She wanted her mother to protest, to beg her not to consider a permanent arrangement with Philip, to tell her that living so far apart would be unacceptable because she loved Jackie too much for her to be so far away and she feared the damage such a physical distance would inflict on their relationship. But she didn't. A dire ache churned inside Jackie to hear those words from her mother. She didn't want to push or prod Janet. No, Jackie wanted the sentiment to bleed from her mother naturally.

"I suppose it's the sort of thing you've always dreamed about, creating a life far—" Janet quietly choked on the word but pretended she coughed, then cleared her throat. "You've always had a misty-eyed, school-girl love for Paris. Living there has probably only enhanced that."

"But you approve?"

"Of Philip? Who wouldn't adore such a man—such security—for her daughter?"

Dejection struck Jackie, and she blamed herself. Pinning expectations on a relationship never proved fruitful. Disappointment inevitably wiggled its way in and caused division. Disruption, even. She couldn't allow that and knew the best reaction was to find satisfaction, to encourage harmony.

"Yes, security. There's that." The flat delivery of her words provided poor camouflage for her true feelings.

"Before we left America, Lee had visited with your Grandfather Bouvier. She said he wasn't all that well and had a ragged cough. I hope you've been corresponding with him, even though he was always a bit of a coot." Changing the subject had long been Janet's forte. Jackie went along, hoping to dull her bruised emotions.

"I think he gets run down in the winter months. It must be lonely at Lasata this time of year especially, when it's so cold and dark. I think it's when he misses Grandma Maud the most."

"Indeed." Janet paused and took a moment to stare at her daughter.

If Jackie had been asked in that moment to decipher her mother's expression, she would have struggled. Usually, when Janet's mouth and shoulders were as taut and tight as they were now, Jackie recognized it as disapproval and would gird herself for the verbal discipline about to follow. But Janet's eyes lacked the fierceness that accompanied such a stance, forcing Jackie to wonder if her mother was holding back what she really wanted to say. Instead of tampering with vulnerability and voicing the opinion that appeared to give Janet mild turmoil, Jackie abandoned her comments and retreated to the only tactic she trusted: propriety. Or so she thought.

"We'd best start getting ready for this evening." Janet set aside her cup. "Tonight's ball is hosted by friends of the Astors, and we don't want to be late."

FIFTEEN

For days, Jackie had tried in vain to reach Paul. She'd left messages for him at the château and at his Paris apartment to no avail, until her mother patted her shoulder, waking her from a blissful sleep one morning with the urgent whisper, "The concierge says a young man is on the line for you down in the lobby. Make yourself decent and hurry down."

Propelled by curiosity but hampered by dread, Jackie dressed quickly and headed to the lobby. She cleared her throat before speaking into the waiting receiver.

"Still in bed this time of morning? What kind of derelict are they turning you into, Jackie?"

"Paul! It's good to hear from you."

His voice energized her as he talked about his latest visits with the de Rentys, Bea, and even Philip.

"It's not the same without you here, Jackie. We've forgotten how to have fun it seems. Politics flavors our conversations more than I care for, and Ghislaine hasn't made a souffle since you've gone. We're a pathetic mess."

"You're exaggerating."

"Only a little."

Jackie let the sentiment sink in, then changed topics. "Claude said she gave you my letter."

"Yes, she did," he said after a beat of silence. "Imagine my disappointment when she told me it was for our mutual friend."

She was glad Paul couldn't see her blush. "I'm awful, I know."

"It's all right. I think I understand, but I haven't seen him. Who knows where he's off to by now. He could be back in the Netherlands, since it's his home."

"Yes." How she hated the way Paul could be so pragmatic and so right.

"If anything changes, I'll let you know."

"You could read it. I wouldn't be a bit upset."

He chuckled softly.

"No, I haven't ventured inside that envelope. Your secrets are safe. I have no desire to insert myself between you and Marceau, and I believe that's why you gave it to me. You've trusted me with a great deal, and I admit, being in your good graces is rather addicting."

"You really are wonderful, Paul."

"It's a terrible character flaw."

They talked about Jackie's travels, and she gave him the rudimentary schedule that Janet had shared with her.

"Philip is supposed to meet us in Munich." She bit her lip after she said it, knowing that it must have sounded like an indication that Paul should join them.

"I imagine you have many details to consider for the ball."

She heard the smile in his voice, even though he spat out the word *ball* as if it left a vile taste in his mouth. Perhaps Claude was right, that Paul still harbored romantic feelings for Jackie, and he was expressing it through thinly veiled bitterness.

"It's going to be a spectacle." Her deadpan delivery ignited Paul's laughter. Exactly what she hoped for. "Paul, I know the rumors are circling like vultures about this whole thing. I want you to know that all I care about is having you and the de Rentys there. Philip can please himself with whatever else." She bit her lower lip.

"Surely you know by now I'm not in the habit of letting you down. I'll be there, Jackie, in any capacity you may need."

She gripped the telephone cord, squeezed her eyes shut. Absorbing the sentiment, she feared the depth of fortitude she might need to survive the impending celebration.

Jackie,

I've heard that you're currently touring Europe with Janet and Hughdie, so who knows when this note may find you. However, I do have a bone to pick with you. Rumors of a romance have reached our ears. It's becoming difficult to sort through, though, as I've heard a vast variety of details, including that you're in love with a French prince (Do they even have a royal house these days?), a famous writer, Charles de Gaul's grandson, or a museum curator. You'll have to clarify for me or let me know if he happens to be all of the above. Did you really find a man that you love? My imaginations are torturing me, so please get in touch—a telegram or phone call may be best—as soon as you possibly can. I could be a stinker, like you, and withhold some exciting news, but I won't do that to you. Charles proposed!! You know how happy this makes me—and how I'm left to wonder if you aren't approaching the same fate, my dear! I've never been good with suspense or surprises and need you to suppress my fear that you might possibly marry without me present—and before I have a chance to give you my opinion of this man. At any rate, I wish you unbridled joy and cheer!! What a man he must be!

With love,
Martha

PHILIP SCOLDED Jackie when she telephoned him from Salzburg, flummoxed and exasperated she hadn't phoned sooner. The chastisement, not harsh but unexpected, made her squirm in her own skin. She was glad to be alone in the hotel lobby as she conveyed apologies and excuses in equal measure. Up until her conversation with Philip, she'd already been taken in by the city, dazzled and awed by its Baroque architecture and friendly people.

When she tired of the sound of her groveling, she pivoted. "How are the party arrangements coming along?"

A mild sigh traveled over the line, which Jackie took as a sign of Philip's forgiveness. He eased into the topic of the party and its arrangements. "It's most impressive. Mother is making herself weary, but she loves nothing more than hosting a grand celebration. She's quite excited for us."

Jackie couldn't pinpoint why, but his mention of *us*, so intimate and conjoined, brought on a light-headedness. Deep breaths kept her from fainting on the lobby's marble floors. "I'm sure the evening will be...so memorable." Her scalp prickled—the same as if she'd been startled or confronted with difficult news.

"Now, the more important matter at hand is when should I join you in Munich?"

Her chest tightened as she worried about having to conceal her true reactions—and what they might be when she saw Philip again. A party in her honor should've enthralled her, but she feared it was too much, being whisked away from Paris and attending balls nearly every night in Vienna. It was growing to be too much showmanship for Jackie's taste and not enough substance. And Philip was going along, only worsening the already-suffocating demands on her. At the same time, she marveled and wondered how her feelings for Philip had diminished so since Christmas Eve, and what on earth could she do about it before the ball.

Dear Yusha,

Since I know you haven't had the extreme pleasure of vacationing alone with Mummy and your father, I know you are craving insights into the experience. For one thing, Hughdie reads excessively, much like he does at home, but here, he has more time as he waits for Mummy to get ready. It seems to take her twice as long. She attributes it to the confined spaces and not having enough room for her things. It would be comical if it weren't detracting from our time here. Europe doesn't agree with Hughdie as easily as it does Mummy and me—both in the delicacies and the prices tags of just about everything.

Have you realized that Hughdie and Mummy have been married eight years this summer? You wouldn't know it, because they fuss and ignore each other as though they've been doing it for decades. Is that what we have to look forward to with marriage? The promise of growing old and grumpy? I've also thought a great deal about the roles men and women are forced to play in relationships. Men get to project their expectations and may even demand certain behaviors from their wives. Women must appease. I suppose such a notion doesn't concern you the way it does me, probably because you're a male. It's baffling, because to woo a woman, a man must do his best to please her and present himself as a marvelous catch. Then a woman loses whatever power she had once she falls for him. Not that I know any of this from personal experience, only deep observations. Perhaps I'm being too harsh, and this melancholy has resulted from this impromptu family holiday. If you feel the urgency to craft a dire emergency—one that demands their presence back home—who am I to stop you?

I still love you even though you let them come,
Jackie

DREAD YOKED Jackie as she climbed into the seat of the taxi, leaving Salzburg. Their journey to Munich would mean seeing Philip in three days, an encounter she wasn't ready for. *The expectations he'll have of me. I'll have to be alight and vivacious, as if his presence has cured the despondency in me created by our time apart. Is that what he will expect?*

"Jackie, you look pale," Janet noted. "Are you up for the train ride?"

"I'm fine, Mummy." She knew better than to pair the remark with too much enthusiasm.

After a curt nod, Janet turned her attention back to the arrangement of the luggage.

Jackie leaned her forehead against the small glass pane in the backseat and welcomed the cold rush to her skin. She longed for an ally, someone she could turn to and share her complaints and worries. In her mind she settled for Charles, but immediately hearing his reasonable, sensible responses, fictional yet true to his character, she exchanged him for Martha, who was eager to hear Jackie's laments and slow to offer advice.

The ninety-minute train ride proved uneventful, though Jackie's racing thoughts allowed her no peace.

Like London, Munich was in the early stages of its restoration efforts, which Jackie and her parents were reminded of as they passed the Residenz palace. Once home to the Wittelsbach royal family, the expansive structure, with portions that dated back to the 1300s, sat shelled from Allied bombs. Long, cold winters, combined with a lack of funding, had slowed rebuilding, or so she had read.

Sunlight punctured the ashen clouds drifting over Munich when they arrived. Just enough light and warmth, at least for a winter day, to lift Jackie's mood. She didn't want to spend the afternoon unpacking again.

Once their bags were delivered to their suite, she piped enthusiastically, "Let's go to Dachau."

"The site of the Nazi camp?" Hughdie asked.

"Yes. We should see it, don't you think?"

"I'm not so sure that's a good idea." Both women looked to Hughdie, which gave him pause. "Well, it's just that your mother, she's the fragile type. I understand your devotion to history, Jackie, and your desire to immerse yourself in the experience, but I don't know what that might do to her...what we might see."

"That's every reason we should go then." Jackie's tone was steadfast yet genteel.

He darted a glance toward Janet and pressed his lips together. "All right, but please keep your mother's sensitivities in mind."

When Jackie met her mother's gaze, Janet toyed with her string of pearls and seemed at a loss for what to make of Hughdie's concerns.

They boarded the trolley the concierge told them would get them to Dachau. Jackie took a seat next to a petite woman who greeted her with a faint smile and a weathered countenance. Gray curls peeked from beneath the faded floral print of her head scarf. Her thinning wool coat, though well-made, concerned Jackie.

Ten minutes later, when Jackie and her family disembarked, the woman joined them.

"Pardon me, but are you here to see Dachau, too?" Jackie asked.

The faint smile returned. "I've already been." A thick German accent laced her soft voice. "You might say I'm here to see what's been done." Solemnness ambushed her expression. "And maybe to look upon my husband one final time."

An icy surge bolted through her. She looked to her parents, who's faces reflected their own dismay.

"May we walk with you, then?" Jackie noted the woman's slow steps and couldn't escape worrying what would become of her with no one to accompany her.

"If you like, and that's very kind of you." She regarded each of them with her sorrow-etched gaze, emitting from dark eyes set in a permanent droop.

"Would you prefer to hold on to me, in case of ice?" Jackie put as much faith in the woman's shoes as she had the coat.

"You are a dear." She threaded her arm through Jackie's. "I'm Yiska."

Jackie and her parents proceeded with introductions as they walked toward the camp's entrance.

"The Jourhaus," Yiska said of the building. "It was once a munitions factory, or so I've been told. The Nazis brought political prisoners here at first. Communists. Members of the Resistance. Others who didn't agree with them. When Levi and I came in 1944, they often picked the Russian prisoners for their tortures. But they didn't stop there. The gypsies, Catholic priests...so many." She shook her head.

Jackie swallowed. "You were...imprisoned here?"

Yiska fixed her somber eyes on Jackie and nodded.

Jackie stole a glance at her parents, who looked as aghast as she felt.

Yiska lifted her gaze to the top of the wrought iron gate that guarded the porte-cochere opening and read the inscription above. "*Arbeit Macht Frei.*"

"What does it mean?" Jackie asked.

"'*Work sets you free'*. As cruel and evil as the Nazis were, one could almost admire their discipline. Meticulous record keepers, they were."

Through the gate and to their right stood an expansive building in the shape of a blocked C.

"This,"—Yiska pointed—"This is where we came, my Levi and me."

"Was Levi your husband?" Janet asked.

Yiska nodded and her eyes glistened with pride.

"Are you sure you want to go inside?" Jackie asked.

Yiska stared at the building stretched in front of her and gave a cautious but solid nod.

Jackie held her closer, and they stepped into a long, dank hallway washed in gray and gloom. Light came mainly from the open door behind them.

"The shunt room." Yiska's voice carried throughout the vast, empty space. She walked ahead of Jackie and her parents and began motioning with her hands. "Tables were here, where the SS sat. They took our names and wrote down what we brought with us. Not that anyone had much. And it didn't matter. They took our belongings and made us shed our clothes. Then we walked to the prisoner baths. We were shaven, showered, and disinfected." Yiska clutched at her chest as the memories seemed to take hold. She turned to face Jackie and her parents.

"I only saw my Levi at roll call after that, because they kept the men separated from the women. He always made sure that we saw each other. Even if it was only for a second, our eyes found each other. Sometimes he would give me that sly grin of his. I took it as a sign that we might get out of this place. Knowing the things I do now, it was foolish to have such hope. But I am grateful. Grateful for those mornings—in the bitter rain or snow at times—when I could see him. He was so strong, and I wanted to be strong for him."

She held her hands in front of her and bent her head.

"Levi and I were in hiding for years. We heard about the terrible things they did in the camps. He feared what would happen to us, and he was right. Levi was shot and killed one day when they lined men up in front of a trench and shot them in the back. Such cowards!" A tear trailed down her cheek as she relived the memory. "Levi—and all the dead—were carted like garbage to the Leitenberg. You can't see it from here, but it's nearby." She patted her chest. "My Levi is nearby."

"Is it...a burial ground?" Jackie asked.

"Yes. The government recently dedicated it as a memorial cemetery. During our internment, coal became scarce at the camp. There wasn't enough to burn the fire in the crematorium, so the SS resorted to using mass graves after executions."

Janet gasped and Hughdie held her. "How appalling."

"Jackie, if you don't mind, I think your mother has had enough. It's probably best if we wait elsewhere for you." Hughdie, his tone soft and laden with concern, darted a glance toward Yiska. "Take all the time you need."

Jackie nodded and joined Yiska as she plodded back outside. Poplar tree saplings lined a walkway that edged the barracks. As they shuffled along, Yiska shared stories about friends she'd lost and the cruelties of camp life.

"How did you do it, Yiska? How did you survive?"

"I had no choice. If I had my way, I would've asked to be in that firing line with Levi rather than live without him. I existed in a fog after it happened. Guards would hit me when I didn't listen. I hoped one of those blows would send me to the afterlife with Levi, or that I would be among the many inflicted with Typhus. But here I stand." She lifted her chin as she gazed toward the hill and drew in a deep breath of Bavarian air.

"How does one overcome such unfathomable agony and find any meaning in life?"

Yiska tried to smile. "You help the others remember."

Jackie wasn't sure she agreed. Looking over the landscape of the camp, Jackie was certain that lost souls were staring back from the empty windows. She worried that people could shut their eyes and ears to the horrors that had happened here and at other camps. But she kept her thoughts to herself.

"This place, who knows what will become of it over time, and what they may do with the remains of those who died here. If I could sift through the dirt and bones and find my Levi, I would. I would bring him back home to Erdweg and honor him with a proper burial. But I won't get to do that. I can come here, see the Leitenberg and know that my Levi rests with many others, and I can tell all those who will listen about what happened here. And when I rise and when I lay down, I will continue to pray that such a thing will never happen again." With tear-stained cheeks, Yiska turned to Jackie. "Don't ever seek to understand a tragedy once it's done. There is no comfort in why, only in doing what we can to honor those we love, those we lose."

REVERENCE CLOAKED Jackie and her parents as they rode the bouncing trolley back to town. Flecks of rain on Jackie's face went unnoticed as melancholy gripped her heart. She had no regrets, walking the grounds of Dachau and escorting Yiska to the Leitenberg, where they both shed tears at the newly erected memorial.

Yiska then rose from her seat to leave at the first trolley stop. Jackie thought she might burst from anguish as she watched her go. She would've given anything to ease the burden of sorrow Yiska would always carry. But Yiska had left her with a gift. As she carefully disembarked the trolley, she turned to Jackie and said, with a lilt in her voice:

"Whatever the days, live them well."

SIXTEEN

Back at the hotel, the concierge held up an urgent telegram for Jackie. She tore into the envelope, probably too anxiously, as her parents hung back. When she realized the telegram was from Philip, the gallop in her chest subsided. In his message, he explained that meeting up with Jackie and her parents in Munich would prove too arduous and demand too much travel for such a relatively short visit.

WILL MAKE IT UP TO YOU. DINNER AT THE RITZ FOR ALL THURSDAY NIGHT. DEEP REGRETS. FORGIVE ME.

A collective sigh escaped her parents when she read it to them, though relief and misplaced anger stirred in Jackie. She betrayed none of her true feelings and agreed with her mother's comment that it was a disappointment.

"Say," Hughdie said, clapping his hands together, "Why don't we head over to that beer hall down the way? Can't say we've had the German experience without kicking back a stein."

Jackie, suppressing a grin, knew what he was up to. Hughdie didn't like the shroud of discomfort and disappoint that had engulfed them since touring Dachau. Philip's telegram had enhanced their dreary postures, so Hughdie hoped his suggestion would give them a boost. And, Jackie suspected, he really wanted a beer.

Rallied by mutual agreement, they set off for Hofbräuhaus, where they helped themselves to sausages and sauerkraut. Though the atmosphere felt old world authentic, with live music and Schuhplattler dancers, Jackie and Janet were ready to leave well before Hughdie. He promised to rejoin them soon, before they scurried out the door and into the cold.

Back in their hotel suite, Janet downed two aspirin, making Jackie wonder if their travels were starting to wear on her mother. She unbuttoned her jacket and sank into a chair, then turned her attention to Jackie.

"Did we do right by you, Jacqueline, sending you here?"

"Of course, Mummy! Travel is vital in shaping one's perspective." Though she regurgitated a customary reply, Jackie suspected her mother was mining for a deeper answer. She let her mind speculate that her mother was realizing that her role in Jackie's life was diminishing—or would be, the closer Jackie came to marriage. Were misgivings creeping up on her mother? Did she wish she'd been a softer, more affectionate parent? Jackie didn't want to take the fantasy too far.

"Is it? After what we've seen...experienced, I've been so worried. I don't want this place to harden you."

Jackie's stomach knotted. She knew what a trial it was for Janet to allow empathy to take hold, for compassion to overwhelm her. Her discomfort a side effect from Dachau and Munich cementing images and memories in her heart.

"It's important that we're here," she said. "That we see and experience the cost of war."

Janet swallowed, nodded her agreement.

She wouldn't dare say it aloud, but Jackie hoped her mother wrestled with regret for her insensitive comments at the de Rentys' home. An apology would never manifest, Jackie knew, but seeing her mother disturbed and her viewpoint enhanced would suffice.

"You know I always hope better for you," Janet said. "I hope that one day your marriage and your life are better than mine ever were. Above all, I hope we haven't damaged you too much. You and your sister." Her tone became firm, and the softness in her eyes morphed into a darkness Jackie had rarely seen. "It's been so hard, watching you both grow and...battling his influence over you girls. He's hardly inconvenienced himself, as far as providing for you goes, and he cares little about how embarrassing his immoral actions are. There's nothing he can do wrong that would snatch away your love for him. While your love for me..." She couldn't finish, the last words clogged in her throat.

Had Jackie been kicked in the gut by Danseuse, it would've had the same impact that struck her now. Hearing how her mother ached for her daughters' unconditional love came unexpectedly. Reflections reeled through Jackie's mind of all the times she'd mocked and ridiculed her mother's corrections behind her back, though she never defied Janet. Jack Bouvier, on the other hand, made no demands on his daughters in the way of etiquette or academics and seemed quite proud when rumors of his womanizing reached their ears.

"I'm sorry, Mummy." Jackie meant it, feeling the stark realization of her devotions clawing at her. "I've always loved you." She went to put her hand on her mother's slumped shoulder, but touching Janet differed little from touching a hot surface. Mostly, she'd slip away from the girls' affections or shrug them off. A form of rejection that had left its scars on Jackie and Lee.

But when her hand connected with Janet now, her mother sighed. A gasp escaped her as if she were drawing her first breaths. Handkerchief in hand, she dabbed at her face, then turned her wounded stare with red-rimmed eyes on Jackie. As if her admission and need for Jackie's love had not been enough of a shock, she added, "Please don't marry Philip."

JACKIE HAD BEEN DUMBFOUNDED at her mother's plea and formed no response. They'd both gone to bed, their last night in Munich, and said nothing else about Philip. The next morning, an early alarm rattled her from a restless sleep, and though she had plenty to read for the long trip back to Paris, she could only focus on her mother's words.

Mild weather welcomed their return to the Ritz once they reached the city. A note from Philip awaited at the front desk, informing Jackie and her parents that an intimate dinner party had been arranged at the hotel for that evening.

Jackie had little time to refresh after the thirteen-hour train ride and feared the musty stench of the car clung to her. The de Rentys, Paul, and the usual assortment of friends from the university cheered when Jackie entered the private room. She made her rounds, greeting everyone, and expressed Janet and Hughdie's regrets.

"Traveling such long hours takes more out of them than it used to," she explained.

As servers dashed in and out, taking care of and delivering drink orders, Jackie led Paul to the side of the room.

"Do you have any news?" She could do nothing about the embarrassment that burned within, having sunk Paul into the situation with her. As well, she worried about how her irrational behaviors must have tainted Paul's view of her. No remedy presented itself—and at the moment she cared more about information of Marceau than Paul's perception.

"Got in touch with several friends of mine. Asked around to see if anyone had run into Marceau or heard any news regarding him. One told me he'd been separated from his wife and had been focused on his family's interests in Paris in recent months. One friend told me he was with the Montmartre Orchestra, which I found hard to believe, until I attended the show at Malmaison. There he was, stroking the violin like he was born to play it."

Jackie recalled Marceau mentioning the performance when she saw him at Nôtre Dame. *His friend didn't return as planned—If he had, Paul may not have found him.*

"We met up after," Paul continued, "and decided to head back to the city and Café Les Deux Magots, a favorite spot of his. We talked for hours. His primary interest was you. I'll admit, I hated how obsessed he seemed. Must have asked a hundred questions about you, and I even thought about not giving him the letter."

Jackie held her breath as Paul gave an ornery squint.

"But I could tell he was miserable. He feared you hated him. I thought it served him right for what he'd done to you, and I wanted to leave him in that state, suffering." Paul sighed. "But I didn't. Well, you can't imagine the look that came upon his face when I told him you'd entrusted me with a letter. I think he wanted to jab me for holding out on him, but he became engrossed. Read it right there in front of me. Then he almost looked worse for it. Why, I feared he was about to break down, but he thanked me for everything and then made a hasty departure."

"You must be teasing. Surely he said something about the note..."

Paul sipped his drink and shook his head. "He didn't share his reaction with me, although he was despondent. I followed him out, hoping he wasn't about to throw himself off Pont Neuf. He knew I was following him, though, and took off. I haven't seen him since. That was several days after I'd spoken to you over the telephone."

Jackie's chest tightened. "I never should've written him that letter. Who knows what's happened to him."

"Don't worry. I'm sure after a bottle of Bordeaux, he forgot all about your letter. He's probably fine. Not that he'll ever recover." A corner of his mouth curled. "Who would ever get over losing you?"

She returned a delicate grin and tried to find comfort in his words but couldn't dismiss the worry that gnawed at her.

"Now don't get in a fluster. This isn't exactly the best time to be thinking about another man."

Jackie caught Philip staring at her and Paul as he sipped his martini. Meeting her gaze, he responded with a raised chin and jolly grin, then lifted his glass. Jackie and Paul held up their champagne cocktails. She couldn't say for sure, but Jackie suspected Philip didn't approve, watching his beloved schmooze with another man during their reunion celebration.

"You're right, Paul." Obsessing over Marceau had no place among the people she'd grown fond of, who were there for her. Before she made her way back to Philip's side, she squeezed Paul's hand. "Thank you. I'd never have gotten through any of this without you."

He returned an affectionate grip and wistful smile.

A pang of fear radiated through her when she thought of the trust she'd put in Paul and his friendship. He could expose her, effortlessly, for the farce she was portraying with Philip. What if he was using her for another purpose or setting her up for a great fall?

She sighed, embarrassed at her own thoughts and fully aware that her predicament was her own fault. Nevertheless, she intended to be more guarded.

LATE THE NEXT MORNING, with a break from frigid temperatures and rain prickling down, Jackie and her parents arrived at Château de Laurent, where a line of servants and the Laurents waited to receive them. Warms greetings emitted from Philip and his parents, Albert and Eustacia, while his sisters, Martine and Tilda grinned and said little.

Dinner that night proved more formal than Jackie wanted. Not that she'd been asked for input, but with the masquerade ball commencing tomorrow night, she had hoped for a relaxed evening. Such as their night on Christmas Eve, when laughter and friendship proved to be the best gifts.

Now, seated at the imposing sixteen-foot mahogany table with servants flanking each guest felt less than ideal. So did the unspoken expectation that she needed to please and impress the Laurents over the next few days. Perhaps too much was at stake for the Laurents to be at ease. Conversations focused on the guests expected to attend, the menu, and what the ladies planned to wear.

Janet naturally held her own and easily impressed Albert and Eustacia. In Jackie's mind, her mother was demonstrating that she belonged there and was worthy of rubbing elbows with French nobles.

Had Jackie's love for Philip been deeper, more consuming, she would've been grateful for her mother's efforts.

When the courses ended and everyone bid their goodnights, Philip asked Jackie if she would ride with him. Nothing could have pleased her more in that moment. She clung to the hope that this was what they needed—a chance to reconnect in private.

After they both changed into riding gear, which Jackie borrowed from Tilda, and met at the stables, two sleek Arabian horses were tacked up and waiting. Philip offered a hand to assist Jackie in mounting the horse, and she laughed at him playfully. Then she slid her boot into the stirrup, hoisted herself up, swung her leg over side of the horse, and settled onto the saddle, all in a swift motion that left Philip slack-jawed and staring. He snapped from his wonderment and mounted his own stallion, then led them from the stables.

"We'll not venture far," he said once Jackie cantered up beside him. "Horses are well-equipped to see in the dark, and the moonlight will help." He glanced at the moon above, with half its orb aglow. "The grounds are still beautiful at night."

"Oh, I imagine so."

He flashed an easy grin, which she returned, despite her tensions bristling. Excitement also surged in her, for how often would she get the chance to ride a horse at night amidst the French countryside? But she felt like a phony with Philip. Too eager, too chipper in a forced attempt at urging her romantic feelings to the surface. It wasn't working.

They galloped around the château, some areas having more light than others, but the horses never faltered. In other parts, the stomping hooves splattered slushy bits of snow and mud. The horses' frosty snorts combined with their own visible puffs of breath in the darkness.

Jackie couldn't believe it had been months since she'd been in the saddle. Naturally, the promise she'd made to her father about not riding while she was away crept into her thoughts. Sitting tall, her back had never felt better—and the small act of defiance suited her. Perhaps one day she'd tell her mother about it.

Philip led them to the top of a ridge overlooking the estate. The moon reflected off a pond below, and light radiated from various windows of the main house, giving it a warm glow. They reined in their horses to stop and savor the view.

"It's beautiful." Jackie looked at Philip when he made no reply.

She took in his striking profile, but slowly realized that being alone with him, after a long absence, even on a moonlit jaunt of horseback riding, had done nothing to stoke her desires for him.

"Something's changed, hasn't it?" he asked.

"What do you mean?"

"Since your journey with your parents. Something has happened between us. I feel it, you know. And last night at the Ritz, it hit me so strongly, almost as if you didn't want to be there or at the very least near me. I don't know a better way to describe it other than a shift."

Jackie had feared Philip's growing ability to sense and see past her cordial personas. She'd failed miserably last night at the Ritz, and she had no readied defense.

"Tell me honestly," Philip implored. "Have your feelings changed for me, Jackie?"

"I wouldn't have taken you as one who's insecure, Philip."

He shook his head. "Don't do that. Don't make this about me."

Jackie hated that she wasn't a better liar—or undeniably suave when it came to crafting an indirect answer to a difficult question. Her body clenched, feeling pressure from every angle. "We're still getting to know each other, aren't we? I doubt we're already able to read each other's moods every second. At least that's true for me."

He turned to her. "But do you love me, Jackie?"

She drew in a breath and scrambled through her mind for the words that would soothe and buy her more time. More time to figure out what she really wanted.

"I've never been good at this sort of thing, Philip—"

"The last time we were alone, here, at Christmas, I asked you to come to my room. You refused me. Said it was too soon. Would it be the same answer tonight?"

A mild fury poked at her. How on earth could he expect a different response? It occurred to her that Philip was no better at loving someone than she was. Not as things currently stood between them. To a degree, his attempt to possess her matched the unreasonable urges she felt for Marceau.

"Is that really fair, Philip? To test me?" *Is that how love works for you?*

His jaw clenched but quickly released. He gently slapped the reins and his horse began to trot. Jackie followed his lead back to the stable, where attendants received them and took the horses, once they dismounted.

Philip touched Jackie's elbow. "Will you come with me? There's something I want to show you."

SEVENTEEN

When they entered the house, the stillness suggested that everyone else had gone to bed.

Phillip took Jackie's hand and said softly, "I promise to be a perfect gentleman."

Though nervous, Jackie nodded.

Wall sconces gave the hallway muted light, enough to see by, and Philip held his finger to his lips, indicating for her to be quiet. They stepped quietly past his parents' bedroom and entered the room next to theirs. Philip carefully poked his head in, then led Jackie inside the small study. He reached for a book on an upper shelf, and just like in the room at Versailles, the book acted as a lever, clicking open a hidden door.

"Not many people know about this room," Philip whispered.

Jackie traded her hesitation for intrigue as they entered an even smaller room that wouldn't allow for more than two adults. The burgundy and gold brocade wallpaper in a floral-medallion pattern was remarkable, even under the single sconce Philip had clicked on by its chain. He removed a painting from the wall, one that reminded Jackie of a Cezanne still life, and placed it gingerly on the floor. The door to a safe was now exposed.

Philip leaned in and spun the combination. Another click and the door opened.

Jackie didn't want to be rude, but she yearned to peek inside at the treasures that surely lay within.

Philip withdrew a box, covered in navy velvet, and the perfect size for the palm of his hand. The tiny hinge croaked when he opened the box, revealing a dazzling ring.

"It belonged to my grandmother, Lisette, my father's mother. She passed on some time ago, but she left me this." A baguette-cut diamond sat in the center and was adorned with smaller diamonds on the side. Sapphires, rubies, and emeralds flanked the smaller diamonds. "My grandfather had this made. The colors represent the family crest, and the large diamond was stolen from Spanish explorers back in the late 1700s. Or so the story goes."

Jackie suspected that even the English monarchy didn't own such a fine piece.

"I've never seen anything like it." She wanted to touch it but didn't dare.

"It's meant to be worn by someone very special."

At that, she met his gaze. He was testing her again. Showing her this ring meant he was considering a proposal, just as Paul and Claude had suspected. She shrank back slightly.

"Oh, Philip, it's...breathtaking. Everything in your world is lavish and refined. The ring," she glanced at it, "should go to someone who belongs here with you and your family, permanently."

"Despite what's transpired between us lately, I think we could have a lasting future together, don't you? If we set our minds to it and gave it a real chance, we could be formidable together. I'm nearly convinced of it."

Jackie swallowed. "You can't make such decisions hastily. You must take your time, and you must be absolutely sure." She wanted to say more, but her thumping heartbeat, the heat racing to her face, made her wobbly. She put her hand against the wall for support.

"What if I already am?"

"Then I would wonder if you're lying to yourself." She delivered the remark with a teasing lilt, not having it in her to be too harsh or too direct. "No one can ever be absolutely sure of another."

Even in the poor lighting, his flummoxed expression was undeniable. His jaw ticked, and he clamped the ring box shut. He put the room in quick order. Jackie wondered if anger fueled his swift actions, but she could think of nothing to say that would ease the situation.

Philip led Jackie back to her room without another word. His eyes were an empty void of emotion as he said an agitated, "Good night," with no offer of a kiss.

JACKIE WAS certain Philip would cancel the ball and have her—and her parents—thrown out onto the lawn by the dawn's light. It was one of the many scenarios that plague her through the night.

Surely, his doubts about me must have surpassed my own after last night's debacle.

She hadn't meant to come across as insensitive or rude, especially when she saw the ring. But Philip had already recognized the disconnect between them. Jackie understood what a proud man he was, and she could envision him casting her aside dramatically in order to save himself. She couldn't blame him or believe that she deserved any better.

When morning broke through the windows with faint rays of sunlight, she dressed and steeled herself for a confrontation. In a way, a sudden dismissal would bring her a sense of relief, since the charade would finally be over.

Entering the breakfast nook, she found most of the family already up and enjoying warm crepes with raspberry filling. The aroma of coffee proved equally strong and inviting.

"Good morning, Jackie," Philip greeted her with a half-grin that contrasted to his grim state last night. He stood to seat her properly, much to the approving smiles of the mothers.

"Good morning. It smells delicious in here." She had to admit, if only to herself, the cheer in the room was as welcome as it was unexpected. Taking her seat, she thanked him and greeted everyone.

"Quite a day we have ahead of us, wouldn't you say?" Philip poured her a glass of orange juice.

"Yes." Her face flushed, more from not knowing what to say than from excitement. Had she merely imagined what befell between them last night?

"Tell us, Philip, what can we do to help?" Janet asked.

"You're to be pampered to the extremes." He sipped his coffee from a small bowl, a custom of château living. "A hairdresser and a seamstress will be here this afternoon, along with a costume designer for any embellishments to your gowns," he held up a finger, "which are to be pressed and primped to your satisfaction."

Eustacia, with diamond bracelets dangling from both wrists and with earrings to match, chimed in, "Lunch will be served on the east terrace and fresh baths will be drawn. We're going to have such a wonderful time. The orchestra will be set up in the ball room, dinner will be served promptly at seven, and we'll have calvados and cigars for the men in the smoking parlor, while the ladies can relax and converse over crème de pêche in the salon."

"And don't forget the fencing," Philip added.

"Fencing?" Jackie's eyebrows raised.

"Oh, yes. Philip can hardly resist displaying his showmanship." Eustacia batted her eyes at her son and flashed a timid but proud smile. "We even included it on the invitations that were sent. Why, I think it nearly goes hand in hand with any large parties we host." She turned her gaze to Jackie. "I hope you'll be agreeable to watching. It is a sophisticated form of dueling and can be invigorating to see, even if you aren't aware of the rules."

"Of course. I would love to watch."

She leaned in to Jackie. "Many of the young ladies become quite breathless and enamored watching him."

"Well, I'll expect quite a show."

Philip gave a coy grin. "In that case, I'd better be off. Several rounds of practice wouldn't hurt." He rose and went to Jackie's side, then bent to her ear. "I'm so glad we talked last evening. It put all my nerves to bed." With a tender squeeze to her shoulder, he left the room.

What...? He's not the least bit discouraged?

Suddenly feeling unsteady, she was thankful for the chair beneath her. With her head down, nibbling on bites of her crepe, she needed a moment to regroup. The ball was commencing...but was Philip seriously moving forward with a proposal?

Jackie shifted her focus. Helpless against any plans or schemes Philip may have up his sleeve, she resolved to simply go along with tonight's events. A gentle peace came in the thought that she could be overreacting.

But when she scanned the remaining faces at the table—all the women, as the men had exited in unison—she wondered if she could fit in at Château Laurent. What role would she fulfill? Philip's sisters had kept their distance and shown no interest in her. Not that she blamed them or put her own energy into breaking down their guards. Perhaps it was a cruel assessment, but Jackie couldn't see herself enjoying Martine and Tilda's company, because it wasn't lost on her, the way they—and Eustacia—doted on and adored Philip as if he could do no wrong.

Philip's accomplishments certainly spoke for him, although Jackie found men with varied interests to be the most intriguing. Was his goal simply to add a wife to his menagerie of admirers? Did she want a life on the fringes of her husband's esteem, or was she wrong to hope that there could be something more equal in a marriage? At the very least, she wondered where her domain would lie in such a union. Would she one day receive full reign when it came to managing the château, for instance? Would Philip care for her opinions when it came to purchasing and caring for the horses? Or would Jackie be expected to wear jewels at breakfast with guests and boast about her husband's fencing abilities?

Am I doomed to morph into Eustacia if we marry?

Careful not to overindulge in the crepes, Jackie joined her mother and Eustacia for a walk after breakfast. The Countess de Laurent spoke of her family's history at the château and recounted stories Philip had shared previously. According to Eustacia's beaming expression when they returned to the house, Jackie surmised that she and her mother had peppered in enough praise and comments and questions to please their host.

Jackie and Janet shared a knowing glance, one that recognized their refined ability of maneuvering into the good graces of a new acquaintance, and Jackie suspected it would be the easiest part of her day.

Dearest Jackie,

I hope this brief correspondence finds you bubbling with anticipation for what lies ahead. I wanted to take a moment and say how pleased I am with how you and your parents have taken to my own. As I stated this morning, I know we have overcome our doubts. Rest assured, my devotions have solidified. I believe we can endeavor on a magnificent future together, and I'm confident this evening will be a night neither of us will ever forget.

With affections,
Philip

JACKIE KNEW BETTER than to soak too long in the lavender-scented bath and risk her skin pruning, but she read and reread Philip's note. Fragrant bubbles edged her decollate and arms, and skimmed her smooth legs, as she ached for a hint of clarity or a glimmer of passion—something, anything real and solid that would get her through the night or alleviate the pressure of an impending proposal.

What does it say about me if I agree to marry a man I don't love passionately?

It was too late, she decided, to ponder such notions. Her only recourse was to move forward.

Though Jackie hadn't told her mother about the ring Philip had shown her, Janet was convinced, based on the extravagance surrounding the ball, that Philip would propose. Despair flickered in her eyes when she mentioned it, though she voiced neither concerns nor outright disapproval, as she had during their holiday.

Her mind racked with indecision, Jackie slid into the black satin gown she'd purchased during her afternoon at the Chanel studio. With a snug fit around the bodice and a portrait collar that wrapped just below her shoulders, the skirt of the dress brushed the floor. She wore more powder and rouge than usual and colored her lips with a berry lipstick that contrasted sharply against her dress. Black shoes with kitten heels, elbow-length white satin gloves, and a diamond and ruby necklace, loaned to her by Eustacia, completed her look. When Jackie took stock of her appearance in the room's gilded mirror, she nearly gasped, finding herself almost unrecognizable.

This is probably what Philip expects.

She dashed to the bathroom, slipped off her gloves and ran water over a washcloth. With vigor, she rubbed her mouth and cheeks until they were stinging and raw and free from the bold colors. Steadying herself against the sink, she breathed deep to settle her nerves. When she glimpsed her reflection in the mirror above the sink, soft curls framing her face and a new self-assuredness resting in her eyes, she decided to give her evening ensemble another try.

HER CONFIDENCE RENEWED, Jackie descended the stairs to join her parents, Philip, and his family. Various expressions and compliments welcomed her, and she couldn't recall the last time she'd felt so comfortable in her own skin.

"You look ravishing," Janet said, her glance dipping to the strand around Jackie's neck, "and my mother's pearls couldn't be more fitting."

Jackie caught the flash of scorn on Eustacia's face when she noticed the pearls instead of the necklace she'd loaned her, but Jackie didn't care.

She drew an unexpected strength from her mother's approval. "Pearls are always appropriate." Then she delivered her own round of compliments to Janet, Eustacia, and Philip's sisters, who preferred wearing masks that tied at the back of the head instead of a mask poised on a stick and held up, much like opera glasses, which had been Jackie's choice.

"Shall we?" Albert held out his hand toward the foyer. "Our guests will be arriving."

Philip leaned into Jackie, dared a kiss to her cheek and whispered, "I see my note had its intended effect."

A welcomed but uncertain flutter tickled her insides as a broad smile stretched across her now pink-stained lips. She slid her hand into his offered, crooked arm. There was nothing she needed to say.

AS GUESTS FLOODED in throughout the evening, Jackie brightened with each familiar face. The countess, Claude, Ghislaine, Paul, Bea, and a slew of others helped her maintain a genuine smile through the endless greetings and handshakes of Philip's friends and family, as well as what seemed to be, the whole of France.

An exquisite dinner of roasted Cornish hen, with all the trimmings followed. When Philip gave a toast to thank everyone for attending and declared that introducing Jackie was the primary reason for the evening's celebration, she blushed under such adoration. Dancing and the filling of champagne glasses consumed much of the night.

The reveling took a downturn for her once Philip changed into his fencing gear and took to sword slapping. Neither Philip nor his opponents were focused on making contact or punctures with the foils, leading Jackie to wonder how much of the display met fencing rules and regulations. Nevertheless, she couldn't deny the athleticism he showed in the fast and furious exchange of the foils shinking and clanging, along with the constant forward, backward, and lunge footwork.

For the fourth time—perhaps fifth, as Jackie had lost count—the gathered audience cheered and applauded as Philip became the self-proclaimed victor of another match. He removed his helmet and found Jackie among the crowd, his forehead shining with perspiration as he scarfed heavy breaths. "Who's next?" He held his arms open wide, his helmet with the meshed face shield in one hand and foil in the other as he extended the invitation.

Jackie released the breath she'd been holding in a slow, silent exhale. Her patience and interest in Philip's display of masculinity also dissipated. Behind her upheld grin, a dull ache pulsed in her head. Was he always this desperate for attention? Was this what parties at the Laurent estate amounted to? If that were so, then Jackie envisioned the need for masks at every event to hide her boredom.

Activity hummed in the room. Mild bursts of laughter, glassware clinks, and a gentle overflow from the orchestra served up soft undertones. People exchanged remarks while Philip, like a showman, beckoned for a new challenger.

A sturdy thump echoed off the wood floor.

Jackie turned, and a hem of the crowd parted to reveal a man, ramrod straight and decked in the fencing uniform that concealed him from head to toe. He lifted his epee—or sabre, Jackie couldn't tell—and pointed it directly at Philip, then bent at the elbow, whipping the epee straight up. The customary acknowledgement of one's opponent. Or so Jackie had been told.

Philip smiled as guests shifted to form an aisle. He replied with the same gesture.

"And who do we have the pleasure of welcoming for imminent defeat?"

Laughter followed Philip's dull attempt at humor.

The man offered no answer. He took his place on the homemade playing area, a strip roughly fourteen meters long and chalk marked with "*en garde*" lines. The crowd closed in and thickened along both sides.

"Very well, then." Philip, smug and obviously irritated by the man's silent rebuke, took his stance.

As did his opponent.

Salutes followed, and Philip yelled, "En garde!"

The bout commenced. Swords clanged. Priority switched rapidly from Philip to his opponent. Swipes and slices by each were blocked and jumped over. It took mere seconds to realize the challenger had no intention of playing gently. Jackie, standing in the front row of onlookers, stood taut with apprehension.

Already winded and with alcohol slogging through his veins, Philip's stamina drained. His lunges became sloppy, and he even dropped his foil once. Reactions from the crowd seemed to recharge him, but it didn't last.

When the bout reached a fevered pitch, Philip staggered backwards. The opponent thrust his sword into Philip's inner thigh. His scream pierced the room, as he fell to his knees, clutching the injury. Aside from his gasps and winces, all went silent. Blood stained his breeches and wet his glove.

Jackie rushed to his side and fell to her knees.

The challenger stood tall, his epee once again poking into the floor. Murmurs and disbelief seeped in, and the man slowly removed his helmet.

"You'll bleed like the dickens but trust me, it's a flesh wound. Some pressure, a few bandages, and you'll heal just fine. Just like I did after you gave me the same injury. Do you remember, Philip?"

Marceau's gaze, mischievous and whimsical, bore into Philip.

Philip's face scrunched hard, as if to force recognizing the man.

"Marceau." Jackie rose to her feet.

"You certainly know how to make friends, Jacqueline." He scanned the room and found Paul, who was nudging his way toward the spectacle. "It seems only the finest men tickle your fancy."

Jackie just stared, unable to form words.

He looked again to Paul and tossed his helmet to him. "It is good to see old friends, though." A look passed between them, one that seemed to acknowledge the depth of their friendship and mutual respect. "And since it's been so long since I've seen many of you, I'd like for you to meet my bride. Sophie, where are you?" Marceau glanced over the veiled faces.

"I'm here." She stepped forward from among the frayed crowd and lifted her mask of feathers and sequins.

"Ah, yes, my dear wife." Marceau took her gloved hand and touched it to his lips. "Most of you may not know this," he said to the crowd, "but my beautiful wife is expecting a child."

Weak and uncertain applause sounded.

He raised her hand. "And what you may also not know is that this woman is a vixen, a conspirator, and a cheat, who would love nothing more than to see me dead."

Sophie snatched her hand from his as if she'd touched a hot stovetop.

Jackie watched in dismay as Sophie's coloring changed from a radiant shimmer to bright scarlet, nearly the same shade as her gown. Partygoers murmured and gasped. Despite the fullness of the dress, her pregnancy was evident. Jackie thought back to her encounter with Marceau and Sophie at the Louvre. She couldn't recall noticing her figure then, but that had been two months ago.

"I know, it's impossible to believe that such an angelic face could be capable of any evil deeds but let me enlighten you. Shortly after our marriage—which, to be fair, neither of us wanted, but ever-faithful to obey the wishes of our parents, we went through with it. Not long after, I found Sophie in bed with her lover. Before I could dismiss her, the war broke out and separated us." He raised an eyebrow in Sophie's direction. "Perhaps we were both grateful. During the fight for my country, I was injured and sent to the infirmary, not expected to recover. Amnesia seized me and kept me from returning home after. My parents and my wife presumed I was dead. No proof could be given otherwise. I came to France, choosing to avoid my life—my duties—back home in the Netherlands. I sent word to my parents, told them of my well-being and that Sophie's heart did not belong to me." He held her furious gaze. "It never had."

"I'll not stand for this!" Sophie's shoulders were taut, and her hands balled into fists at her side.

"Yes, you will!" He took her by the wrist and kept her from escaping into the crowd. "Because there's someone here tonight whom I care about deeply. Someone who's rescued me from the pit of despair that became my life. She has no idea what her presence has done for me, and she deserves to hear everything." His eyes went to Jackie, who feared she might drown from the exhilaration swirling inside her. "I'm alive—truly alive—because of her."

Marceau turned back to Sophie. "So you see, it's fitting, even necessary, that all the world knows what you've done. How you almost ruined me. Because when you realized I wasn't dead, as you'd hoped, you tried to poison me! But, oh, sweet Sophie, how could you know that the heat from my coffee would lessen the lethal capabilities of the ricin from those castor beans?" He released his hold and slid his fingertips along her clenched jawline.

The crowd responded with gasps and a flurry of awestruck expressions. Jackie suspected hers looked the same.

"Why —one might ask—Why are you so desperate to be rid of me?" Resolve replaced the pained expression on Marceau's face and his eyes narrowed. "Because of the baby growing inside you. The baby that belongs to your lover!"

Exclamations and raised furor took over.

"My dear, consider this declaration my petition for divorce."

Incensed, Sophie huffed in his face as she trembled with anger. Her only other retort was a glare of fury before she turned and began shoving her way through the bewildered throng.

Marceau walked to Jackie and dropped his epee. He took her into his arms and kissed her like a man awakened from a slumber of depravation, hungry for affection. More exclamations rippled through the gawking audience, but Jackie heard nothing. Her senses, her body became electrified by Marceau's intensity. When he released her, she had to catch her breath.

Marceau held his hand to her cheek briefly, then turned and disappeared into the crowd.

EIGHTEEN

Jackie, Paul, and several others, moved Philip to a private room. A doctor was found to examine him and confirmed the wound was insignificant.

"Almost as though he knew what he was doing. Knew right where to puncture you and how deep. It's quite brilliant, if you ask me."

Philip found no amusement in the doctor's words and didn't share his—or Paul's—smirk. After the wound was tended and bandaged, Philip went to his bedroom and changed back into the suit he'd worn when the evening began.

"Are you all right?" Jackie asked when he returned.

"I haven't seen Marceau in ages, probably not since boarding school." Philip ran a hand over his locks, the perspiration of sheen now gone from his face. "He was right. I served him up first, you know. Years ago. A competition at Aix-en-Provence, I believe. Poked him straight in the...."

Having seen Marceau's scar the night she sketched him nude, Jackie knew.

"Incredible, wasn't it, the story he unfolded?" Philip downed a shot of calvados.

Jackie nodded and looked to Paul instead.

"How did you come to know him?"

She couldn't avoid an interrogation, not after the kiss Marceau left her with in front of dozens of people. Jackie hoped the alcohol and pain medications would cloud Philip's head.

"I hardly know him. We attended an art class together." Sticking to the truth—the minimal truth—was best.

"But the way he took you, kissed you...there's a connection between the two of you." Philip couldn't finish the thought.

Again she glanced at Paul, perhaps for a dose of strength—or to gauge how far Paul would go with her version of truth. She worried that he would expose her, tell Philip about the letter she'd written to Marceau, and admit for her that she did indeed harbor an infatuation for the man.

"I suppose I was nearest him." Jackie shrugged a shoulder. "He made a dramatic entrance and wanted to make sure he left on an equally dramatic note, I imagine."

Her heart pounded. Could she really play off Marceau's actions? Would Paul allow it?

"But he was speaking of you, wasn't he, when he spoke of caring deeply for someone?"

"He seemed ravaged with betrayal." Frustration riled in Jackie and translated into her voice. "I can't fathom what he must be thinking, nor pretend to understand his intentions." It was an honest answer. Too honest, as she wrestled inwardly with not being able to converse with Marceau—to hear it from him directly, that his feelings for her matched her own in passion and unreasonableness.

Philip seemed to relent. He held out his hand to Jackie, and she obliged.

"This isn't the way I wanted this evening to end. I...I had something I wanted to ask you." His jaw clenched. "I've never wanted to be another man...but when you looked at him, in that instance...I almost wanted to kill him. It felt as though he'd robbed me of the thing I've desired most, which is your complete adoration."

Her pulse ramped, harder than she thought possible. "Philip—"

"Don't say anything, Jackie." He let go of her hand and shook his head. "Please...just don't."

JACKIE EXCUSED HERSELF.

Outside the room, Philip's parents and sisters waited, not having seen him since Marceau inflicted the injury. Jackie calmed a fretful Eustacia and informed them that Philip was all right, then stepped aside as they stampeded in.

Janet and Hughdie also stood there, bound up with concern.

"He's seen a doctor, and he's fine," Jackie repeated.

Janet let go of the breath she was holding while Hughdie nodded with relief.

"Jacqueline, who on earth is this Marceau?" Wonderment sparkled in Janet's eyes.

She noticed other partygoers approaching. "I'll have to explain later." An empty remark, she knew, without an ounce of guilt.

As other guests zipped toward her, she gave the same pronouncement she'd shared previously, then excused herself from the growing crowd, as if she had an emergency to tend to.

Her escape successful, she aimed to make a quick search and see if she could find Marceau, but Bea caught hold of her and scurried her around a corner. Black feathers along the drop-shoulder neckline of Bea's black dress fluttering as they hurried.

"That was unbelievable." Bea kept her voice subdued. "Are you holding up?"

"I'm a bit overwhelmed." Jackie found she needed that small release.

"How's Philip? Is he angry?"

Her tension returned as quickly as it had left. "His head is spinning, or it will be if he keeps drinking." A fair assessment, she believed.

A devilish grin curled on Bea's cherry-colored lips. "What's it like, having these men lose themselves over you?"

The comfort she'd hoped to gain from Bea deserted her. Much like the hope she'd held for convincing Philip that Marceau meant nothing.

"You may not believe me but it's not an enviable position." The urge to abandon Bea's company, the same as she'd abandoned Philip and Paul, consumed her. "Not the way you might think." Whether or not Bea picked up the intended yet mild insult, she didn't care.

Bea piped a mild guffaw. "And you said he was a friend of Paul's."

A clamor of voices and motion rustled from around the corner. Jackie and Bea peeked and saw Philip emerging, a flock of guests at his heels.

She left Bea and went to him. "What are you doing? Shouldn't you be resting?"

"Nonsense." Philp buttoned the cuffs of his shirt. "I'm not going to miss the rest of my own party on account of a little mishap. Wouldn't want Marceau to think he got the best of me. And, more importantly, I must assure my guests of my good health. Show that it takes more than sword to take me down."

Jackie forced a thin smile.

With an arm around each of his sisters, Philip led them and the rest of his adoring audience to the ballroom. Jackie followed, uncertain how far Philip would go to prove his virility. At the same time, she paid no attention to her parents or Paul, who were among the crowd.

Philip entered the ballroom with both hands in the air as he declared, "Here, here!" He insisted the orchestra strike up a peppy number, which they complied with by playing the overture from Glinka's opera. Pleased by the selection, Philip spun, then swiped a glass of champagne from a nearby table and downed it. He swept his mother, stunned but laughing, onto the dance floor. Boisterously, he encouraged others to join in, commented that the night was still young.

Jackie watched in muted awe for a moment. She fixed her expression, made sure that she appeared delighted and agreeable to Philip's antics, because she felt the eyes of every guest dart her way. She spoke congenially with everyone who approached her, though she was a shell of herself. When conversations went limp, and she was satisfied she'd done her duty as Philip's ornament, she slipped from the room.

Nausea threatened. Not from anything Philip had done, but from the fear that she might have missed the chance to catch Marceau. Scant and illogical as that hope was.

He must be gone by now.

The thought ached her but didn't diminish her desire to search through the rooms of the château. There was a chance, she believed, that he'd stolen away somewhere and was waiting for her to find him.

Jackie headed to the second floor, intent on making sure no one came after her this time. She ducked in and out of rooms but was forced to reconsider her reckless tactic when she suddenly heard muffled voices. Carefully, she leaned against the door and attempted to listen, but the mahogany yielded nothing coherent.

She decided to enter the room beside it and see if she could pick up the conversation between the walls. It was petty, listening in on others, but nothing could dull her resolve for finding out anything she could about Marceau. She gathered a fistful of the skirt of her gown and slinked inside the room.

A fire blazed, providing her enough light to see that no one else was in there. Delight surged in her when she noticed a door connecting to the other room. But once more, she couldn't hear as clearly as she wanted with her ear pressed to the door, so she turned the knob. Delicately, she inched the opening wider but only enough so that she could peek inside.

Two people were in the room. A man, pacing, and a woman, seated on a couch with her back to Jackie. Their words were tempered.

Jackie leaned in more, and just then, a cat leapt at her from the shadows of the room. Startled, she half fell, half jumped into the next room. The man and woman, startled and both now on their feet, turned to face her.

"You!" Sophie's jaw hung slack after the exclamation.

The man's expression looked equally mortified.

Jackie straightened as the cat lifted its tail and rear in front of her and padded away. "Hello, Sophie." Disgrace blazed her face as she pinched and twisted her gloved fingers. "I apologize for barging in like this. I was looking for the water closet." Her words trailed off, as did her stout effort to support the lie.

Awkward glances made their rounds.

"This is Victor," Sophie announced.

Victor and Jackie traded nods.

"Victor, give us a moment." Sophie kept her gaze on Jackie as he made haste.

"You might as well join me, now that you're here." Sophie returned to the sofa.

Though Jackie thought every muscle in her body was frozen and knotted, she went and seated herself next to Sophie. They said nothing as they quietly sized each other up. Jackie noted her astonishing beauty with her red-rose lips, plump and puckered, her crystal-blue eyes, hauntingly bright, and her golden hair spun into thick, perfect ringlets.

Jackie's gaze dropped to the bulge of Sophie's abdomen, which was more noticeable as she sat. Sophie caressed the red silk covering her growing baby.

"Marceau is right about the baby. It isn't his. We tried when we were first married, both of us believing that a baby would bring us together and fix everything. Only God knew then how hopeless we were." Sorrow twisted her face. "I should've known that afternoon at the Louvre that you were special to him." She spoke with little bite or energy. "The way he looked at you that day—and again tonight. It's been years since his eyes have gone so...lovesick."

"He never told me he was married." Jackie hated the admission, along with the fount of humiliation exploding inside her.

"So you slept with him?"

"No!" Her embarrassment deepened. Had there been a chance of intimacy, she would've made love with Marceau. She wanted to believe that knowing he was married would've deterred her, but she wasn't certain, which added to her shame. Her life had largely been built on the shattered remains of infidelity, and she had no intention of duplicating that kind of pain and destruction, for herself or others.

"It's not that I care. Well, I'm not entitled to care anymore. We're far from being a devoted couple."

"I'm sorry." Jackie squeezed her clasped hands sitting in her lap. She had no other release for the nagging nervousness.

"I can only imagine what you must think of me." Sophie thumped her head against the back of the couch. "You and the whole of France, after the things he said."

"Was it true?"

A snide expression crossed her face. "That I tried to kill him? He's irresponsible—always has been. He had no right to air those accusations."

Jackie held steady.

"We'll call it a misunderstanding." Sophie sounded dismissive. "He has a talent for overreacting. I blame it on the years he spent with that traveling theater company, which might explain his need for such a show tonight."

"What will you do now?"

"You mean what will become of me after the divorce?" Sophie's tone bordered on comical, but then she sighed. "I'll return home to Luxembourg and build a life on the fringes of my parents' estate. I'll have my marriage annulled, then marry Victor." The corner of her mouth ticked upward. "We won't be poor, but I'll never be a duchess."

To Jackie's surprise, she stifled a snicker. Sophie suddenly reminded her of wealthy girls in Newport, the ones who complained that their future husbands preferred a yacht over a summer home. The ones who planned to spend their lives displaying their wealth and who pinned their happiness solely on achieving more wealth and more status.

"Marceau's not a bad man," she remarked. "He just isn't my ideal husband. I never should've married him or allowed my parents to control me. You probably don't understand what it's like, having no choices that are your own."

Jackie resisted the chance to correct her. While empathy sparked within her, she knew they could never be friends, and that no matter what she said, it wouldn't compare to the turmoil of Sophie's current circumstances.

"This will sound strange, but I suppose I owe you thanks. Because of tonight, Marceau and I can finally be rid of each other and our parents' ideals." Sophie laughed, then narrowed her eyes. "I think he's in love with you, and it almost makes me sad for you, because I wonder if you could've loved each other well."

Jackie's throat tightened, and she swore inwardly to hold back the tears that threatened.

JACKIE LEFT SOPHIE SOON AFTER, convinced the broken pieces of her heart would tumble out. She composed herself as she made her way back to the ballroom, hoping Philip hadn't grown wary of her absence. The orchestra was still thrumming strong and the floor filled with waltzing couples.

"Ah, there she is!" Philip stretched out his arm, as if directing everyone's attention to her. Heads in the room turned. "Jackie, please, join me if you will."

The activity in the room came to a clumsy halt, as the music bumbled and screeched while couples lost their rhythm.

The mild commotion caused a pit to form in Jackie's stomach. She kept her smile pleasant and readied herself to play his pawn. Making her way to his side, she was grateful to glimpse the de Rentys and her parents among the gathered. When she reached his side, Philip put an arm around her waist, which unleashed wrathful glares from Tilda and Martine, which Jackie ignored.

"Ladies and gentlemen, may I please have your attention?" he bellowed. The heavy stench of alcohol on his breath made Jackie rear back, though she was careful not to seem repulsed.

"I'm sure you'll all agree with me that tonight has been full of surprises." Philip paused and stole a glance at her.

Soft chuckles purred from the guests.

"Of late, I've been thinking about my grandmother, Lisette. This estate and many treasures within," he stole a glance at Jackie, "are part of the legacy she left behind. My family and I shared in her hope, that one day these halls would echo with the sounds of children's laughter and bare feet slapping against the marble floors. That together, we would continue to build upon the reputation and prestige she held dear. I must say, it's no easy task, searching for someone you want to spend the rest of your life with."

Jackie drew in a silent breath and tucked her clenched palms behind her back. Her eyes raced over the dozens of faces staring at her, ripe with anticipation. She began to tremble as her pulse throbbed in her ears. Seeing Claude and Bea's wide-eyed expressions didn't help. Neither did the stress mounting on Janet's face.

Can I go through with this? Can I accept a proposal from a man I don't love? Love or not, she couldn't humiliate Philip—or herself—with an honest answer.

He faced her. "Jackie, I have no doubt Grandmother would've adored you. Your beauty and grace are enchanting. Dare I say, she would've approved, possibly even encouraged our relationship."

She made herself breathe slowly, to avoid fainting.

"But...Grandmother isn't here tonight." Philip turned back to his audience. "Perhaps it goes without saying, but the war has taught us, cruelly in some ways, not to take life or any of its beautiful moments for granted. Tomorrow is never promised." He offered Jackie a somber expression paired with a thin smile. "So, let's share one last toast for the evening, and let us celebrate one another tonight." Philip made a *come hither* motion with his hand.

A waiter stepped up to them, holding out a tray of champagne cocktails. Philip and Jackie each took a glass.

"Here's to those who can't be with us, and to our futures, however marvelous or uncertain they may be."

Cheers followed.

Jackie touched the champagne to her lips but didn't drink. Instead, she upheld her pleasant expression, though she didn't bother looking at Philip. Moments later, when the orchestra began to softly play again, she casually left his side to be with her parents. When he made no move to stop her or to speak to her, she burned with animosity.

That was the most ridiculous toast and one of the most embarrassing moments of my life. Given the choice, she now would have preferred being arrested with Marceau, and the inner chaos that had developed in her head, over anything that had to do with Philip.

"Are you all right, dear?" Janet took Jackie's hands into hers.

"Yes, Mummy. I'm fine."

"I thought...for a moment..." She shrugged, as if finishing the thought might injure Jackie even more.

"I had wondered myself, but honestly, Philip and I don't know each other well enough to...take such a broad step. It's much too soon." To her surprise, Jackie found her own words soothing. Believable even.

Janet stepped closer. "I never felt he was right for you."

"Well, it's over now." The sentiment made her throat constrict. For she realized it wasn't just the evening careening to an end, but also her time with Philip.

Despite the whirlwind of doubts and dread that swam in her mind only moments ago, relief wasn't the overriding sensation for Jackie. Whether it was regret or sorrow, she couldn't tell. What had propelled Philip to make a public disgrace of her? Why had he felt it necessary—or acceptable—to shame her? She had to know, and she wouldn't sleep until he came clean.

THOUGH NO ONE asked her to, Jackie joined the Laurents in bidding goodnight to their guests. Janet and Hughdie accompanied her, and Jackie could feel her mother's pride in the fact that she hadn't let the embarrassing toast triumph over a show of good manners. Yes, she wouldn't let Philip make the last impression for her, even if she never saw most of these people again.

Curiosity also had a role in Jackie's decision, as she wondered if Sophie and Victor would file past her with the others. They didn't, leaving her to believe they had left shortly after their encounter.

Immediately after the last guests departed, Jackie exchanged goodnights with her parents and the Laurents, then excused herself. She wouldn't confront Philip now, and she craved a moment to smoke alone.

Once she was in her room, she removed her gown and washed her face. As she checked her reflection, she braced herself against the sink. A tidal wave of anger, pain, and regret crashed over her. Tears streamed down her cheeks. She sank to the floor, impervious to the cold marble against her bare skin. Sobs escaped as she tried to fathom where she'd gone wrong with both Philp and Marceau. Would love always be this fleeting? This cruel?

Before her sorrow mixed with exhaustion and lulled her to sleep, she rose from the floor, dressed, and smoked a cigarette to calm her tattered nerves. Moments later, a gentle knock sounded at her door.

"Jackie, are you in there?" Claude asked.

Suppressing a groan, she let her in. As far as she knew, the de Rentys, Paul, Bea, and other guests were still staying overnight.

"I just wanted to see if you're all right." Despite the late hour, Claude appeared wide-eyed.

Jackie let her shoulders sag. "I'm too tired to hash over things tonight."

Her hands flew up. "I completely understand. It's just with your parents and Philip, I...wanted to be here if you needed me."

Jackie hated herself for wanting to cast Claude aside. "You're too good, Claude." She embraced her and told herself she'd find a way to improve their relationship, once they were back in Paris and her parents had returned home.

After Claude left, Jackie felt renewed. She planned to wait a bit, allowing for others to be in bed before she went to Philip's room. Perhaps it wasn't the best strategy, showing up in the dead of night at his bedroom, but she knew it was the only way to assure they were alone—and to get answers.

An hour later, she padded barefoot up the stairs to Philip's door. A dim light escaped under the threshold, confirming that Philip was still awake. *Good. He shouldn't be able to sleep after all he's put me through this evening.*

How she wished she could turn her frustrations into courage. Standing at the edge of his door, she considered going back to her room, forgetting everything and simply packing so she could be ready to leave first thing in the morning.

No, I want to hear straight from the horse's mouth what prompted him to be so heartless.

If he were infuriated by his jealousy of Marceau, Jackie didn't need to be the one to suffer—and she planned to tell Philip. It wasn't her fault, that Marceau loved her. Nor should she be demeaned for loving him, a feeling she couldn't control, despite trying. Even though her devotion to Marceau did her no good, and would amount to nothing, she hoped it would hurt Philip worse than the puncture wound Marceau had inflicted.

Jackie rose up on her toes, prepared to knock, but the tension roiled inside her. She was setting herself up for an argument, one that promised a string of unkind words. Accusations even. Sparking an altercation held no appeal for her, but she had to see this through, and she wouldn't give Philip a chance to turn her away.

Forgoing etiquette and a knock, she palmed the knob and turned. Finding it unlocked, she pushed the door open.

"Philip, we need to talk."

When Jackie stepped into the room, her resolve melted.

Philip, rumpled in silk sheets, bare skin aglow in the firelight, was also tangled in the arms of Bea.

JACKIE SCAMPERED BACK to her room, dumbfounded, seething with anger and working to breathe through the heartbreak. Back in her room, she locked the door and sank to the floor. Her hand over her mouth stifled her erupting sobs.

Fearful that someone might overhear, she didn't stay on the floor long. Still, a whirlwind of thoughts stormed through her mind. Mainly, how could Bea and Philip betray her so?

After she calmed herself and splashed cold water over her puffy face, she packed—furiously and not without bursts of anguish that she muffled. She didn't touch the immaculate bed, knowing sleep wouldn't come. And when she ran out of menial tasks, she sat on the ledge of an opened window and smoked, ignoring the cold that crept in.

When the sky transformed to a dull winter morning, Jackie, dressed and treaded lightly to her parents' room. She hoped, achingly so, they would be as anxious to leave the château—and the Laurents—as she was.

Hughdie opened the door after her gentle rap and welcomed her in. She found they were both packed and ready, which helped her breath easier.

"I thought it best we make an early departure," Janet said, as she appeared to fiddle and squeeze her fingers, much the same as Jackie did whenever her nerves boiled over.

Downstairs, they found Albert and Eustacia, sans jewelry, in the breakfast nook. Janet took the lead, thanking the Laurents profusely for their generous hospitality and diplomatically explained how they needed to be off, as they had already planned to spend their last day together shopping in Paris.

The Laurents seemed numb and agreeable, though they encouraged them to stay for breakfast, perhaps out of implied etiquette. Janet humbly refused, citing that it was best to abstain after last night's fares and with a car ride ahead.

"Well, I'm sure Philip will be beside himself that he missed seeing you off," Eustacia said, again, a likely obligatory response.

Jackie's chest tightened at the mention of Philip and she hoped—no, prayed—she could escape without facing him, not knowing how well she could hold up at the sight of him.

Their bags were retrieved and loaded, and Jackie and her parents put Château Laurent, and Philip, behind them.

NINETEEN

A degree of guilt nagged Jackie at having left the de Rentys at the château without a mention of her early departure. With her head against the back seat of the car, Jackie knew reparations were needed. She pictured her beloved host family, gathered around the breakfast table with Philip and the somberness of Albert and Eustacia, and the shock that would settle over them once they heard the Bouviers had gone so abruptly. She didn't envy their chore of tolerating Philip's smugness—or whatever phony display he would project for the sake of his *valiant* reputation.

Little was said during their ride back to Paris, and Jackie wondered if her parents had endured a restless night as well. Her mother could've used the time to question her about Marceau, but thankfully, Janet seemed equally as lost in her thoughts as Jackie.

When they arrived at the Ritz, Janet instructed the bellhop to take care of their luggage and suggested to Jackie and Hughdie that they take advantage of the early morning hours to shop. He agreed, which Jackie recognized as their attempt to distract her from dwelling on last night's debacle. Their concern eased the hurt coursing through her, but her zeal for shopping didn't manifest.

Later, as Hughdie paid for their purchases at Guerlain, one of the many fine shops they visited along the Champs-Elysees, Janet took Jackie aside.

"I know you're struggling a bit. Love is never easy. I've learned that forgiveness is paramount."

Had she been herself, Jackie might have remarked, with obscure sarcasm, how Janet had yet to forgive her ex-husband, and possibly how such an endeavor could have made life easier for her daughters. But she didn't. Because she realized that her mother's noble revelation of forgiveness could be new—a tender shoot working and growing—one that could easily wither under criticism. Defeated and with her exhaustion deepening, she also lacked the mental fortitude to be contrary.

"Now," Janet continued, "that doesn't mean you overlook what's happened or allow someone to go on hurting you. Doesn't mean that the relationship may even be salvageable. What it does mean is that you'll be released. It's the only way to recover, to lighten the burden on your heart. Forgive him, Jacqueline, truly forgive him. Then see if it's something you can move past."

Jackie imagined her parents quarreling. She'd always pictured Janet as too hard to please, too demanding. Rarely had she considered the hurt her mother endured with every fling, every affair, every suspicion that contributed to the disintegration of her marriage. Rather than live as a constant victim of her husband's betrayals, Janet had conjured up a great deal of mettle to leave and divorce Jack Bouvier. High society proved unkind and unwelcoming to such women—especially one attached to a crumbling fortune and with children in tow—but Janet, knowing she deserved better, overcame her circumstances and established herself as a respected wife and mother. It was nothing short of courageous, now that Jackie thought about it. Shame needled her as she realized she'd never given her mother enough credit for her strength.

"You're right, Mummy." A true smile formed on Jackie's face. "You've always been right, about everything."

They enjoyed their afternoon and evening together, with a light dinner in their suite.

Goodbyes didn't come easy the next morning, as Janet and Hughdie stood at their cab.

"It wouldn't be the end of the world if you came home with us." He ran his hands along Jackie's arms, a feeble attempt to battle against the brisk wind that had kicked up.

Her shoulders sagged slightly. Because the temptation to fly home and hole herself up in Newport or Manhattan or Poughkeepsie was strong. If she returned to Vassar, or transferred elsewhere, she would eliminate the possibility of running into Philip—or Bea—ever. But such a move also risked labeling her as a coward.

"I would consider it the end of the world. If I ran home because a boy stopped liking me, just think how Lee would relish that. I wouldn't be able to live with her gloating at me non-stop." While it was an effort to make things light, Jackie knew it was true.

"You have a point." He hugged her tightly, the way he always did when he didn't know what else to say. Jackie thought of all the things he didn't know, the things that would've made him feel so much worse for her. She was glad that he didn't, glad that he didn't have to know.

She faced her mother.

"I feel terrible, leaving you just now. It seems we should stay and help you work through things." It was the first mention Janet had made that referenced the difficulties Jackie faced in repairing her Paris life.

"I'll be fine, Mummy. It's best if I do things on my own now."

Janet replied with a tight grin and worry-laden eyes.

"Promise me you won't fret and fuss," Jackie said.

"Impossible."

"I know, Mummy, but promise me anyway and let's pretend."

Jackie held her mother in a strong embrace, knowing that tangible feel of her mother's love would need to last her for months.

With last goodbyes and well wishes, Janet and Hughdie hunkered into the cab. Jackie waved from the sidewalk as the car blended into the traffic.

She drew a breath. If Yiska could rebuild a life after surviving a concentration camp and losing her husband—the same of which could be said of the countess—then Jackie could go on. She'd find a way to fulfill the promises she now made to herself—that she'd return to university blissful, even if she ran into Bea; that she'd enjoy her social life, even if she happened upon Philip; and that she'd give love and romance a chance, and not cling to the idea that she could never duplicate or exceed the feelings she'd had for Marceau.

The last item was most out of her control, but she'd try.

Promise me anyway...

JACKIE RETURNED to Mozart Avenue and the de Rentys' apartment that afternoon. They welcomed her with open arms and few questions. She settled in her room, alone, and welcomed not only the reprieve from the explanations that were due, but also the familiarity of the space. She lay atop the cool duvet, as the wind seeped in past the aged windowpanes, and stared at the ceiling for several moments before joining the de Rentys for lunch. Over piping bowls of navarin stew, though sparse on mutton, Jackie shared that her relationship with Philip was over.

"We're so sorry, dear," the countess said. "I felt simply awful for you."

"I don't know how you did it, standing there beside him while he rambled," Ghislaine said.

"Maybe he was drunk, and he didn't know what he was doing," Claude added.

"Oh, I'm sure he knew what he was doing." Jackie wouldn't expound upon the last time she saw Philip, entwined with Bea. "It's for the best, really it is. I'm ashamed to say it, but I never really loved Philip, not enough to become his wife one day."

She wanted to leave it at that, to shoulder much of the blame even, if that's what it took to rest the subject of Philip forever.

They discussed other aspects of the evening, including Marceau, but Jackie downplayed their interest. She stuck to her usual rhetoric that she'd met him in an art class and hardly knew him. It was true, and she didn't want to revisit how heartbroken she'd been at learning he was married.

Fortunately, Claude didn't bring up the letter Jackie had written to him before her journey with her parents, and whether or not she had read the letter, Jackie didn't know. She hoped Claude would ask her in private, if it came to that. Jackie would honor Claude and endure her questions, but she hoped Claude would let it go and afford Jackie the space she would need to move forward.

Whatever that meant.

March 1950

WARMER TEMPERATURES HERALDED in along with more chances to explore the city again. Classes resumed at the university, but Bea was in none of her lectures.

One way Jackie aimed to put the calamity of Philip and Marceau behind her was to fill her schedule.

A favorite activity became the pottery classes she and Ghislaine started taking one night a week. Claude joined her in a watercolor art class that wasn't part of the Sorbonne's program. In some ways, Jackie preferred Ghislaine's company the most. Unlike the countess and Claude, she kept to benign topics, such as Jackie's studies and her own quest to find suitable work.

The more time that separated Jackie from the night of the ball, the more at ease she felt. She considered what would've happened, if Philip had proposed. She would've said yes in the moment. Being overly accustomed to pleasing others—and having an aversion to public spectacles—she might never have found the nerve to save herself. What would it have taken, she wondered, to break off an extravagant wedding? For all she could figure, it would've required Tilda and Martine tying her up and throwing her into a broom closet. She wanted to believe she was cured of that ailment now.

The hurt that lingered most, aside from having no future with Marceau, was the loss of Bea's friendship. Gone was the kinship with the lone confidante she'd needed among a group of girls she otherwise felt distanced from. None of the other girls appreciated Jackie's wit or pranks like Bea had. She felt Bea's absence when they went to Elephant Blanc, one of their favorite clubs. When her grief amped up, Jackie wondered if Bea had suffered too, and if that notion of forgiveness had any chance of salvaging such a fractured friendship.

TWO WEEKS after the masquerade ball, Paul rang the de Rentys' doorbell, much to Jackie's surprise and welcome. Claude and Ghislaine were out for the evening with Christian, and the countess excused herself to her room, leaving Jackie and Paul to themselves in the parlor.

Jackie stole into the kitchen and attempted to make a tray with refreshments and snacks. She returned to Paul with a bottle of red wine, crackers, and cheese.

"I wish I were a better hostess." Her nerves were apparent, as she almost slid the contents of the tray onto Paul's lap. She sat and went to work, fiddling with her fingers.

"It's fine," he chuckled. "I'm more concerned about how you're doing, after...."

She couldn't face him, the weight of her disgrace nearly too heavy to bear.

Paul cleared his throat. "What I meant was, I was worried about you. Philip had no right—"

"He had every right. It was his home, his party." Jackie sprang to her feet and went to the fireplace. She wanted to drop her face into her palms and sob.

He went to her side.

She apologized, which did nothing to dampen her escalating embarrassment.

"Am I on the brink of losing your friendship too?" Jackie asked without pretense.

His face became awash in dismay. "Not a chance. I didn't come sooner because I was afraid you wouldn't see me, that you needed time to...decompress and clear your head."

She exhaled and returned to the settee. He joined her and gave her a moment to unwind.

"Shall I?" He indicated the bottle of wine.

Jackie nodded. She hadn't meant to create an outburst, but she'd had no true release for the vehemence that had built within.

Paul poured them each a glass and handed her one. "To true, lasting friendship."

Jackie touched her glass to his and sipped. "I'm sorry, Paul."

"You can stop apologizing. I'm here to check on you, not to strain you."

Finally, a smile teased the edge of her lips. "I should know better."

"Yes, you should."

They diffused the unnecessary tension with more sips of wine and carefree chatter about their lives since the ball. Then Paul veered into precarious territory.

"He's back in the Netherlands, in case you hadn't heard."

"Marceau?"

Paul nodded. "Divorce proceedings are underway. He didn't waste any time."

The news didn't enthrall her, since she couldn't imagine divorce ever being a good thing.

"Why do you think Marceau made such a show that night, Jackie? Exposing his wife, practically telling the room he was in love with you?"

Goosebumps prickled her flesh. "I don't know."

"If you ask me, he did it to protect himself. All those things he said about Sophie, how she was in love with someone else and had once tried to kill Marceau, if that were true, then dozens of people heard it, and he disarmed her from trying to hurt him again."

Jackie thought back to her conversation with Sophie. She didn't deny that she'd tried to poison Marceau, only called it a misunderstanding.

"It's possible." She had spent no time musing over Marceau's marital woes, but Paul's theory made sense.

"In any event, I hope those two can move forward, apart from each other."

"So do I." Jackie meant it.

"You know, I almost went to your room that night," he said, though he couldn't meet her eyes. "I was so worried about you, and I didn't think you should be left alone, but I didn't want you to think...And I can't swear that I would've been precisely what you needed, but something in me told me not to go. I've wrestled with it ever since, and I've wondered if I was wrong, not being there for you."

When Jackie considered the litany of complications that could've unfolded, had he shown up at her door...

"You're here now, Paul, and that's what matters most to me."

TUCKED IN BED ONE NIGHT, neither Jackie nor Claude could sleep. They both agreed a smoke might settle them, so they opened the doors to the Juliet balcony and sat on the wooden floor while they puffed. Aware of the hour, they kept their voices to a whisper.

"How are classes?" Claude asked.

"Challenging. I didn't expect it to be so intense, but it's...helped." Jackie doubted she'd chosen the right word.

"I know you've had a rough time, with Philip...out of the picture."

She nodded as she considered whether to tell Claude everything, from her fickle, lackluster feelings toward Philip to her desire for Marceau. She held back, apprehensive of the emotions such raw truth could bring forth.

"It hasn't been easy for you, has it? Being so strong while you feel everyone's watching?"

The accuracy of Claude's observation smacked Jackie even wider awake. Had she failed miserably at fooling others? Was she so unconvincing that she could withstand the torment that had been placed on her shoulders?

"I understand it's hard for you to share your feelings," Claude went on, "and I can't say that I blame you. It's easier that way, I suppose—and maybe there's a lesson in that for me. You're a lot like Ghislaine in that area, you know? She's good at pushing me away."

"I'm sorry, Claude, I've never meant to hurt you—"

"Oh, I know. I'm not trying to make you feel worse, it's just that...."

Jackie waited.

"I just wanted you to know that you don't have to suffer. That," she shrugged, "I wouldn't mind being there for you, if you ever needed me."

A sigh escaped Jackie, and pride stretched her grin wide. "I don't know what I've done to deserve your friendship, Claude. You're right. I'm not the easiest to be around when I'm hurt. It's like I want to curl up into a shell and never let anyone near me again. I'm sorry if I've been insensitive and cruel."

"No, never cruel. It's just that you've been good to me when I was in a bad spot, and I wanted the chance to do the same for you. Show that I can be a good friend."

"You already are a good friend. The best. I probably trust you more than my own sister."

"Really?" Claude stifled a laugh.

Jackie nodded. "I haven't told anyone about Marceau. Well, Paul knows a bit, but no one knows the whole story and what's happened between us."

Her eyes lit. "He's dreamy. I'd give anything to be kissed like that one day."

The mention of Marceau's kiss brought back every tingle and sensation that his lips had sent through Jackie's body. A kiss she felt in her soul and would never forget.

"If I tell you everything, would you promise not to tell another living person, ever?"

Claude nodded.

With a deep breath to prepare herself for the flood of emotions, she proceeded to share everything about her encounters with Marceau. Claude hung on her every word. Their pack of cigarettes dwindled, as did their need for sleep. Hearing the tale aloud, feeling her heart race inside her chest as she relived those moments, Jackie wished she would've known that the night of the ball was her last chance to say goodbye. If she had, she would've returned the passion in his kiss.

WHEN JACKIE ENTERED the apartment late the next afternoon, her arms loaded with a haul of books, Claude jumped in front of her, holding out an envelope.

"This telegram came for you today." Her crinkled brow and panic-stricken eyes made Jackie pale with sudden worry.

"Have you read it?" She toppled the books onto a nearby couch and wiped her palms over her wool skirt.

"No, but the courier said it was urgent."

Jackie ripped into the envelope.

JACKIE. SAD NEWS. YOUR GRANDFATHER HAS PASSED. BAD BOUT OF PNEUMONIA. WILL SEND MORE DETAILS IN A LETTER. KNOW THAT HE LOVED YOU WELL. MY DEEPEST LOVE TO YOU.
DADDY

Tears were falling when she finally tore her gaze from rereading the message and faced Claude and the countess. She couldn't bear to repeat the words and handed Claude the telegram. After reading it, Claude snatched her into her arms and held her tight. Jackie wept. Words of sympathy poured from the ladies. Jackie nodded, more as a reflexive response than an answer, because she heard nothing. Sounds muffled in her ears.

When she reached for the telephone, with permission from the countess to make the trans-Atlantic call, she phoned her father. The de Rentys left her in private.

Hearing his voice made the news real and penetrate with merciless despair. Feeling like a little girl, she wanted nothing more than to climb in her father's lap and bask in his soothing words. But she was thousands of miles away, both from her father's presence and from being a child. It intensified her ache.

Her father assured her at length that he and his sisters would take care of burial arrangements, and that he would take special care of Lee, who had taken the news hard.

Later, when she needed to escape the well-meaning sympathy of the de Rentys, Jackie headed to the sculpture gardens at the Rodin

Museum. Warm sunbeams and the park's solitude provided the healing balm her soul craved. She wished the rose garden were in bloom, but the dormant vegetation, dull and silent, felt appropriate. For her it seemed the ideal place to mourn both of her grandparents. Memories of Grandma Maude surfaced. Jackie was certain she would've loved the Rodin garden, and it would've reminded her of Lasata. The same could've been said of Grampy. Peace washed over her when she pictured the two of them together, reunited in Heaven.

Before returning to the apartment, Jackie visited Our Lady of the Assumption, where she lit a candle and prayed. How she wished for her family.

FOR THE NEXT WEEK, the de Rentys gave Jackie a wide berth. She kept to her schedule and missed no classes, including her pottery lessons with Ghislaine and painting lessons with Claude. Being unable to attend the funeral chiseled the broken pieces of her heart, but so did guilt for bringing her sorrows into the de Rentys' already grief-stricken home.

Maintaining my dignity is the best tribute I can give became her inner mantra.

In a gesture to thank the de Rentys for the ways they'd cared for her, she picked up fresh eclairs and mille-feuilles, Claude's favorite, from a bakery near the Sorbonne. She'd popped in after lectures had finished, feeling more chipper than she had in days, and hoped the sweet treats might cure the gloom hanging in the apartment.

As she was about to catch the metro at the Cluny stop, her stride lost its gusto and the air abandoned her lungs.

Bea stood before her.

"Hello, Jackie." Neither venom nor arrogance laced her tone. In fact, her cherry-painted lips stretched in a casual smile and she seemed genuinely pleased to see her.

"Hello." She barely managed the word as several emotions vied for center stage inside her, namely fury, a nagging curiosity for answers, and a storm of humiliation dashed with sadness.

"Do you have a moment? I'd appreciate it if we could talk." Her confident poise lacked any trace of guilt. Offered no hint of regret.

Jackie nodded. In her mind, she had imagined this encounter several times over. It usually played out with Bea falling at her feet, begging for forgiveness with a fit of shameless weeping. She had also rehearsed the things she'd say to Bea, given the chance, but the harsh, spiteful words she'd prepared clogged in her mouth and dissolved. Her curiosity won out, though she intended for it not to show.

Their aimless stroll took them to the Thermes de Cluny, the ruins of a Roman bathhouse dating to the third century. They'd visited before with the Smith girls, and Jackie thought the site fitting. Crumbling ruins for a devastated friendship.

They settled on a bench outside the main bath, an open-aired space that could be mistaken for a courtyard. Patches of grass covered what was once the bottom of the pool. Visitors weren't permitted inside the area, and a black iron fence protected what was left of the structure. Kingfishers and pigeons sang as Jackie and Bea loosened up by asking after one another, each replying with similar responses that focused on their studies. Their banter, forced as it was, wore thin quickly, and Bea abandoned the ruse.

"You'll never forgive me, will you?"

The shift from the cordial to the still-painful, tender truth jostled Jackie. How could she answer one way or the other, when she was hardly able to believe that she and Bea were having a conversation?

"It's not that I can blame you," Bea said, not waiting for Jackie's response. "What woman could forgive such a thing?" She looked at her. "But let's be honest. You'll never lack for men lapping at your heels. Rich ones at that."

"Are you two in love?"

She guffawed. "Hardly. We slept together. Doesn't mean we're getting married." She ran her fingers up her neck and fluffed out her hair. "But I was there for him. He came to me in the ballroom, after he made a show of returning. He'd wondered where you'd gone. I didn't know, of course, but he grew fairly agitated and didn't understand how you could leave his side. Men are the worst when they whine for attention." She spoke her last sentence like an inside joke that Jackie was in on.

"Anyway," Bea continued, "he started in on Marceau. Rambled about how Marceau always flirted with girls he liked and did his best to woo them away. You know, I won't lie to you, Jackie. There's no need. Not now. I played my part perfectly that night. I listened to Philip whine and told him all the things a man like him wants to hear." She cocked her head. "I wanted to take advantage of him, see how easy it was to lure him away and convince him you were no good."

Jackie didn't bother restraining the perturbed expression that took over her face. "Why would you do that?"

"The opportunity was there. You won't believe me, but it really wasn't personal." She laughed. "Well, maybe it was, but we'll get to that. So while I consoled Philip, stroking his hair as I agreed that you shouldn't have left him, I casually mentioned that I'd seen you with Marceau before, that day we were at Nôtre Dame. The attraction between you two was obvious, fiery even. Philip didn't like hearing that. I think he assumed you two were seeing each other, since he mumbled something about betrayal."

"Bea, that's not true! I told you he was a friend."

"Oh, Jackie, I know what you said." Bea waved her hand in the air as if she were shooing her comments away. "But set aside your feelings for now. Listen to what I'm really telling you. I already knew you didn't love Philip. How many times had we been together when you preferred or enjoyed Paul's company more? You and Philip never stole away for kisses, you never reached for each other under the table—and you *never* looked at Philip the way you looked at Marceau. I hated you a little for that, having fine choice men eating out of your palm while I had no one. I wondered, if you were out of the way, could I have a chance with Philip? It seemed only fair, knowing what I did, to find out."

Jackie bit the inside of her lip a moment. "All right. Suppose I indulge your logic. Go on." She girded herself as one who'd asked for a punch to the stomach.

Bea offered a wry grin. "Since I'm bearing my soul here, you might as well hear everything. It's childish, perhaps, but I was spying on you two Christmas night, when he asked you to come to his room."

Her jaw went slack.

"You stumbled through some excuse about not being ready, and I knew it would be a perfect time for me to step in. So after you parted ways in the library, I waited until Philip was in his room and knocked on his door. I confessed, sheepishly of course, that I'd overheard your conversation, and that unlike you, I was more than ready. Do you know what he said?"

Jackie shook her head, almost imperceptibly, the shock sinking ever deeper.

"He told me he would wait for you, that he really was in love with you. Didn't want anything to sabotage his relationship with you, and that he intended to make you his wife. Can you believe it? Turned me down flat."

Jackie sighed and held her eyes shut for a long second.

"Don't flatter yourself," Bea whispered. "I think he suspected it was a test, that you and I were in cahoots. Gauging his loyalty. Who's to say. But on the night of the ball, when I stepped into the role you should've been playing, he relented. He sent a note to my room, asking if I might comfort him. An hour or so later, you found us."

The image of the two of them together flashed before Jackie.

"Was it worth it?" She swallowed to combat the lump in her throat. "Did you get what you wanted?"

Bea snickered again. "Hardly. We used each other for different reasons. Philip told me he'd planned to propose that night. Even showed me the ring. He was fairly drunk by then but wasn't out of his mind. He was flustered and angry. I meant nothing to him, just as he meant nothing to me. But after you walked in on us, we were both troubled. Philip was terrified you'd take revenge, wake the whole house and tell the world what you'd seen. I knew right then he was ashamed to be seen with me, that there really was no chance that we'd be together. Not permanently. I hated him for that, for using me so easily. And I hated that you let him get away with hurting you. Why did you do that, Jackie?"

"I suppose because you were right. I didn't love him. Not the way he wanted or deserved."

"I left the château early, before dawn, and I haven't seen him or spoken to him since. It's no loss, though. His sisters hated me, and his mother would have me boiled in oil before letting her son fall for the likes of me. If anything, I should be mad at you."

Jackie whipped her gaze toward Bea. "How are you entitled to be upset?"

"Because I slept with the man and took him off your hands. You didn't have the nerve to break it off with him, so I sacrificed myself for your benefit. I hadn't intended to do you such a favor, not for that lousy sex."

Though she tried, Jackie couldn't suppress her laughter for long. Bea joined her. Their cackles escalated to a raucous level, causing the birds to squawk and scatter. They doubled over, leaned into one another, their foreheads touching. When they became breathless, they each found the other's hand and their bodies relaxed.

"Is the damage too great for us to be friends anymore?" Bea asked quietly.

Jackie considered that. On one hand, she was grateful. Bea had saved her from accepting a proposal insincerely—and from the eventual fallout of canceling a grand wedding. Conversely, she doubted she could trust Bea again, not only when it came to men, but also when it came to their friendship. After all, fierce loyalty ranked high among qualities Jackie demanded of those she trusted most.

"I don't know what will happen, Bea." It was the best response she could muster. "Once the semester is over, we'll go our own ways. I don't feel callus toward you, though, not after today."

"That's good enough for me, for now." Bea rifled in her handbag and withdrew her lighter and cigarettes. She gave Jackie a smoke, then lit each of them. "If Philip had gone through with the proposal, there were a few things I wanted you to know. Sometimes, the way he spoke about you when you weren't around bothered me. He couldn't stand how much you loved reading. Said it was unnatural for a woman, how you could spend hours with your nose in a book. He also didn't like how you always knew more than he did when it came to history, or that your political views had no backbone. His words, not mine."

Again, Jackie absorbed the revelations like a punch square to the chin. Whether Bea intended to plumb the well of Jackie's injuries further or thought she was rebuilding their fractured relationship by exposing Philip, she couldn't say. Instead, she focused on the moment and the incredible sense of freedom and release she felt, no longer housing pent-up anger.

"Tell me something, Jackie, why did you come to his room that night? Were you planning to sleep with him, to save the relationship?"

Instinct cautioned her and reminded her that Bea no longer deserved insights into her. Restricting people who had hurt her, would be a delicate skill that required time to refine.

She shrugged a shoulder and exhaled a puff of smoke. "Having always dreamed of horseback riding naked across the French countryside by moonlight, I needed him to play Leofric to my Lady Godiva."

TWENTY

Dear Philip,

It's been weeks since we've spoken. Although I wish our relationship had a more amicable conclusion, I do realize it was for the best. Time has a way of healing and providing perspective. I'm sure we can both see it now, that we weren't suited for marriage to each other. Such a commitment demands love and respect but with a mix of compromise, I believe. For no one is perfect in this life, and one must swallow the faults he finds in another while accepting that he also provides a bitter pill for his companion.

In light of our parting, I feel it's best to return your gift, though I savored every page as I read it. Books are such a passion of mine, as you know. It's a shame we couldn't share a mutual love for literature and learning, among so many other things. Perhaps Hugo was right when he wrote: "To love or have loved, that is enough. Ask nothing more." I will always speak well of you and wish you contentment.

Jackie

Jackie's heart smarted as she handed over the carefully wrapped package to the postal worker. Philip would never treasure such a book the way she would, and giving it back to him seemed a disservice to the world of antiques and even to Victor Hugo's memory. Keeping the book, though, would lump her into the same category as Bea. At least in Jackie's mind. She'd never intended to use Philip, but she'd rarely turned down his gifts and expensive outings. This was one way she could demonstrate a morsel of self-control. Prove, if only to herself, that she wasn't lorded over by materialism.

Perhaps it no longer mattered, what Philip and his family thought of her, and she had no control over such notions, but returning the book was an undeniably classy move. Jackie hoped such actions defined her, outshone whatever missteps she made along the way.

"Please, please be careful with this," she said as she hesitated letting go. "It's rather delicate."

The gentleman on the other side, spectacled and with wispy white hair, met her gaze. "Will do my very best, miss."

His words, backed with genuine conviction, brought a smile to Jackie's lips as she paid the postage and left.

Yes. Moving on, I will do my best also.

April 1950

CLAUDE SPOILED JACKIE for the next couple of weeks, taking her to every spot Paris had to offer with raging cherry blossoms in full display. Strolling Rue Monge and the orchards in Sceaux became particular favorites, followed closely by the Luxembourg Gardens and the Jardin des Plantes. Jackie's time in Paris was coming to a close, and she preferred spending time outdoors and soaking up as much of the city as she could, which helped lessened the time she could think about Marceau.

One of her most cherished days with the de Rentys came when they picnicked in the Bois de Boulonge, a nearby park. Jackie attempted to teach the family how to play kickball, but Christian lost interest in running to bases and liked running and kicking the ball as he pleased while Jackie or his mother chased him. He switched to chasing ducks when they neared the lake, giggling all the while. After the ducks paddled away, they settled along the water's edge, with Christian throwing rocks into the water—though not at the ducks. The glorious warmth of the sun combined with the breeze-laden fragrance of magnolia blossoms solidified Jackie's long-held belief that no other place compared to Paris in springtime.

As the afternoon dwindled, along with Christian's rambunctious energy, Jackie and the de Rentys headed back to the apartment. Ghislaine carried Christian most of the way since he complained that he was too tired to walk. He was asleep in her arms before they made it home.

There, Jackie sifted through the mail while the countess and Claude headed for the kitchen. When she came to an envelope addressed to her, she froze. Her chest tightened and her throat clenched as she recognized the familiar handwriting.

"What is it, dear?" the countess asked, having returned to the parlor. "Is something wrong?"

She held up the letter. "It's from my grandfather."

Bewilderment struck the countess. She took the letter and examined the post stamp. "It's dated over two months ago. Must have gotten lost in the mail." She pressed her thin lips together as she handed the envelope back. "Can I do anything for you, dear?"

"Thank you, but no." Jackie drew a breath to keep her emotions from spilling over. "I think I'll step out for a walk, find a spot to read it."

The countess nodded, her eyes glistening with empathy. "May be best not to wander too far, but take the time you need, dear."

Jackie gave a slip of a smile before darting out the door and down the street. The countess was right—she'd be in no condition to maneuver unfamiliar streets once she read the letter—but she didn't want to remain in the apartment, putting her host family on edge.

She found a bench along the Seine, not more than four blocks from home. Ache swelled in her chest as she opened the envelope knowing she was about to read the last sentiments she'd ever receive from Grampy. A gift and heartache in one.

My Dearest Jacqueline,

I've spent much of this winter trying to shake a cold. It's drained the sap out of me, I must say. Nevertheless, I'm anxious to start discussing your return. I think we should hold a grand celebration at Lasata. Your grandmother's flowers should be in full bloom by then, and we'll have the whole family over. I miss everything about those days gone by, when your grandmother wore that ridiculous hat to tend the garden and children were always running amuck. I'm not made for a quiet life. Perhaps you might consider boarding your horse here—or we could buy a pony, several ponies, all thoroughbreds of course, and you could offer riding lessons this summer. I know I'm getting ahead of myself, but the hope of seeing you puts vigor in my bones.

What have you learned while living in Paris? I do hope your time there has enriched your love for poetry. I am most anxious to hear you read aloud some of our beloved poems in your perfected French! Dare I confess how much comfort Second April *is giving me these days, as I am cooped up in bed.*

Your aunts have been by often and always ask after you. Your father seems to prefer telephone calls over visiting, as I have not laid eyes on him for several weeks. Even your sister has grown stingy with her presence, but I will ring her up and bait her with the promise of a trip to Bloomingdales just as soon as my strength is up.
There are few pleasures that rival your company, my Jacqueline. Although it is some time before you set off, I wish you Godspeed on your return journey home. Remind me in your next correspondence when you will be docking. I should like to be there and perhaps be the first to embrace you.

Your Ever Loving,
Grampy

ANXIOUS EYES GREETED Jackie when she returned to the apartment shortly after dark. She countered with a somber grin and shared how wonderful it made her feel, knowing her grandfather had passed peacefully, his stout, animated personality still intact. A tear escaped as she spoke, though she kept her tone cheerful.

"I was fortunate to know him and to be raised in his love," she told her host family. "You have all been so kind and patient with me through this, and I could never thank you enough. I...I don't know how I'm going to leave you in a few weeks."

The next evening, the countess and Ghislaine surprised Jackie with an extravagant meal. Coq au vin, soupe à l'oignon, and Ghislaine's better-than-any-bakery-made chocolate soufflés. They even used bowls Jackie and Ghislaine had crafted in their pottery class. When the countess shared that coq au vin had been her husband's favorite, other memories flowed from both the countess and the girls.

Jackie reciprocated with her own recollections of her grandfather. Hearty laughter and tender healing filled the modest apartment that night. They discussed plans for just the four of them. A tour of Madeline de Galea's doll collection close by in Auteuil, which the countess had been dying to see. Ghislaine suggested they share a final night at the opera, since *Les Misérables* was featured.

Despite the miseries that marred her time in Paris, Jackie couldn't have asked for more in that moment. She had become a better person from her experiences, most notably from being loved by her host family. And family they would always be in her heart.

WELL BEFORE DAWN on Saturday morning, Jackie coaxed Claude out of bed and took her to Canal Saint-Martin. She'd convinced Claude the canal provided the ideal scenery for painting a sunrise, a skill she wanted to refine. Having walked through the area on occasional, aimless afternoons, Jackie had found a spot she wanted to capture on canvas, with a pedestrian bridge arching over the water and wisteria plants embellishing the scene.

As they set up their easels, tufted ducks clamored and streaked through the water. Cool morning temperatures invigorated them as pale blue skies promised a beautiful day. Jackie couldn't escape thinking of Marceau and their morning at the Trocadéro. Nor did she want to. She replayed every bit of advice he'd given, and then shared his knowledge and techniques with Claude. Though she made no mention of Marceau, Jackie felt as if she were honoring him as they dabbed and brushed and created in joyful silence.

After a while, Claude's frustration reared its head with a groan. "I'll never get this right." She put down her brush and stepped back from the easel. She tilted her head, as if trying to appreciate her design, but her brow wrinkled. "I just don't have the knack for it like you do."

"Art is subjective, you know that," Jackie said.

"No. I know I don't have the talent to paint a scene. Just look at that." She motioned toward Jackie's canvas. "There's no way I could make the sky like that."

Pride swelled in Jackie, knowing Marceau deserved the credit. His patience, along with his technique of blending colors, had elevated Jackie's talent. *I'll always have that to show from our time together.*

"Maybe you're more of an abstract artist, then," Jackie said.

"Ah, well, that explains it. Wait till Picasso hears." They laughed as Claude began to clean her brushes. "Only a few more weeks of classes."

Jackie nodded. The approaching end of the academic year had been an impending topic. One that gave her knots of uncertainty in her stomach.

"I'm not ready to go back," she admitted.

"No?" Claude's surprise was genuine, probably since Jackie had avoided discussions about returning home.

"Now that Grampy has passed, I don't think I can spend the summer on Long Island, or even in Newport for that matter. I'm not ready for the ambush of memories and people's sympathy."

"I can understand that." Claude's words were sympathetic. "I've been thinking about something, so tell me your thoughts."

Jackie's shoulders tensed. Claude hadn't been one for the best ideas.

"I've always wanted to drive down south, explore the country. I have loads of cousins who live all over, but I haven't seen them for years. Now that I'm older, and if you'd be interested in going with me, maybe Mother would let me go."

"Really? You'd let me tag along?"

"Now, it wouldn't be anything fancy," Claude added quickly. "No restaurants or operas or art galleries. My relatives lead a simple life. No châteaux. It could be rough. If I remember correctly, some of them didn't have running water in the house. Chickens were rampant. Might have to wash in the streams we find. And you'd be stuck with me for weeks on end."

Jackie grinned. "That sounds absolutely perfect."

WHEN JACKIE and Claude presented their plan to visit relatives in the countryside, the countess wasn't easily won over. On a whim, Jackie said that she could call her brother and see if he could join them. Though she faltered, the idea seemed to ease the countess's concerns about two young ladies traveling alone.

Claude dashed a side glance Jackie's way, one that expressed both her approval and awe at her quick-thinking skills. Once the countess and Claude left the room, allowing Jackie her privacy, she dialed home.

She coiled the telephone cord around her fingers, the strain turning them purplish-blue within seconds. She tapped her feet and chanted to herself, *Please, be home. Please, be home. I need you to be there.*

One of the kitchen servants answered at last, and to Jackie's relief, Yusha was there. Jackie skirted around the usual chit-chat and forged to the pressing issue.

"So I was thinking about staying." She again twisted the cord around her fingers as the tension rebuilt.

"In France?"

"Yes, through the summer, to do some traveling, and I thought maybe you could join me. Actually, it'd be me and Claude." She peppered her pitch with hearty enthusiasm.

Silence beat from Yusha's end. "And why would I want to join this caravan?"

"Why wouldn't you?" She punctuated her comment with a giggle. "It would give us a chance to catch up...away from everybody."

"Mm-hm. Have you mentioned this excursion to your mother yet?"

Jackie hesitated now. "No. I wanted to talk to you first."

"Ah. Didn't learn your lesson from the last time you made big plans without consulting her?"

"I never told her when I was coming home. Not exactly." Jackie recalled the last time she'd seen her mother, when she waved at her from the rear window of the cab as it drove away that slushie winter morn. Warmth radiated through her when she thought of how they bonded over the wrongness of Philip.

"Convenient, for you anyway," Yusha said. "I'm not sure Janet will see it that way. But listen, I'll do what I can here and see about making a few arrangements. I've been wanting to head to Ireland. Maybe this will work as a precursor. No promises yet. In the meantime, you'd better make it a point to speak to your mother."

Yusha's firmness was unmistakable, and Jackie couldn't blame him. She wasn't sure she'd want to be around Janet either once she heard Jackie's summer plans. Even rehearsing it in her head made her pulse quicken and her chest tighten. Mostly, she worried that the progress they'd made in their relationship would unravel, that the news would make Janet revert to her domineering ways again, but no worthy alternative bloomed in Jackie's mind. Now that she'd already dreamed of living like a bohemian, she'd accept the cost however steep, because it was her very own decision to make.

May 1950

JACKIE SPENT her last night in Paris sipping champagne at Elephant Blanc, her favorite jazz club, with Claude and Paul at her side. With classes concluded, the other girls from the Smith program were set to return home in the morning. They knew Jackie wouldn't be joining them, and she couldn't help wondering if they had told Bea, and if Bea was missing her, even if just a little.

Jackie missed Bea—or the Bea she had known in Grenoble, in Sassenage, and when they first arrived in Paris. As she tapped her fingers on the tabletop in tune with the music, she smiled at how Claude and Paul were also enjoying it, with Claude lobbing her head side to side and Paul snapping his fingers. She wondered if this was the way it should have been from the beginning.

Her thoughts shifted to tomorrow, which held its own excitement. Jackie and Claude were set to start their road trip, and Yusha would meet up with them the next day in Orleans.

"I can't believe you won't be in Newport while I'm there." Paul swigged his soda water as if to soothe his mild irritation.

"Not this time anyway. But you should call on my sister, Lee."

"Is she anything like you?"

"She's only seventeen. Hardly cares a thing for horses and wouldn't dream of spending an afternoon reading. She might enjoy sailing with you, though."

"Sounds more like a babysitting assignment."

Jackie laughed. "Lee is a handful. Not that I want to spoil it for you. She never turns down a party invite and she's likely to know everyone, every place you go. You won't be bored."

He placed his hand on top of hers. "I'll miss you, Jackie."

"You'll have my number, so you can ring me when I get home." She took his hand and squeezed it. "And I'll look you up when I visit again."

"The city won't be the same without you."

"A long summer, a few pretty girls to flirt with, and you'll forget about me."

"Never. I only wish that...." He looked away for a moment, strangled by unspoken words.

"I know, Paul, but you can't force things." She smiled playfully, hoping her sentiment carried no condescending tone. "We've had an easy connection, right from the start, and I know we'll always be friends." Her gaiety took a downturn. "Philip...will never be part of my life again." The remark held more sting than expected. Too much for her to add, *And neither will Bea*.

"Believe me, I'm grateful not to be in Philip's shoes." Paul looked past Jackie and sighed. "I shouldn't be doing this." He shook his head slightly. "But I think you deserved better than that night at the ball."

Jackie glanced at Claude. Her eyes seemed locked in a hypnotic trance. When Jackie turned to see what had confounded her friend, her eyes blurred, and her head felt dizzy. Then her vision settled—and she realized he was truly standing in front of her.

"Marceau." Her breath caught.

"Jackie."

He looked similar to the night he had at the École des Beaux-Arts, his hair longer and curled at the ends, his jaw peppered with stubble. Gone was the caginess she'd seen in his eyes that afternoon at the Louvre, when Sophie had been by his side.

Paul properly introduced Marceau and Claude, then Marceau, his eyes on Jackie, said, "Paul got a hold of me, told me this was your last night in Paris."

They both looked to Paul, who wore an expression of mild defeat on his face. "I thought you two might want to clear the air."

"Would you mind terribly if we stepped out?" Marceau asked him.

"Go on," Paul said. "I'll see to it that Claude gets home safely."

Jackie kissed his cheek, her joy palpable. "Thank you for this."

They made their way to the Jardin des Tuileries, an expansive garden between the Palace de la Concorde and the Louvre. Void of tourists now, it proved tranquil at night.

Their hands laced together effortlessly. Jackie held his arm with her other hand and leaned her head against him.

"I owe you an apology." Marceau spoke softly, almost as if he didn't want to disrupt the silence between them. "I never should've put you on the spot that night at the ball. Kissing you was selfish of me. I had no right to endanger your relationship with Philip, or to leave you to deal with the fallout on your own. Paul told me what happened after I left, and I'm ashamed of the humiliation you endured because of me."

Her cheeks ablaze, Jackie cast her gaze to the ground. She didn't want Marceau to regret kissing her. His bold affection had been the best part of the night.

"I don't really care about the ball," she said. "Not anymore. I cared about what you'd been through, and what would happen to you and Sophie."

He snickered. "It's played out as you might've suspected. Our divorce is officially in the works. She's gone back to Luxembourg, and we haven't spoken since. I'm not sure she truly loves Victor, or that Victor's intentions are genuine either, but it doesn't concern me anymore. We had no business getting married."

She looked up at him. "What will become of you, Marceau?"

The corner of his mouth curled. "You don't need to worry about me. My family's busy trying to decide for me."

"But isn't that how your troubles started?"

"Yes, but moving forward, we're all a bit wiser." He draped his arm around Jackie. "When you come from a family such as mine, there's no likelihood of living far from their influence. Some see it as a curse, but it's all I've known, and I don't begrudge my future. How could I?"

Jackie's chest squeezed. She could possibly say the same about her mother.

"So there's little chance I could persuade you to run away with me?"

He grinned, drew her body closer to his. "Tell me, where would we go? What would our life look like?"

"Perhaps we should live on a boat and spend our days sailing in and out of exotic ports. That way, no one could ever find us."

"It does have a certain appeal." He looked to the stars gleaming above and became pensive.

"But?"

He met her gaze. "What good would it bring to the world? I guess I'm not one for creating strife and division in a family. Perhaps I'm being too severe, but now isn't the time to cower and hide away. I've done enough of that. History is calling for leaders, and the legacy of my family demands that I do my part, whatever that may be." Against the direction of the breeze, he tucked strands of Jackie's hair behind her ear. "I don't think you're meant to skim along the edges of this earth either. I'd give anything to be the man destined to be by your side, Jackie."

She considered that. "Anything...except everything, because that's what it would cost you, isn't it?"

He sighed. "I can't afford to make another mistake, not that a life with you could be a mistake, but...."

Marceau didn't need to say it. She already knew, and the pain of that knowledge pierced her deeply. She buried her face in his chest and breathed him in, hoping to burn the scent of him, aspen trees mixed with paints—and a hint of lavender—on her brain.

"We'll always have Paris." He held her close. "And I'll *always* have my sketch of you in the moonlight."

EPILOGUE

September 1950

Dear Grampy,

I know you'll never read this, but I have to write it anyway. I'm sitting on the deck of Liberte in my lounge chair, soaking in the sun as we sail back to New York. Yusha is napping or off flirting with a girl. We spent a wonderful summer together, exploring southern France with my dear friend Claude. Just like you wanted, I visited our ancestral home in Pont Saint-Espirit. It's just as quaint as you might imagine, and the people I met, some distant relatives, are as happy as anyone could be.

We had so many adventures—they'll never fit into a letter—but I became such a bohemian, and I loved it! Picnics, sleeping outside (only a few times), and bathing in a creek. I'll treasure the moments always. Then we drove Claude back to Paris and Yusha met the rest of my host family. They got on beautifully, as I knew they would.

Yusha and I spent August in Ireland. Oh, it would pain you to hear it, but I fell in love with the never-ending hills and clifftop castles. Mummy has an ancestral home there, which we came to adore—along with the people! I may have made a life-long friend in Father Leonard, a priest we met, who took us to the Blarney Stone and other sites. We spoke of so many things, and since your passing, it was one of the few moments I felt a sliver of peace about you leaving me. He promised to write me, and I hope that he does.

Yusha arranged for us to meet the prime minister, and we attended a play at the Abbey Theatre. I could go on, but I know how you prefer to do most of the talking.

We toured Scotland and London before boarding the ship, and now our course is set for home. It has been a whirlwind of excitement and unforgettable memories. In your last letter, you asked me what I had learned while living in Paris. It's a lengthy answer and one I'm likely to blather my way through, but I wanted to share it with you.

It's possible that I may have cried more tears in Paris than anywhere else. Losing you, losing a man I never really had, as well as bouts of humiliation, and bidding farewell to the de Rentys all took their toll.

I've learned that true friendship is hard to come by. People can be so self-centered and focused on their own needs—and willing to hurt you to get what they want or what they think they want. I've found true gems in Claude and Paul, but trusting others with my heart will not come easy for me. It never has. Not at boarding school, not at Vassar, never at our social events or in riding club, and not in Paris.

I've learned that I need to look out for myself when it comes to love. There may be times when I need to do something hard, or when I must tell others NO. I need to do things that may seem too difficult but will save me from greater heartache. I should've been more straightforward, even courageous, when it came to Philip. I almost let others carry me away into a decision and a future that were not wholly my doing. What would have become of me? I would have only myself to blame for the destruction that would have inevitably followed, namely divorce. If there's anything I wish to have power over in this world, it's that I would never know the pain of divorce—or put my future children through such an ordeal. Is that too much to ask?

I don't know that I'll ever get over Marceau. It's an immature notion, I know, to fantasize about a relationship I'll never have, one that could never be. Perhaps I have read too many books. I keep telling myself there's no point in idolizing Marceau and the mere moments we had together—that someday, I'll open my heart to a man who's available to love me.

Which reminds me. Before setting sail, a letter came from my friend Charles Bartlett. He's anxious for me to return home and said he can't wait to introduce me to a Congressman from Massachusetts. He and Martha seem to believe we'd hit it off. I laughed to myself because a Congressman sounds terribly boring—and I've been told my politics have no backbone—so I can't imagine what we would have in common. Then again, being in Paris has taught me that love—being in love, falling in love—has a way of surprising you, and you never know exactly how it's going to happen. I only hope—hopelessly so—for an everlasting love.

Since I began this journey, I've encountered so many people and emotions, from princes to women who've lost their husbands in the worst way. Each of them have left their mark. Spoken words I'll carry with me.
Daddy said we must sell Lasata....

I'll miss you always, Grampy. Edna St. Vincent Millay said, "Childhood is the kingdom where nobody dies". Your passing makes this resonate in my soul. Change is an ever-present, hungry beast that's never satisfied. It seems to devour the things we hold dear and at times when we are most vulnerable. I've learned to be strong when my world is shattered and broken, so even in death, you are teaching me still, and much of your lessons will always reside in me.

Forever and lovingly yours,
Jacqueline

AUTHOR'S NOTE

This is a work of fiction. Jacqueline Bouvier did spend her junior year of college in Paris, but many of the characters and events depicted here are fabrications. One of the biggest deviations from fact was the death of her beloved Grampy. In real life, the Major passed away in 1948, well before Jackie set sail. Otherwise, there is a generous mix of 'creative liberties' and truth. This book is for entertainment purposes only and is a fictional tale.

ACKNOWLEDGMENTS

I'm very grateful for the talents of Hannah Linder and Christy Distler. Both added coats of polish to this book. Big thanks to my writing buddies at Buckeye Crime Writers. Much gratitude to Alicia Anthony, one of the few who truly understands the work, devotion, and pinch of crazy it takes to write and publish a book. Thanks to Twila Kolda, who's always there for me. A shower of confetti and honors to the 'real' Jacqui in my life, Jacqueline Conforti Barnett, who provides valuable insight. Very special thanks, as always, to my family. Oh, the things they endure for my sake...

—*MK*

ABOUT THE AUTHOR

A founding member of Buckeye Crime Writers, Mercedes King is a Columbus, Ohio, native. With a degree in Criminology from Capital University, she enjoys combining her love of pop culture with history and exploring the depths of deviant behavior. Since her stories often mix fact with fiction and are shaped by not-so-distant decades, she refers to many of her works as Modern Historicals. In 2016 and 2017, Mercedes was a finalist for the Claymore Award. When she's not elbow-deep in research, reading, or enjoying the local bike path, she might be at Wrigley Field or sinking her toes into the sand somewhere along Florida's coastline.

BOOKS BY MERCEDES KING

The Jacqueline Bouvier Kennedy Onassis Collection

Jackie's Paris

Jackie's Camelot

Jackie's Greece

Jackie's New York

Historical Fiction Titles

A Dream Called Marilyn

Plantation Nation

Crime Fiction / Mysteries

Every Little Secret

Grave Secrets

Columbus Noir

Newsletter subscribers receive a FREE e-book for joining. Sign-up here.

Printed in Dunstable, United Kingdom

70949968R00160